One oblique one

The killing of the Marriott family was a particularly brutal one: asphyxiation, a savage clubbing and what looked like rape.

The 'one oblique one' call swiftly brought DI Stark and the Scenes of Crime squad to the death house at 43 Maple Close, where a forced window and a missing video recorder were the immediate clues in what was to become a protracted and torturous murder investigation.

Why did the killer disguise his entry to look like a burglary? If not burglary, what was he doing in the house? Had he gone there specifically to rape and murder the promiscuous Faye Marriott? Why hadn't she struggled? And why did he remove the video after the murders?

Two men were seen running from the house – in opposite directions. But they were not the two men most closely connected with Faye. Winston Kelly, West Indian pimp and Faye's sadistic lover, looked the best of the bunch of suspects, yet moneyed, foppish Charles Lyon, who had been enraged by the girl's sexual taunts, ran him close.

This immensely exciting, fast-moving and professionally plotted first crime novel is by a young, serving CID detective. It gives readers a rare chance to follow the detection of a murder in authentic, albeit fictional, circumstances.

ONE OBLIQUE ONE

Keith Wright

Constable · London

First published in Great Britain 1991
by Constable & Company Ltd
3 The Lanchesters, 162 Fulham Palace Road
London W6 9ER
Copyright © 1991 by Keith Wright
The right of Keith Wright to be identified
as the author of this Work
has been asserted by him in accordance
with the Copyright, Designs and Patents Act 1988
ISBN 0 09 470330 2
Set in Linotron 10pt Palatino by
CentraCet, Cambridge
Printed in Great Britain by
Redwood Press Limited, Meltsham, Wiltshire

A CIP catalogue record for this book
is available from the British Library

To my beloved wife Jayne
and to all wives and loved ones of police officers,
the unsung heroines who have to put up with our lifestyle
and without whose support 'the job' could never be done

1

'One murder makes a villain, millions a hero . . .'
                    Beilby Porteus (1731–1808)

The police radio crackled out its final instruction to the young
uniformed officer, breaking the monotony as he sat staring at
the crowds of people, busily hurrying to their various desti-
nations, from his position in the car-park of the Swan and
Peacock public house. He turned on the ignition of his panda
car as he repeated the message to himself. 'One oblique one'
had only one meaning – sudden death; his heartbeat quickened
as he realised its full significance. While driving to 43 Maple
Close he wound down his window a few inches, allowing the
breeze to blow through his blond hair, cooling his now flushed
face. The policeman was only twenty years old and although he
had known that one day he would be confronted with a
situation as serious as this, he certainly hadn't expected it to be
today. He felt alone as he attempted to concentrate on his
driving, his newly given responsibility hanging around his
shoulders like a lead weight which he couldn't shake off.
    Within minutes he had left the office buildings behind, and
as he turned into the tree-lined Maple Close, the subdued quiet
of a middle-class suburban estate emphasised his feeling of
loneliness. He turned left, slowly manoeuvring the Ford Escort
between the two large pillars on to the gravel drive which led
to the large, four-bedroomed detached house. It was a 1950s
design with a garage and a beautifully mown lawn sheltered by
conifers and shrubs. As promised by the officer in the control
room who had issued the radio message, he could see a
milkman standing outside the wooden front door. As the officer
drew up, the milkman came forward to greet him and the two
met as the policeman stepped out of his car. The milkman, one
Norman Price, was a short, stocky man of about thirty, with

7

long, brown, curly hair that rested on the collar of his white 'Co-op Dairy' waist-length jacket, contrasting with the scruffiness of his jeans. Norman appeared fairly calm, which unnerved the probationary PC further as he wrestled with his emotions in a vain attempt to give off a more confident air.

Norman had to arch his neck as he addressed the six-foot-tall policeman. He pointed toward the house, illustrating his observations.

'It's in there, mate. The door was open a bit so I just put my head around and there it was. Pretty gruesome, I'm afraid.'

The PC set off, without speaking, his shiny boots hard on the gravel drive that led to the brass-handled, oak front door. His heart raced into top gear, pumping out adrenalin, his mouth became uncomfortably dry as he made the lone journey. Norman did not follow; he had seen enough, settling instead to lean on the police car, arms folded, watching the officer from afar.

The PC paused and glanced hesitantly through the open door into the hallway, his feet rooted to the spot. He craned his neck – he could see nothing. He would have to go inside. He took a deep breath and swallowed hard before stepping in.

'Jesus Christ!'

Detective Inspector David Stark was the sub-divisional CID boss. He appeared troubled. His large, muscular frame moved easily in his well-pressed grey suit as he strode boldy down the dimly lit corridor. He passed the CID general office to his left, pausing only to shout to his Detective Sergeant: 'Nobby, I want to see you in my office now!'

'Coming, boss,' came the gruff reply.

Stark was a kind, approachable man and warmth emanated from him despite some twenty years as a police officer. Today, however, was different. He puffed on a long-stemmed pipe, smoke billowing out, leaving a trail behind his visibly angry stride.

Detective Sergeant John 'Nobby' Clarke rose tentatively from the plastic chair. His handsome but rugged face grimaced as he anticipated the worst. He had used his charismatic air to manipulate women of all ages and to evade all sorts of problems in the past. Stark in this mood, however, was a different proposition. Nobby started his excuse immediately upon entering Stark's bright, roomy, modern office.

'Look, boss, I can explain. I couldn't turn her down, I didn't leave her apartment until after four . . .'

Stark cut him short. 'Nobby, I am not going to argue with you. You are a grown man. I know you like the nightlife – God knows I used to – but I've got a department to run, and this is the second time this week! Now if you, my best DS, can't get here for eight o'clock, how can I expect my DCs to?'

'Fair comment, boss, it won't happen again . . .'

The apology was cut short by the ringing of the telephone. Stark looked at Nobby as he spoke and listened to the voice on the other end of the red plastic scoop.

'DI Stark . . . You're joking? . . . Bloody hell, and we're sure the PC has checked all three are dead? . . . Right, we're coming down. I want you to tell the copper who is there to double check that there isn't an offender on the premises and then seal it off, touching nothing until we get there, OK? Cheers, Bob.'

Stark replaced the receiver. Nobby was curious.

'What is it boss? A murder?'

Stark looked grim. 'It's a murder all right – the murder of a family in their own home by the looks of it. It's a Mr and Mrs Marriott, apparently, of Maple Close and their daughter Faye. You'd better get your coat.'

Stark and Nobby were in the black Cavalier. Stark was driving.

'Number 43 Maple Close, Dave.' Nobby felt that he could call him 'Dave' now that the reprimand was apparently forgotten.

'It's there, look.' Stark pointed at the house. He parked on the gravelled drive and the two got out.

The young policeman looked flushed as he stood outside the door. Stark approached him. Perhaps he was getting old, but the kid looked not much more than sixteen.

'What's happened, then?' Stark asked him.

The PC's reply was excited but nervy. 'There's three of them, sir, the whole bloody family by the looks of it!' He fidgeted his feet about, his shiny black shoes scraped on the ground and his

9

chubby face continued to glow red as the blood rushed uncontrollably to the surface of his skin.

'How did we get to know about it?' asked the Inspector.

'The milkman knocked on the open door for his money. He didn't get a reply so he looked through and saw the old man croaked inside.'

'Have you got the milkman's details?' Stark asked as he looked at the front door, which stood slightly ajar.

'Yes, but he's pissed off now, said he'll be late finishing his round!'

'So the front door was ajar when you arrived?'

'Yes.'

'How long have you been here?' Stark enquired.

'About fifteen minutes, I would think. Nobody else has been in apart from me, and I've only touched the door handles. I had my gloves on.'

'Good lad. Anything else?'

'No – apart from the rear window's been forced.'

'Did you see anybody around when you arrived?' Nobby asked, feeling slightly redundant in the shadow of his Detective Inspector.

The boy diverted his stare to the detective. He seemed to be looking at his moustache.

'No, nobody at all. It was like . . .' The boy hesitated. '. . . a morgue!'

Stark gave his instructions. 'I want you to start a log of every person who enters this house and the time they arrive and leave, understand?'

'Yes, sir. Does that include you and DS Clarke?'

'Yes, it does.' Stark glanced at his silver-linked wristwatch. 'Right, it's 8.52 a.m. and we're going in. Come on Nobby.'

The door would not fully open. The legs of the dead man lying in the hallway were in the way. Stark stepped rather gingerly into the hall, carefully avoiding the considerable area of carpet that was soaked in blood. He could never decide whether it was a smell or an atmosphere or a mixture of both, but almost every 'death house' had that 'air' about it – an indiscernible, unnatural feeling as if one were a trespasser, an uninvited guest to something intimate and private. His heart beat faster as he uncomfortably took in the disturbing scene, leaning closer to examine every intricate detail of the terror frozen in time.

The dead man in the hall was not young, probably in his mid-forties, and slightly greying around the sideburns. Stark was unsure about the hair colour as the blood had matted it into a dark claret. The man lay face down. There was a large hole in the back of his head. The side of his face was silhouetted against the Axminster carpet. It wore an expression of apparent surprise. The dead man was wearing a suit and tie, and next to him lay a Yale door key; the open door seemed to indicate he had not had time to close it.

Stark turned the gold-coloured doorknob and entered the living-room. He looked straight into the unseeing eyes of a young girl in her late teens. She lay on the floor, on her back. Her head was tilted and resting against the black hi-fi stacking system. As he approached for a closer look, Stark noticed that she had a peculiar lop-sided grin on her face, but he failed to see the joke. He could not fail, however, to see the large hole in the crown of her head, not dissimilar to that of the man in the hallway. The girl's breasts were exposed, her dress pulled down to the waist and folded up on to her stomach, her white knickers twisted around her left ankle. Her legs were wide apart, displaying her black triangle of pubic hair to the two detectives who scrutinised her vagina, which appeared sore and moist. It looked as if the girl had had sexual intercourse before she died although necrophilia could not be ruled out.

'Not so much blood in here, boss,' Nobby observed, his voice seeming like a shout in the hushed atmosphere.

'No. It's interesting that she's lying on her back, and there appears to be no sign of a struggle at all. I suppose she could have been asleep or drunk when the attacker struck.'

'True. At least it would have been over quickly for her,' said Nobby reverently.

Stark shook his head. 'I'm not so sure.'

'Why?' asked Nobby. 'You've seen the wound on her head – the first blow would have killed her or rendered her unconscious at least.'

'What about her eyes?' asked Stark, slowly removing his pipe from his jacket pocket.

'What about them?' asked Nobby, as he leaned closer towards her face as if to kiss her.

'Petechial haemorrhaging, caused by lack of oxygen,' Stark commented.

Nobby stepped back. 'Yes, but we all die of lack of oxygen!'

'Very funny, Nobby. I'm talking about asphyxiation. When a body has been asphyxiated, there are tiny red spots in the whites of the eyes, where the tiny blood vessels have burst through . . . lack of oxygen.'

'I didn't know that,' Nobby confessed.

The two tall men surveyed the antique-filled living-room. Stark felt as if they had walked into a freeze-frame of a reel of film, with inanimate objects surrounding them, the only movement emanating from themselves. It was as if real life had been suspended and they were ghosts, intruders.

Nobby's powerful voice again seared through the silence, making Stark jump physically. 'I see the hi-fi is still on.'

'Yes, I had noticed that. See anything else?'

Nobby's eyes lit up. 'Ah yes, the video.'

'What about it, then?' Stark asked with a smile.

'Well, whoever did this must have taken the video after the killings.'

Stark tapped his pipe against his mouth in thought. 'Yes, the spattering of blood from the girl's head is on the carpet and telly but there's none where the video must have been, even though there are tiny spots of blood on the carpet in front and behind.'

The two men ventured into the open-plan kitchen, which was decorated in pastel shades. There were no signs of violence in this room. The focus of attention lay at the wooden transom window which was ajar and swinging on its hinges, letting in the morning birdsong and the faraway sound of a lawnmower, which disturbed the otherwise tranquil morning. Closer examination of the window by Stark revealed that it had been forced with a blunt instrument, approximately half an inch wide, near the handle, about half-way up the side. It appeared that the window had been the point of entry for the sinister visitor or visitors.

With nothing else of note, Stark and his associate returned to the living-room. Stark's face screwed up, disgusted at the realisation of what he saw. He shouted out his instructions: 'Oh bloody hell, Nobby, quick! Shut that pissing door! A fly's come in – oh shit, it's feeding on her wound, look!'

Nobby hurriedly shut the door and they went upstairs, leaving the fly seemingly rubbing its front legs in glee at the welcome sight of the slowly festering flesh.

Out of the corner of his eye, as he drew level with the landing floor, Stark caught sight of the third body: a woman in her forties, in a blue dress and cream cardigan. The two men stood, looking down at the pathetic sight. Her skin was grey and sallow, her lips blue, her eyes bulging. A foul smell assailed the insides of Stark's nostrils – the smell of human excrement, some of which was visible on the carpet in a sticky liquid mess. Stark put his hand quickly to his nose. It looked as though the woman had been on her knees and knocked over to one side. Her eyes were open, and there was a gaping hole in her head.

'That looks like the murder weapon at the side of her.' Nobby said, his voice muffled through his white cotton handkerchief.

'That certainly looks as though it's been used to hit her,' said Stark.

The two men stared at the brass ornamental clown on the plain light-blue carpet. It was about fourteen inches long and smeared in blood and tissue. Stark noticed that the upper half of the clown was very clean with a definite line, a cut-off point where the blood started.

'It looks as though the killer has wiped it,' he said. He noticed a small patch of blood smeared at the edge of the woman's dress, somehow alien to the rest. 'Yes, the bottom of her dress – look, Nobby, that's where he wiped it.'

The men checked the other rooms, which appeared undisturbed. Stark made a mental note of a blue diary in a room lined with posters of the latest rock stars, then they trooped downstairs. Stark pressed the button on the side of the radio.

'DI Stark to Control.'

A lilting Scottish accent was quick to reply. 'Go ahead, sir.'

'Yes, start a computer log, please. You might not believe this, but it's a triple murder. I'd like the Detective Superintendent here, please, and two DCs, Scenes of Crime, the police surgeon and the undertakers. Nobody else – it'll be enough of a circus as it is.'

'Ten-four, sir. Superintendent Wagstaff is already on his way.'

Stark and Nobby went back outside to the front garden for a smoke and to gather their thoughts before the cavalry arrived. Stark asked his friend, 'What do you make of it then, Nobby?'

'I don't like it. It stinks, doesn't it?'

The two men walked around to the back garden. A neat, mown lawn with a flowery moat was all there was. No footprints, nothing. They returned to the front of the house just in time to see the rather portly figure of Detective Superintendent Wagstaff struggle out of his Rover Vitesse.

Stark had always considered that Wagstaff looked like an outraged, retired Wing Commander, and Wagstaff did little to change the image as he marched briskly up the drive in his dark-blue three-piece suit, twitching his well-trimmed white moustache. Stark nudged Nobby, who was leaning against the wall. Nobby straightened himself up and held his cigarette behind his back.

The Detective Inspector greeted his senior officer. 'Morning, sir.'

'Is it, David? Tell me what the position is, then.'

Stark related the grisly details and then the enquiry began in earnest. The two DCs arrived next, young Paul Fisher and his older and uglier colleague, Jim McIntyre, later followed by Scenes of Crime. The two detectives presented themselves to Stark. Paul was fresh-faced with blond curly hair. He wore a light-blue suit and a green tie, and regretted being paired up with Jim McIntyre, whose pock-marked face did nothing but moan and complain from dawn till dusk. Everything was an effort for Jim. Paul was keen to start. This was only his second murder and he wanted to throw himself into action. Jim, on the other hand, had wanted to finish his cup of tea before leaving the station. Paul had stood impatiently at the door, waiting for Jim to drag his shiny-seated backside off the chair. 'Let them wait,' he had said. 'They're dead, aren't they? They're not going anywhere, are they? What's the rush?' Jim's logic had been lost on Paul.

Stark issued his instructions. 'Start house-to-house, just in the immediate vicinity for now, and ensure that there is nothing of burning importance staring at us; and Paul, keep a record of who you see and what, if anything, they know.'

'OK, sir.'

Jim, who had paid little attention to Stark's orders, was true to form. 'Are we going to be wasting our time with this all day or what?' he asked.

Stark replied 'Well, that depends. Are you a bloody detective or aren't you?'

'All right, keep your hair on. I was only asking,' Jim's voice croaked. He cleared his gullet and spat out a ball of phlegm on to the drive, where it glistened in the morning sun.

'We'll have a bit of a briefing at half-past three, back at the nick.'

'Right, see you later, sir,' said Paul. He and Jim turned and made their way down the drive. Neither spoke to the other.

'Come on, Nobby, let's have another look around the back,' said Stark.

43 Maple Close backed on to Yew Tree Gardens, the main road for the estate. A small gate led into the road.

'Careful where you tread, Nobby.' The men's eyes scoured the ground.

'I still can't see any footprints, can you, Dave?' Nobby asked.

'No, nothing; just small fragments of wood where the window's been forced.'

Stark looked through the glass pane into the house. He could see Wagstaff and the police surgeon. 'Come on, let's go and join Tweedledee and Tweedledum!'

As Stark and Nobby entered the living-room, the police surgeon left, having performed the perfunctory task of pronouncing life extinct in the three bodies. Wagstaff addressed Stark. 'Right then, David, once Scenes of Crime have finished, we'll get the bodies shipped off for the post-mortems. Sergeant Clarke can be Exhibits Officer.'

'But, sir, that's usually a DC's job!' exclaimed Nobby.

'Well, now it's your job. It's going to be a complex one is this, so I want it doing right from the word go.'

Wagstaff turned to Stark. The Superintendent's white moustache twitched again. 'David, keep me posted as to how things develop. I'll be in my office for the rest of the day.'

'Very good, sir,' said Stark, nodding his head in a semi-bow.

With that Wagstaff left the room. Stark peered through the bay window to watch him puff and pant back into his car before driving away.

The space he left was quickly filled by the arrival of the plain white Scenes of Crime car. A grandfather clock in the corner of the room chimed the half-hour. The bell seemed excessively loud for the size of the clock.

'For whom the bell tolls . . .' said Stark before continuing. 'Well, it looks like you've drawn the short straw, Nobby, so make sure you do a good job of it. Remember, every fibre, every loose hair, every minuscule item has to be packaged and labelled correctly. I'll take young Fisher to the post-mortem with me. It'll be good experience for him. He'll sort out the exhibits there for you.' Nobby looked miserable. Stark tried to reassure him. 'Don't worry, there'll only be a couple of hundred exhibits!' he laughed. Nobby didn't.

'Cheers, boss. See you later,' he managed to say.

The two men parted company, Stark heading for the hall and Nobby for the kitchen. Suddenly Stark stopped and caught Nobby's attention before he disappeared behind the kitchen door. 'You know, the thing that bothers me is what sort of idiot steals a poxy video after killing three people?'

Nobby shook his head as he stood in the doorway. 'I don't know. It's beyond me too.'

As he stepped outside on to the drive, Stark brushed past a Scenes of Crime officer in a white boiler-suit holding a metal suitcase. He caught hold of his arm. 'Excuse me, I'm DI Stark. Do you mind doing me a favour?'

'What's that, sir?'

'Well, I've seen a diary upstairs that I'd like as soon as I can. Will you dust and examine around there first so that I can take it?'

The officer looked thoughtful, and slightly put out. Already someone wanted to disrupt his routine before he'd even started.

'Oh, OK, if you're running the show and you think it's that important, yes. Show me the way.'

Stark patted him on the back and smiled. 'Good man.' He led the balding officer up the stairs into the second bedroom and indicated the dark-blue diary resting on a white dresser.

'We'll have to wait for the Sergeant to come up with the video before we touch anything. I'll start with my magnifying glass,' said the officer. He opened his box of tricks and went straight for the large glass, which he used to examine the area where the diary lay. He could see only dust, and a tiny spider which struggled over the obstacle course of cosmetics that adorned the dresser. It looked as if the diary hadn't been moved for a couple of days.

Stark noticed another white boiler-suited figure progressing slowly up the stairs with a video camera, recording the grim scene for posterity, evidence and spotty-faced trainees, who in years to come would have nightmares about its contents.

Once the bedroom scene had been recorded, the magic box was again opened. It held an array of brushes, and plastic tubs containing white, silver and black powder. There were small plastic squares, cellophane, sticky tape, scissors, a small knife, a magnifying glass, several plastic bags and a small torch. The man took out a well-worn brush and a plastic pot of aluminium powder which he painted over the diary, having picked it up carefully. Its shiny surface was a good one; there were three clear fingerprints. The men were confident that these would be those of the dead girl.

After lifting the prints, the Scenes of Crime officer threw the diary at Stark, who caught it at the second attempt. 'It's all yours.'

Stark didn't look in the diary until he had carefully negotiated his way past the dead woman on the landing and down the stairs. He walked out to his car and leaned against the side before thumbing through the list of names and telephone numbers in the diary. He estimated twenty or so male names, but there was only one female name, written in capital letters in red ink and underlined – 'CHANTELLE NAYLOR'.

2

'I'd rather have a free bottle in front of me
than a pre-frontal lobotomy'
Unknown

Stark glanced at Paul who was biting his lip in the passenger
seat as they turned the left-hand bend in the busy afternoon
traffic. Only the ticking of the indicator broke the uncomfortable
silence. Struggling with the black leather steering wheel, Stark
said, 'You're very quiet. What's the matter?'

'Nothing, sir. Well, to tell you the truth, I've never been to a
post-mortem before.' Paul tapped nervously on the dashboard
as he spoke.

Stark reassured him. 'You'll be OK. I'll give you a tip: if you
feel you must look but daren't, focus on something beyond it
and break the image in gradually. That'll help you get used to it
first.'

Paul sought a justification for the visit. 'What's the point in
us going, sir? Why don't we just wait for the report?'

'Because,' said Stark, 'we get instant answers to questions
and if we have any particular points of enquiry we can pass
them on to the pathologist. It'll be good experience for you
anyway: these things can be quite interesting.' Stark nodded at
the pedestrian who waved his thanks at him as he walked
across the pelican crossing, then glanced in the mirror before
pulling away.

'Is it like an operation or what?' asked the increasingly
nervous DC Fisher.

Stark gave a wry smile. 'Well, it is, but it can be a lot more
brutal as they know they can't damage the . . . "patient", for
want of a better word.' The silence between the two men
returned momentarily. 'It's left here for the mortuary side of
the hospital, isn't it?' asked Stark.

'Yes, I've been here a lot – it's the butchery part I've not encountered.'

Stark laughed out loud as the memory struck him. 'It's not so bad nowadays, though, Paul. You want to think yourself lucky.'

'How do you mean, sir?'

'Well, when I first joined the job the old-timers would play all sorts of tricks on us. I remember when I was on nights once, they locked my mate in the mortuary all night.'

Paul winced. 'Christ.'

'The poor guy woke up all the neighbourhood, banging and screaming. He was quiet at first, but when his eyes became used to the darkness he could make out the silhouettes of the bodies.'

'Bloody hell.'

Stark continued his memories. 'He was still all right, but, as you know, dead bodies let their gases out gradually, and when the first one farted that's when the screaming started.'

'The bastards! Fancy doing that to him.'

'He went sick for a week after that.'

'I'm not surprised,' said Paul.

'This is it here, on the left.' Stark's black Cavalier pulled into the parking bay marked 'Morticians'.

'This'll do here – we're the Queen's men, aren't we? . . . Are you all right?'

Paul's face was as white as a sheet as he stared vacantly at the plastic fascia. He answered honestly, 'I don't fancy doing this, boss.'

'You're not going to let this beat you, are you? Come on, mate, you're a bloody policeman. Once it's over you'll wonder what all the fuss was about.'

Paul's stomach churned, his mind chased back to when he was a frightened eight-year-old sitting outside the dentist's. He made a decision. 'Oh bollocks to it – in for a penny, in for a pound!'

Paul and Stark strolled over to the drab brick building. The cold chilled Stark's bones as he walked into the white interior.

'It's colder in here than it is outside,' said Paul. 'Why is there that constant trickling of water, sir?'

'They're the post-mortem tables. It keeps the blood washed away.' Stark grew conscious of Paul's nervousness. The two detectives allowed themselves a cursory glance around the room. The main area was quite large, with whitewashed walls and concrete floor. There were three slabs; only one of them was vacant. The first was occupied by the naked body of a man of around sixty, the purple staining of his skin showing along the base of the body as it lay on its back. On the third was a girl of about nine, whose mangled legs gave reason for the look of abject terror etched on her face. Paul didn't dwell on the sight; he took a deep breath.

Off the main room were what appeared to be an office and two smaller annexed rooms. In them stood white ceramic tables. A loud, booming voice made Paul jump. 'Hello, the audience has arrived early. I take it there's no queue outside then? People are dying to get in here, you know!' His raucous laughter was enough to wake the dead – well, almost . . .

'Paul, this is Tony the mortician.'

Stark wondered what Paul would make of the thirty-year-old mortician. His off-white coat and black, matted, unkempt hair advertised his obvious lack of hygiene and Stark noticed Paul's reluctance to shake hands with the apparition.

Tony sensed nerves tingling in the hand of the young detective. 'You look a bit white, son. It's not your first time, is it?' A gleam appeared in his eye.

Stark interrupted hastily. 'No, he's been here quite a few times, actually.'

'The butcher won't be here for about ten minutes, Mr Stark. Do you fancy a cuppa?'

'Yes, go on then.'

The three walked across the concrete floor into the surprising heat of the mortician's office. The opaque windows which surrounded it were gaily decorated with nicotine-stained net curtains and Page Three pin-ups. As Stark chatted to the mortician, he noticed Paul fidgeting in his seat, his cup and saucer rattling between his tentative sips.

After what seemed an age, the pathologist, Dr Disney-Hargreaves, and his assistant arrived. When the formal introductions were over and Disney-Hargreaves had ordered the first 'contestant' to be brought forward, he enquired after Paul's health. The young man's embarrassment couldn't disguise his pallor. Disney-Hargreaves was a man of around fifty, with short, straight, brown hair and gold-rimmed spectacles. He was ex-public school and spoke with a plum in his mouth. His reputation as a pathologist was unquestioned in the highest medical circles. His assistant, a young registrar, hung on his every word.

Tony and the assistant crossed to the wall lined with refrigerators with metal doors. 'We'll get the young tart out first,' declared Tony in his best bedside manner. 'It's drawer eight, Jim.'

They pulled the drawer open and the cold air streamed out, clearing to reveal the body of nineteen-year-old Faye. There were see-through bags on her hands and head.

'Shame about the hole in the head: she's quite tasty,' said Tony, out of earshot of Disney-Hargreaves.

Stark shook his head at the distasteful comment. 'You're sick – you know that, don't you?' Tony grinned broadly at him. He and the assistant dumped the body that had once been the beautiful Faye Marriott on to the white ceramic slab in the annexe room. The men assembled round the body. It's soul long gone, it literally was a lump of meat and organs.

The pathologist's assistant took up a large pad and pencil and Disney-Hargreaves began the well-rehearsed spiel. 'I am commencing the post-mortem of Faye Marriott, nineteen years, of 43 Maple Close, Nottingham. The time now is 10.32 a.m. on Friday, 4 August 1990.'

'Here we go. Keep taking the deep breaths, Paul,' thought Stark. The annexe was not particularly large and there was no hiding place for the young DC; however, he stood furthest away, close to the doorway.

Disney-Hargreaves's voice was cold and calculated. 'External examination reveals a large wound at the top of the deceased's skull, revealing part of the brain.' The pathologist's assistant removed the head bag and Disney-Hargreaves placed a ruler at the side of the head wound, while photographs were taken of the wound showing its dimensions.

'The wound is 3.2 inches in diameter and does not appear to have clotted too well . . . I'll take the scrapings off each hand and from underneath the finger-nails once we have removed the bag, Mr Johnson.' Disney-Hargreaves turned to the assistant on his left, who hurriedly removed the left-hand bag and

21

subsequently sealed that inside another bag so that any debris in it would be preserved. The pathologist then took the relevant scrapings and gave the implement and cotton wool to the assistant, who packaged them in separate bags. They then repeated the process on the other hand.

'I also note that there appears to be blood and fluid in the left ear, petechial haemorrhaging to the eyes. There is a bruise to the left forearm. Now, turning the body over, there is a one-inch graze at the base of the spine in the coccyx region.'

'Looks like she's been screwed,' Stark whispered over his shoulder to Paul.

'Quite right, Mr Stark,' commented Disney-Hargreaves, 'and so beautifully put, Inspector . . . which leads me to the vaginal area.'

The pathologist took a smear from the entrance of the vaginal walls and then inserted a large swab. He then proceeded to do this with every body orifice. Stark's mind wrestled with the sudden mental image of Disney-Hargreaves telephoning his wife: 'I'm sorry, I'll be late at the orifice.' A grin tickled his face.

All the hair, including pubic, was combed for loose hair samples; then samples were plucked, and each comb and hair was packaged separately. It was time for the blood and gore. Stark focused on the scalpel as it sliced easily through the skin. The pathologist cut in the shape of a large Y, starting at one side of the neck and moving down the front of the girl's chest. He then cut down the other side of the neck and joined it into the cut on the chest. Stark couldn't help flinching, even though the girl was beyond pain. He glanced at Paul and saw he was sweating despite the coldness of the room.

Disney-Hargreaves peeled back the layers of skin and yellow fat, with great aplomb. The girl's breasts lay sagging down by each side of her body, her sternum and rib cage exposed. Stark saw Paul wince, his eyes screwing up, his lips a thin red line on his increasingly wrinkled face. With great physical exertion the top flap of skin was pulled up over the front of the girl's neck and chin, revealing the bone and muscle of her chin and neck in its red-and-white glory. Stark knew Paul would simply have to endure the horror he was witnessing; the churning in his stomach would not go until a few more post-mortems had been attended. Paul's eyes screwed up again as he watched the assistant do the labouring job of sawing through the rib cage whilst his white-gloved mentor looked on. The noise of the sawing was a new one to the young officer's ears. Small chippings of bone flew on to the slab and floor, and the Detective Inspector noticed Paul take a conscious step back so that none would land on his suit. It was like some perverted horror story. Paul didn't know what he had expected, but it certainly wasn't this.

'If you can suggest any other way of getting to the cardiovascular organs, I'll gladly try it,' said Disney-Hargreaves, who must have seen the look of disdain on Paul's face.

Paul stumbled over his reply: 'No, sir, of course not.' Stark could only watch as the detective's face changed from ash-grey to bright red in an instant.

Once the small hack-saw had finished, a chisel and mallet were used to prise open the rib cage, which was then fully opened manually by the assistant. A vast dormant pool of blood was revealed, which was ladled away, some of it sucked up by a tube similar to one a dentist might use to remove saliva. There followed a thorough dissection of every individual organ. Each organ was removed from the body on to a trestle table, then cut into pieces, and the pathologist commented on its condition. Each organ was then thrown into the space where the stomach had once been. Part of the spleen was dissected and stored in a container; it would have to be frozen so that it could be used for any later DNA profiling. Other samples of blood would be sent away to be given a grouping; these needed only to be refrigerated.

Although the proceedings were gruesome beyond compare, Stark could see that Paul had become slightly more interested. He had begun to crane his neck to observe each organ: the miracle of life was suddenly brought home to him. Once the disgusting smell had cleared, he found it interesting to see that some of the food the girl had eaten was actually visible in identifiable form. The contents of the stomach were emptied for the toxicology lab to examine at a later date.

The last part of the butchery was the worst, as Paul was introduced to another new implement – the trepan, similar to an electric drill but with a circular 'bit' one and a half inches wide. The shrill sound of sharpened steel screeched into the

23

ears of those watching as it progressed around the forehead to the back of the head. Mercifully, the drilling stopped, to be replaced by a dull thud as the chisel and mallet prised off the top part of the skull to reveal the brain. This was quickly snipped out, dissected and thrown into the stomach area with everything else. The empty shell of a skull was filled with a large piece of cotton-wool wadding and the top of the head crudely sewn back on.

'Thank God that's over. One down, two more to go!' Stark's and Paul's thoughts coincided.

Disney-Hargreaves and Stark strolled through the car-park discussing the results of the post-mortems. Stark had his hands in his pockets; the pathologist carried his large black briefcase.

'Well, sir, now that you've finished all three PMs, can you tell me what's what?' asked Stark.

The cultured voice was unhurried in its reply. 'Well, officially the results aren't ready, but I'll tell you whatever I can with any degree of certainty. Faye Marriott was asphyxiated to death – '

Stark was keen for answers and interrupted the slightly overbearing doctor. 'How?'

'She wasn't strangled. Probably a hand or some article held over her mouth and nose for a long enough period of time. She'd had sexual intercourse prior to her death, although I didn't find any semen traces. She hadn't been forcibly raped, although that doesn't discount fear as a weapon, obviously.'

'What about the gaping hole in her head?' asked Stark.

'The blow that caused such a wound would undoubtedly have killed her outright. That wound was definitely inflicted after her death, there is no question about it. It was made with a heavy blunt instrument.'

'So the head wound was an attempt to cover up the asphyxiation?' Stark enquired.

Disney-Hargreaves laughed. 'That's for you to find out, fortunately. It is feasible that the killer went into a frenzy and didn't realise that she was already dead.'

'What about her mother?'

'She, like her daughter, died from asphyxiation, but this was due to actual manual strangulation.'

'Can you be certain?' asked Stark.

'Absolutely. The bruising and striation marks showed quite clearly around the neck. I would say your killer is right-handed.'

'Well, that narrows it down.' Stark forced a grin.

'The head wound again was caused after the death had taken place.'

'Now that definitely sounds like a cover-up to me.' Stark's voice became louder as his certainty increased.

'The woman was completely terrified immediately prior to her death,' Disney-Hargreaves said as the two men reached his Mercedes.

'How can you be so certain of that, sir?'

'Because, Mr Stark, the woman had defecated prior to her death. She'd shit herself, to put it crudely.'

Stark nodded. 'Yes, of course she had. I remember the smell.'

'I suppose the only consolation is that she wasn't interfered with sexually before she died.'

'Anything else, sir?'

'No, not really. I would say the killer was very strong.'

'Why?'

'Well, he almost put his thumb through her trachea. There's substantial damage in that area.'

'What about the dead man?' Stark asked. He had produced a pad of paper and began scribbling now that they had stopped at the pathologist's car.

'He's slightly more straightforward. He was killed by a single blow to the top of the head, apparently with the same blunt instrument.'

'Lucky him. Anything else?'

'A few scratches on his back – you probably saw them. I don't think that they were caused by the killer, however!' Disney-Hargreaves smiled for the first time.

'Yes, it's surprising really: his wife didn't look the passionate type,' Stark commented.

'It doesn't have to be his wife, of course,' the pathologist said wisely.

'True.'

'I'll get the full report to you as soon as possible,' said Disney-Hargreaves. 'It depends how long forensic and the toxicology department are. I'll try to hurry them up for you.'

'Thank you, you've been most helpful, sir,' said Stark as the two men shook hands and parted company. Stark returned to his car, met half-way by Paul Fisher.

'Come on then, Paul, let's take a drive back to the nick.'

Paul seemed in high spirits, pleased at having survived the ordeal. 'What did the doc say?' he asked.

'It's a long story, Paul. I'll tell you on the way back, in the car.'

Stark explained the complicated details as he drove through the city-centre traffic. His account drew to a close as the Cavalier's tyres struggled to grip the loose gravel on the police-station car-park.

'Did the pathologist give a time of death?' asked Paul, somewhat naïvely.

'Oh, come on, Paul, that's for Hercule Poirot! Pathologists can't give an exact time of death; all they can do is give a rough estimate based on a table drawn up after a series of thermometers have been thrust up the deceased's backside on an hourly basis. All we know in this case is that it was some time last night.'

'Can I ask just one more question?'

'Of course you can. What's that?' asked the Inspector, interested.

'Who's Hercule Poirot?' Fortunately Paul's nimbler legs evaded the swift kick aimed loosely towards him by Stark.

The two men used their master key to gain entry to the large sub-divisional headquarters. They passed along the corridor into the spacious canteen. Two uniformed officers sat at a table to the left, speaking in hushed tones. Unusually, the slot machine sat redundant, flashing out its attractive message. Paul and Stark walked up to the serving hatch and studied the small menu stuck to the wall with a drawing pin, while the canteen staff, two girls, busied themselves and a pall of smoke rose from the area of the deep-fat fryer.

'Ah, liver and onions!' said Stark.

Paul looked disgustedly at his senior officer. 'You're joking, aren't you? I've seen enough of those today. What else have you got cooking, Margaret?' Paul directed his question to the brunette in the light-blue apron.

She replied in a broad Nottingham accent, 'You can have either liver and onions or steak-and-kidney pie!'

Paul winced. 'Give us egg and chips, will you, love?' Margaret tutted her agreement to the breaking of her usual routine.

Paul looked drained as he shuffled to the nearest table and sank low in the chair. He forced his hands into his pockets and let out a loud blow that would have done Moby Dick justice.

Margaret shouted from behind the counter: 'What's the matter with him today?'

Stark called out his reply with a half-laugh: 'He's all cut up about something!' Paul grimaced before Stark continued the diatribe: 'Like somebody else I know, he hasn't got the stomach for it any more!'

Stark handed Paul his egg and chips before sitting down next to him and devouring his liver with relish. The feast was interrupted by a voice with a Yorkshire accent behind Stark.

'Scenes of Crime, sir. Can I join you?'

Stark turned round, some potato still on his fork. 'Yes, of course you can. Stuart Bradshaw, isn't it?'

'Yes, sir,' answered the gangly, freckle-faced officer, drawing up a chair.

Stark continued eating. 'So what's happening down at the scene, Stuart?' he asked, after swallowing a particularly sinewy piece of liver.

Stuart leaned forward, intent on holding the Detective Inspector's full attention. 'I'll give you the full report later, but I can tell you what I know so far. It looks as though the house, as you no doubt saw, was entered via the rear kitchen window. We've taken a plaster cast of the marks left by the tool, so if you find any burglary tools about half an inch wide during the course of the investigation, they can be forensically examined. The instrument used to gain access doesn't appear to be in the house.'

'It'll be interesting to see what the Special Operations Unit discover when they start their fingertip search of the area,' said Stark.

Stuart nodded his agreement, his long thin legs uncomfortable under the low-slung table. 'Did you notice that the video was taken after the killings were committed?'

27

'Yes, we noticed that.' Stark concentrated on spearing more potatoes on to his fork.

Stuart continued his report. 'The girl was actually struck as she lay on her back – you can tell by the direction of the blood spattering. It looks as if she didn't move at all to defend herself. I think she must have been dead or unconscious when the blow was struck.'

'That's what the pathologist said.'

'Did you notice the petechial haemorrhaging?'

Stark placed his knife and fork together on the plate and wiped his mouth with the paper serviette. 'Yes I did, Stuart. I was there, you know.'

'Sorry, sir. It looks as though the killer was standing on the stairs when he attacked the man. The Yale key at the side of the dead man fits the door, which tends to confirm that they were just returning home and possibly disturbed the killer. I have a theory about the older woman.'

'What's that?' Stark asked, lighting his long-stemmed pipe.

Stuart was now in full flow. 'I think she walked in first, and then, realising her husband had been attacked from behind, ran into the kitchen, no doubt hotly pursued by the killer. She then must have doubled back, when she found the back door locked, and tried to get back out through the front door. It looks as though she couldn't get it open enough because of her dead husband's body being in the way, so she quickly ran upstairs and was caught by the killer on the landing. It looks as if she went down on her knees to beg for mercy, shit herself and then was attacked by the killer. How does that sound to you, sir?'

Stark blew out some smoke. 'It sounds about right to me. It's early days yet, but that's more or less the scenario I'd conjured up. What about the screams, though? Surely both mother and daughter screamed?'

Stuart shrugged. 'We'll have to see what the house-to-house teams discover.'

Paul ate his last chip. 'We got no reply either side when me and Jim tried,' he said. 'What about Lockhart's theory?'

Stuart laughed. 'See thee, tha's trying to be clever. Is that the only thing they teach you nowadays?'

Stark interjected. 'Now come on, Stuart, we've all been where Paul is now.'

Stuart quickly apologised. 'Only kidding, Paul. Right, Lockhart's theory, as you obviously know, is that every object or substance, no matter how minute, that comes into contact with another object or substance, leaves its trace. Now the only thing we've got so far is that we've found some red fibres on the carpet next to the dead girl and on the older woman upstairs, her dress. Nobby's labelled them anyway.'

'He's never still there, is he?' asked Stark.

Stuart's face creased into laughter. 'I'm afraid so. You can hear him cursing and swearing as you walk up the path to the house!' The three laughed in unison.

Stark rose from the table. 'Right, I'm going to ring the missus. It's going to be a long day today.' He walked back down the length of the canteen. 'See you later, Margaret,' he shouted, the double doors carrying the call further into the room as they rebounded into place.

Stark leaned back into the black swivel chair and gazed out through the venetian blinds that hung over the window, masking the sunlight. He held the red plastic to his ear, waiting for his wife to answer the phone. His heart warmed at the thought of her lively, excited face, the sparkle in her eyes, crowned by the closely cut hair that gave her a 'pixie' look.

'Hello.' Her voice had a ring of happiness in it.

'Carol, it's Dave.'

'Hello, love. I've just put dinner on. It's your favourite, lamb.'

'It sounds great, but I'm afraid there's a slight problem with that . . .'

Carol guessed the implication. 'You're not going to be late again, are you? You know your mother's coming for dinner.'

'I'm sorry, Carol, but there's been a murder – three in fact – so I'm going to be late for the next few days at least.'

'Three murders? Sounds horrific. Are you OK?'

'Yes, there's no problem – don't worry about me,' he reassured her.

'It's a shame about your mother. She's coming up to see you, not me.'

'Don't be silly. You know she thinks a lot of you.'

Carol laughed. 'Great! We'll sit looking at each other all night then.' The sarcasm displayed an obvious disappointment.

'Well, ring her up then and tell her to cancel!' Stark had enough on without a whingeing wife. An annoyed tone had crept into his voice and it rose a pitch or two.

Carol backed down. 'Oh, I'm sorry, Dave. I was just looking forward to seeing you. I hate being on my own all day and all night.'

'Well, there's the kids,' Stark offered.

Carol was feeling a little sorry for herself. 'It's not the same, you know that.'

He tried to cheer her up, adopting a lively tone. 'Hey, listen, I'll make it up to you when I get home, honestly.'

'Now come on, David, you know damn well that when you get home you'll be too knackered to do anything!' The hint of a reluctant smile had returned to her voice.

'Perhaps you're getting to know me too well, but I can definitely promise a cuddle. Will that do for tonight?'

Carol had accepted the inevitability that she would not see her husband as planned. 'That's fine. I shall look forward to it.'

Stark leaned forward on to his desk and began doodling with his pen on the white blotter that covered most of its surface. 'Don't wait up, Carol. I'll probably be very late. I've got a funny feeling about this one.'

'I'm not surprised, with three murders. What sort of funny feeling have you got?'

Stark smiled to himself as he continued his aimless scribbling. 'I think it's my mysterious powers picking up strange vibrations.'

Carol laughed. 'I think you've been working too hard lately.'

Stark glanced at his watch. 'How's your day been?'

'OK. Nothing fantastic has happened. Laura and Christopher are sitting glued to the goggle-box. It's the Hit Show – they've taped it. Who invented school holidays?'

'It sounds really exciting!' said Stark, mockingly.

'All right, I know it's not as exciting as you Supercops, but it's all I've got and I'm stuck with it.'

'I know – I'm only joking. Listen, I'm going to have to hang up now.'

Carol gave her plea. 'Try not to be too late, Dave. You know I don't like going to bed on my own.'

Stark felt sorry for his wife stuck at home and was thankful for her understanding. 'I know. Listen, I'll see you later, OK?'

Carol sounded concerned. 'I love you. Be careful, darling.'

'I will, don't worry. Bye.'

'Bye.'

Stark put the receiver down. He would now be involved in a hectic enquiry. His wife would have to cope on her own at home. He wondered which was the harder.

Stark entered the CID general office and spoke loudly above the clatter of his fellow policemen. 'All right, quieten down.' The noise subsided. He focused on each of the ten or so detectives, scattered around the room between the wooden desks and chairs. A pall of stale smoke hung in layers throughout the room, emphasised by the rays of sunlight which shone in strips through the broken slatted blinds, strobing the assembled officers.

Stark knew he was in line for promotion and wondered if that was the reason Superintendent Wagstaff had given charge of the enquiry to him. Wagstaff had twiddled his moustache as usual as he broke the news. 'David, this enquiry is down to you now. If you can sort this mess out, you can sort anything out. I'll be available as officer in the case on paper, and give you a guiding hand where necessary. I've told those in the ivory towers that you're up to it, so don't let me down.'

Stark was running the show, at least for now, and it was for that reason that he addressed the disparate group of men and women in the room. He studied each person there – all of them different, but with one common goal: to find the killer before he struck again.

Stark looked at Steve Aston, the young aide to CID, an unlikely candidate: ginger hair, suede sports jacket, baggy trousers. He was a timid boy in many ways, a vegetarian who cycled to work most days. For some reason, though, he had an ability to communicate with criminals and to track them down, a sort of 'Midas touch'. In contrast was Ashley Stevens, a man of twenty-nine whose expensive suits and jewellery put Steve to shame. His hair was beautifully styled and he drove a Porsche. The guys were certain he received a private income from his wealthy father.

The DI addressed Steve. 'Go and get Special Operations Unit up here, will you? They're in the canteen.' Steve scurried out.

'And put the bloody kettle on!' shouted rotund Charlie Carter, a man in his forties with greying hair and a twinkle in his eye. Stark smiled to himself; he had been a DC with Charlie in 1975. Charlie had lived and worked on the patch for twenty-four years – everybody knew Charlie. He looked like a village squire as he sat back in his chair, puffing on a cigar.

Stark's attention was diverted by the sound of swearing from behind a wall of large, brown-paper bags. He knew that voice well. 'Haven't you finished that bit of a job yet, Nobby?' he said, laughing.

The voice sounded desperate. 'I'll tell you what, boss, I reckon I'll still be here this time next week at this rate!'

'Don't worry,' Stark replied, 'a DC from headquarters is coming to relieve you.'

Nobby's hard features emerged from behind the packages. 'Brilliant! Someone to relieve me. Couldn't you let Stephanie relieve me instead?'

The inevitable whoops and catcalls resounded. Detective Policewoman Stephanie Dawson sat smirking on a side-table, her slim body leaning forward, causing her long blond hair to cascade downwards, shielding her firm breasts. Over the years she had learned to use her beauty and sensuality to the maximum. 'It will have to be somebody better equipped than you, Nobby!' She emphasised the 'Nobby'.

Nobby hadn't finished. 'Come on, give us a kiss!' He walked towards her, arms outstretched, ready for the embrace. The whoops rose in volume as Steph turned to evade the oncoming advances of her Detective Sergeant.

A voice in the doorway halted proceedings. 'So this is what the CID gets up to, is it?' In walked the SOU, led by the inimitable Sergeant Tuckworth, every man in a blue boiler-suit and carrying a navy-blue beret. Some of them had bags, containing various paraphernalia. The Sergeant was of obvious military bearing, a barrel-chested hard case.

'Grab a chair, or sit down where you can, lads,' Stark

instructed. 'Right,' he continued, somewhat over-loudly. He sat on the desk at the far side of the office, all eyes on him. 'This isn't going to be a lengthy briefing. I've prepared a rough copy of the parts of the enquiry which will be of use to you. We'll have a full briefing tomorrow. I just want to highlight the crux of the investigation as it stands at the moment. The Marriott family have been murdered. Man, wife and teenage daughter – Faye. The killer has forced a rear transom window with a half-inch blunt instrument to gain access to the house. Faye Marriott has been asphyxiated, but prior to this she had sexual inter-course in the living-room of the house. This means either that the killer knew her, or that she was raped, or that there is a third party who has yet to be traced. It looks as though Mum and Dad interrupted proceedings and paid dearly for it. It looks as though the sex act was interrupted as there are no traces of semen at the scene. Necrophilia cannot be ruled out. Walter Marriott was killed by a single blow to the back of the head by a brass clown ornament which is about fourteen inches long. It appears that Audrey Marriott, in an obvious panic, ran into the kitchen, doubled back and eventually ended up on the landing. The killer then strangled her to death. For some reason the killer then took great trouble to hit mother and daughter with the same brass clown. Presumably this was done to disguise the mode of killing. Our killer then unplugs the video recorder and makes good his escape, taking the video and the implement he used to get in with. We've found the operating manual for the video: it's a Matsui and we have the serial number should you require it. The hi-fi was still switched on when we arrived at the scene this morning. Any joy with the house-to-house enquiries, Paul?'

All eyes turned to Paul, who was sitting at the back of the room. 'No, sir, nothing of any use. Most of them were out, and those that were in haven't seen anything.'

Stark swung his legs as he sat on the desk. He continued: 'Right, SOU can finish off the house-to-house – three streets in every direction for now – and a fingertip search of the gardens please, Sergeant Tuckworth.' Tuckworth nodded. 'Some red fibres have been found which we believe could well belong to the killer or the third party, so please bear that in mind. I think the key to this lies with Faye Marriott. Myself and Nobby, when

33

his replacement arrives, will team up, and Stephanie and Ashley Stevens, if you team up also. We'll look into the background of Faye; Ashley and Steph can hang loose and tidy up any enquiries that come up. Charlie and Steve, you can look into Walter and Audrey Marriott. Paul, can you contact Force Intelligence regarding the same *modus operandi*, and any other comparisons with other features of other murders. I'll arrange a liaison man at that end. Jim, I want you as office manager for today until the HOLMES computer starts tomorrow, and all the menial thousand-to-one-shot enquiries start. We have a diary belonging to Faye Marriott, and everyone in it will have to be interviewed. The lads and lasses in this room, Steph, will involve themselves with enquiries of some importance: the rubbish can be done by a squad set up at headquarters. Right, that's about it. Any questions?'

The heads shook in unison.

'Right, crack on. Back here at 10 p.m. for a debriefing. Overtime's been organised, so don't worry, Jim, you'll get what's due to you. Let's go and see who would want to kill a nice girl like Faye Marriott.'

3

'She has two complexions – a.m. and p.m. . . .'
Ring Lardner (1885–1933)

Stark and Nobby stood on the pavement and stared up at the sign: 'Squires Turf Accountants'. The betting shop stood on the corner of Victoria Street and Main Street. Its large front window hadn't been cleaned for weeks, but the black cardboard silhouette of horse and rider was still visible behind the glass façade. As Stark opened the door a cloud of smoke billowed out, and the two detectives stepped from the comparative brightness of the bustling street into a seedy world. The tinny voice of an announcer heralded their entrance: 'The two thirty at Chepstow, three to one favourite Misty Morning, seven to two L.A. Girl, ten to one bar six.'

Smoke stung Stark's eyes as he tried to focus on the images within the dingy den of iniquity. A man of about sixty stood, hands in pockets, staring at the extracts from various racing papers which festooned the walls. He had a stubbled chin and a dirty cloth cap resting well back on his head. A cigarette was smouldering its life away in a nearby aluminium ashtray. Another man of about thirty stood close by at a side wall-counter; he wore a smart three-piece suit and looked worried. His eyes flicked from a scrap of paper to the newspaper on the wall and back again.

To the left of the detectives were six television screens screwed to the wall, with lists of horses' names displayed on them. One screen was host to the tinny announcer, with his bland expression. A fat, middle-aged woman with a beehive hairstyle and a beauty spot stared disdainfully at the list of runners and riders. Her short, tight-fitting black skirt revealed a glimpse of her varicose veins, and thankfully little else.

A heavily tattooed young man of around twenty leaned back

against the wall, scowling at Stark and Nobby as they entered; but he became distracted as the loudspeaker recommenced the high-pitched tirade: 'Nottingham results. First place, Ben Hur, seven to four . . .'

At the far side of the betting office was the main counter, with a perspex shield. Two notices gave the simple instructions 'Bets' and 'Pay Out', and an electrical cash-till was positioned under each sign. The carpet beneath the 'Bets' counter was considerably more worn than that beneath the 'Pay Out' counter. Stark focused beyond the cash-tills to the woman sitting behind them. They walked over to her; she had now taken notice of their arrival. Her name, Stark would discover, was Sally Lawrenson; she was around twenty-five years old and stunningly beautiful, with long, flowing, jet-black hair and full lips which pursed to form the question: 'Police?'

'Yes, love. Detective Inspector Stark, Nottingham CID. I'd like to see Faye Marriott's boss, please.'

Sally answered in a soft, slow voice, which Stark strained to hear. 'I'm sorry, but Bernard Squires is unavailable at the moment. Can he call you on his return?'

Stark allowed himself a glance at Nobby. 'Bernard Squires, eh? Well, will you tell Mr Squires that unless he gets his backside out here sharpish, I'll lay some odds. Ten to one that he doesn't keep his bookmaker's permit long.'

The door to the rear quarters had been ajar; now it was opened wider by the forty-year-old body of Bernie Squires. Gold-rimmed, light-sensitive spectacles adorned his balding head, setting off the white shirt and red bow-tie of one of East London's villainous sons. Cockney charm oozed from the ex-boxer's gnarled face.

'Sally, don't be silly, love. Course I'm here, ain't I? Hello, Mr Stark. How are you? Sorry about that little misunderstanding – you can't get the staff, see?' He shook Stark's hand warmly and then Nobby's. 'And Mr Clarke too! My, we are honoured. I didn't know you were betting men?' Bernie's furrowed brow and raised eyebrows emphasised the question in his voice. He was a big, powerful man, quite an imposing figure, a hard nut. Stark remained unmoved by the purposeful pressure Squires applied during the hand-shaking ceremony. Turning round to see that the shop was now empty, he nodded to his DS. Nobby

36

returned to the door, flicked the catch and turned the yellowing cardboard sign, 'Closed', to face the street.

'It's been a long time, Bernie,' said Stark. 'I'm afraid it's not a social call. Can we talk privately?'

Squires adjusted his glasses unnecessarily. 'Yes, sure, but I have got a business to run, Mr Stark – let's play fair.'

Stark addressed Nobby. 'If you'll talk to the young girl, Bernard and I will use the back office.'

Nobby nodded in agreement. Stark followed the by now sweating Bernie into the small office and closed the door behind him. It was a very small office for such a big man. A tatty old school desk supported a telephone and a flexible lamp. The only other furniture consisted of two PVC-covered chairs and a black plastic swivel office chair, upon which Bernie sat down. A pile of loose papers headed 'Squires Turf Accountants' was strewn messily around the desk. Dusty, wooden-framed certificates hung on the wall next to a picture of Her Majesty the Queen, who looked down regally at her two subjects. Stark, warm in his grey suit jacket, sat on one of the chairs, resting a foot on the other. He lit his pipe, ignoring Bernie, who obviously felt it was for him to break the silence.

'Trouble, is it, Mr Stark?'

'You tell me, Bernie.' A cloud of smoke escaped from the corner of Stark's mouth.

Bernie was getting impatient; he fidgeted in his chair. 'Let's not play games with each other – what's the SP?'

'Murder!' said Stark rather melodramatically.

It had the desired effect. 'You what? It's a joke, ain't it?'

Stark remained serious. 'I'm afraid not, Bernie. You see, it's Faye Marriott.'

'What about Faye? Here – you don't mean . . . What – it's her . . . what's been done?'

'I'm afraid so, Bernie. At home – suffocated.'

Bernie got up from his chair and paced the floor. 'Flaming Nora, I don't believe it! She was here only yesterday. I thought she was ill when she didn't turn up today. Bloody hell, straight up?'

Stark nodded. 'Straight up, Bernie, last night.'

Bernie returned to his chair and buried his head in his hands.

He removed his glasses and wiped a palm over his closed eyes. 'I still can't believe it . . . Have you got him?'

Stark shook his head. There was a pause. Bernie suddenly peered at the detective through a gap in his fingers. 'Here, hold up – you don't think . . . Nah, you can't think . . . Well, in case you do, I was with Tommy Slater in his pub, the Red Lion, till closing time and then I went straight home to bed!'

Stark could see that Bernie was getting bull-faced. 'Nobody's thinking anything at the moment, Bernie. I just want to get to know what I can about the girl. What was she like?'

Bernie shook his head again. 'This is crazy, absolutely crazy! This'll crack our Sally up. I hope your mate breaks it to her gently!'

Stark reassured him. 'He will, don't worry.'

Bernie lit a Park Drive cigarette with a slight tremble in his hands. He blew out a lungful of smoke. 'Well, what do you want to know then?'

'Did you say "our" Sally?' asked Stark.

'Yes, she's my niece. A nice girl is Sally. She's a student working the holidays. She's stony broke, so I bung her a few notes up front and I get the brains where it matters – behind the till.'

'What sort of girl was Faye, though, Bernie?'

'Fifty-two-carat diamond – straight up, mate, she wouldn't hurt a fly. I'm telling you, she was always polite, friendly with the clientele. Pure gold she was, straight!'

'So who would want her dead, Bernie?' asked Stark, chewing on his pipe stem.

'Nobody. There can't be. Listen, it must be somebody what don't know her. She was an angel, gospel truth, Mr Stark.'

'Any boyfriends?'

Bernie looked thoughtful, staring at the ceiling. 'No, I don't think so. Sal will know more about that than me.'

'What about aggro? Do you know if she was in any kind of trouble?'

Bernie shook his head. 'No, she wasn't like that, I've told you – she was just a kid.'

'How did you get on with her, Bernie?'

'Fine. We used to have a laugh together, me and Faye, a bit

of a mess about, slap and tickle, bit of a cuddle . . . You know me, Mr Stark. I love a bit of a giggle.'

'Have you had any problems with her, at work I mean?'

'No, none at all. Oh, I tell a lie – she had a go at me once, in the shop, packed with customers it was as well. I think it was the wrong time, if you know what I mean. She took exception to my bit of fun. I got a knee in the knackers for my trouble too!' Bernie laughed out loud.

'How long has she worked here, Bernie?'

'About eight or nine months, no more. That was another thing, come to think about it.'

'What's that?' asked Stark, interested.

'Her mum and dad didn't take to her working here. I think they were a bit stuck up, but Faye, she used to love the job, she was a happy girl, everyone liked her, especially the boys.'

'Did she enjoy the attention then, or what?' asked Stark.

'What woman doesn't?' said Bernie, smiling.

'How did she get the job here?'

Bernie laughed. 'She just turned up, out of the blue, asked for a job and got one. She even brought a couple of references, but I told her I didn't need any: if she worked hard, she stayed; if she didn't, she went.'

'Who were the references from, can you remember?'

'Oh Gawd, now you're asking. Let me see.' Bernie put his thumb and forefinger on the bridge of his nose and closed his eyes to concentrate. 'One was from her bank manager, whoever he was, and, let me see – yes, the other was from Florence Hodge, one of her old teachers. I'll tell you how I know, because her husband comes in here for the odd flutter on the QT.'

The telephone on Bernie's desk rang. Bernie quickly glanced at his watch and then scowled. He looked at Stark. The phone rang twice more. Bernie still didn't move. Stark, puzzled, looked at Bernie, who smiled back at him nervously.

'Aren't you going to answer it then, Bernie?' asked Stark, intrigued by his reluctance to lift up the receiver.

'No, leave it, I'm busy.' Bernie rubbed the flat of each palm over the tops of his thighs, rocking his upper body. The phone still rang.

'You can't just let it ring,' said Stark.

Bernie's voice was louder, annoyed. 'All right then.' He

picked up the receiver two inches, then dropped it back down again. 'There, that's solved that! Now I hate to hurry you, but I have got a business to run. Are there any more questions, Mr Stark, or is that it?' The telephone bell still resonated in the background.

'No, I think that's about it, Bernie. You could have answered the phone, you know.' Stark was puzzled at Bernie's sudden display of anger.

'Well, that's me – impetuous. If I hear anything that might be of use, I'll be straight on the dog and bone.'

Right on cue the telephone rang again. This time the Inspector was too quick for Bernie and answered it himself, lowering his voice. 'Hello?'

'Yes, Bernie, it's me, old son. I've sorted that little problem out for you, as agreed.' Silence. The voice continued: 'Well, aren't you pleased? You're clean now, Bernie?' No reply. The line went dead.

'Interesting call, Bernie,' Stark observed as he put the phone down.

Bernie attempted a half-smile. 'Who was it? A crank? I've been on to the operator about them. It'll be some nutter – forget it.' He toyed with his watch.

'Oh, I shan't forget it, Bernie. He seemed to know you. Come to think of it, the voice was familiar to me . . . I just can't put a face to it – it'll come to me. You know, it's always amazed me how you ever got a bookmaker's permit,' mused Stark with a wry smile.

Bernie pulled his shoulders back exaggeratedly. 'Upright citizen, Mr Stark, not one conviction to my name. I've been in – what shall I say? – some disagreements with a number of hard men, Jack Tarquin and Sonny Capola to name but two. Yet never once have I been convicted of a criminal offence. And I'll tell you something else: I'm proud of it!'

'What's your secret, Bernie?'

He smiled and winked at Stark. 'Like all good businessmen – delegation!'

Stark laughed and shook his head as the two men returned to the betting office proper. Stark was met with the sight of Sally being comforted by Nobby. He held her tight against his shoulder, patting her head as she drew another hesitant,

gasping breath, crying incessantly. Bernie eyed him suspiciously.

Nobby spoke to the girl. 'There, there, Sally – it's all right.'
He gave Stark a rueful glance.

Stark slapped Bernie on the back. 'There you are – I told you
he'd be gentle with her! Have you finished here, Nobby?'

'Yes, boss, all done. Now listen, Sally, don't forget to give me
a call in three or four days' time and I'll take you for a drink and
we'll talk some more, OK?'

'Now just a minute . . .' started Bernie.

Sally looked up at Nobby from beneath long eyelashes. 'OK,'
she sobbed. 'Thank you, Sergeant Clarke.'

'My pleasure.'

A wall of sunlight hit the two detectives as they stepped out on
to the hot pavement, and the noise of the traffic heightened
their speech into shouts.

'I might have bloody well guessed!' Stark remonstrated.

'What now?' enquired Nobby incredulously, extending his
open palms rather over-enthusiastically.

'You bloody well know what. I leave you for five poxy
minutes and you've all but got your cock out!'

'Oh come on, boss – I was only sympathising with the girl.'

The two men crossed the street, heading for Stark's Cavalier.

'Sympathising! That's what you call it, is it? That's a new
word for it.'

'The girl was upset, for Christ's sake!' exclaimed Nobby.

'Not as upset as she'll be when you dump her in a month's
time for some other tart.'

'Now don't be like that, sir. I'm just a caring, loving
policeman.'

'Yes, whose brains are in his cock!'

Nobby put his arm around the wide shoulders of his Detective
Inspector. 'Do I detect a little jealousy?'

Stark shrugged off Nobby's arm. 'Look, you're starting on me
now! That's about all we'll detect at this rate. Of course I'm
jealous – she's a cracker.'

The two men reached the car and they both leaned against it
while they continued the banter.

'Some of us have got it, some of us haven't.'

Stark laughed. 'Philosophy as well! Where will it all end? I don't suppose you found anything out while you were snogging with Miss World, did you?'

Nobby lit up a cigarette, stepping back to avoid an old dear with a shopping trolley. 'As a matter of fact I did. Apparently Faye had a boyfriend, somebody called Charles. I take it we will pay him a visit next?'

'You don't think it's Charlie Carter do you?' They laughed. 'We'll go and see him once we know where he lives.'

Nobby had his uses. 'That shouldn't be too difficult: he should be in Faye's diary so if we shout Happy Jim up on the radio this Charles should be in it and Jim can pass us the details.'

The two men got into the Cavalier and hastily wound down the windows to let some air into the car.

'DI Stark to Control.'

'Go ahead, sir,' came the reply.

'Talk through with DC McIntyre, please.'

'You've got it, sir.'

'DI Stark to DC McIntyre.'

'Go ahead, David.'

'Yes, Jim. Get hold of Faye's diary – it's in amongst the exhibits. Look for a Charles in it and get back to me with his details.'

'Ever heard of please and thank you? Stand by.'

'God, he's a miserable bastard,' said Stark, annoyed at the DC's disrespect. He started the car and waited for Jim to get his act together. He passed another observation to Nobby. 'You're a jammy bleeder with women.'

'Luck doesn't enter into it, Dave. You've either got it or you haven't.'

Stark's imagination was working overtime. 'I bet she screws like a jack rabbit!'

Nobby looked sideways at Stark. 'I'll let you know.'

The Inspector confided in his Detective Sergeant. 'It'd be nice to solve this one, Nobby. It wouldn't do my promotion prospects any – ' The crackling of the radio cut him short.

'DC McIntyre to DI Stark.'

'Go ahead.'

42

'There was only a telephone number for this Charles, so I've had to mess about ringing Telecom.'

'You poor baby,' thought Stark.

McIntyre continued. 'He lives at 14 Sunrise Cottages, Arnold – it's quite a select area. There's no trace on the Police National Computer for this guy: looks like he's been a good boy. His full name is Charles Edward Lyon.'

'Ten-four, Jim. Any other news?'

'Negative. Nobody's got back to me yet, but I'll keep you posted.'

Stark nudged Nobby; he was smiling.

'DI Stark to DC McIntyre.'

'Go ahead.'

'Yes – in future use "sir" when you address me!'

There was a pause.

'Did you receive, Jim?' Stark wouldn't leave it.

'Yes . . . sir.'

Stark's smile stayed with him as he pulled away in the car. 'We are going to have to get Bernie looked at very closely. What do you reckon, Nobby?'

'I couldn't agree more. I'll look at Sally in great detail.'

'Oh, piss off!'

The detached six-bedroomed house stood palatially in its landscape setting. The big white door displayed a large brass horse's head as a knocker. It was too stiff for Stark to use properly, so he merely hammered on the door with his fist. There was a pause. As he reached to knock again, the door opened. A rather elegant middle-aged woman, wearing a flowery silk scarf and a long, blue corduroy dress, greeted the two strangers.

Stark introduced himself and asked to speak to Charles Lyon. The lady answered in a well-educated voice. 'I'm afraid he's still out, but he is due back at any time now. You are welcome to come in and wait. I hope it isn't anything serious?'

The men didn't answer as they stepped into the hall. The smell of polish on wood underscored the cleanliness of the house. The chime of a grandfather clock emphasised the quietness that embraced the cold living-room into which the two men had been ushered. The décor was lavish; five china ornaments were shelved against the oak-panelled walls; a tiger-skin rug guarded the Adam-style fireplace, the coal in it unlit.

'I'm Mrs Lyon, Charles's mother, in case you hadn't realised. Would you like some tea?'

'Yes please,' Stark replied politely.

'Thank you,' Nobby reinforced.

Mrs Lyon left to prepare the Earl Grey. The two men sat down, each in a high-backed chair that squeaked at the slightest movement.

'What a miserable place this is,' volunteered Nobby.

'It's colder in here than it is outside,' whispered Stark.

Nobby continued his critique. 'They haven't got a television here at all, just a piano – look.'

Stark arched his neck and saw the writing desk over-shadowed by the baby grand piano, complete with silver candelabra.

'I bet they have wow parties here, boss.'

'Everybody isn't such an ignoramus as you are; some people live a more sedate and sophisticated lifestyle,' said Stark.

'Boring you mean,' said Nobby.

Stark felt as if he were in the study of his headmaster, who had just left momentarily. Silence befell the living-room; a far-off chinking of pots indicated the imminent arrival of refreshment. Mrs Lyon re-entered the room and set the silver tray down on the occasional table as she had done on dozens of previous occasions, only this time she knew the conversation would differ from that of the Women's Institute meetings and the vicar's visit the previous Sunday. She felt unusually uncomfortable with her company, as she settled herself in the leather chesterfield.

'What could Charles possibly do for you, Inspector?' she asked.

Stark explained, 'Well, it's to do with his girlfriend, Faye Marriott.'

'Dreadful girl!' interrupted Mrs Lyon. 'Well, no, I don't want to appear unfair, but she was definitely beneath Charles's bracket, if you understand me, Inspector.' Mrs Lyon sipped at her fine china cup.

'I take it you've met her then?' asked Stark, a little peeved at the pomposity.

'Oh no, I haven't met her, but I told Charles from the start not to entertain the likes of her. What is she? Some betting-office clerk or something. How awful! I knew she'd bring trouble!'

'Might I enquire what Charles does for a living?'

Mrs Lyon placed the cup and saucer delicately back on the table. 'He's just started his own business – he can't fail to succeed, he's an absolute darling. I just wish he'd come out of himself a tiny bit more.'

Stark couldn't avoid the mental picture he had conjured up of Mummy Lyon wetting her handkerchief in her mouth and wiping some imaginary mark off the young Lyon's face. He spoke.

'I think we ought to explain the purpose of our visit. It's about Faye Marriott, as I started to tell you – she's dead. Murdered.' The Inspector's face remained emotionless.

Mrs Lyon raised a hand to her mouth. 'Oh, how terrible!'

Stark continued, drily watching the expression on the woman's face. 'In fact, the whole family have been murdered.'

'Oh, how shocking!' Mrs Lyon stood up. 'Who could do such a thing? When was this, Inspector? Today?'

'Last night, we think. Obviously we want to speak to Charles as a matter of routine.'

'Of course, but all last night he was playing bridge with myself and the Crawford twins – they will confirm that.'

They heard the sound of the front door slamming.

"Tis only I, Mother,' came the theatrical, high-pitched greeting.

Charles Edward Lyon entered the room in a blaze of glory. Had it been the eighteenth century he could only have been described as a fop. He wasn't a tall man, and he had about him that immaculately clean look, as if he groomed his curly brown hair every hour on the hour. His turquoise velvet waistcoat and gold watch-chain went well with the silk cravat and stud.

He appeared shocked. 'Good heavens! Company!'

Stark rose from his chair and offered his hand. His compara-tively gruff voice slightly intimidated the sensitive boy. The hand of the former divisional boxing champion met a well-manicured, soft hand that should have belonged to a woman.

'Hello, Mr Lyon. I'm Detective Inspector Stark and this is Detective Sergeant Clarke.'

Stark broke the news as gently as he could and watched the devil-may-care cavalier turn into a quivering wreck. It transpired that Charles had grown to love the betting-shop girl. He'd known her for three months; they had met in the Café Victoria and he had wined and dined her ever since. Embarrassed, he accepted that they had a sexual relationship. They hadn't talked about marriage. She was such a demure girl – carefree. Charles had stayed in all last night playing bridge, as his mother had said previously. He gave the address of the Crawford twins, which would later be positively checked. He saw Faye only two or three times a week, at most. He had last seen her on Tuesday and was supposed to pick her up for a meal tonight at seven o'clock. She had seemed in good spirits when he left her on Tuesday; she didn't appear to have any problems at all. Charles stated that he was her only boyfriend as she didn't mix particularly well; she certainly didn't mention anybody else to him. He occasionally burst into tears whilst answering Stark's questions; he continually mopped the corners of his eyes with his sparkling white, initialled handkerchief. He said that they had discussed spending a couple of weeks in Miami next month, at Charles's expense of course. Faye didn't have many friends – in fact, Charles knew only of a Sally at her work and another girl whom she mentioned a couple of times, a Chantelle Naylor.

Assembled in the cold living-room, they spoke for over an hour. Stark briefly contemplated arresting Charles, to give them something to work on, but Charles's reactions seemed authentic; he had a good alibi and Stark wanted something more positive before diving in with both feet. He wasn't surprised at Charles breaking down; Stark decided, rather harshly, that it was the obvious result of a spoilt, sheltered upbringing, and he gave thanks for the struggle his own life had brought him. Charles was so indecisive, such a mummy's boy, cocooned by suburbia's shell in a naïve sense of security – and yet he was terribly insecure and timid. Stark felt that Charles was afraid of him.

'Fop' looked concerned as the detectives got up to leave. 'Does this mean I'm a suspect, Inspector?' he asked red-faced.

Stark lied. 'Of course not, Charles. You've been a great help.'

They made their farewells and the two men walked down the sheltered drive. Nobby grunted out of the side of his mouth, 'What a bloody wimp!'

'Seems like a nice boy to me,' Stark replied, 'and nice boys don't commit murder, do they?'

Stark and Nobby joined their colleagues and sat around the wooden desks in the CID general office. Everybody had arrived back safe and sound, and began to relate their experiences to each other in a loose debrief. Steph and Ashley related how they had visited Faye's old school as a matter of course and had in fact already spoken to Florence Hodge, the teacher who had given Faye the reference for her job. She agreed with everyone else that Faye was a quiet, fairly intelligent, but selfish girl. She often, surprisingly, appeared a trifle 'snobbish', her former schoolfriends had told the detectives, and a bit of a dark horse. Some still kept in touch with her. Apart from that, very little information had been forthcoming from other members of staff or old schoolfriends whom they had been able to contact.

Charlie and Steve told the group that Walter Marriott was a senior bank clerk who had worked his way up through the ranks of banking the hard way. Walter wasn't a particularly interesting person; he had little social life and spent most evenings either reading or watching television. Enquiries at the bank to see if there were any major customer vendettas had so far proved negative.

Audrey Marriott was a housewife who buried herself in work for the Salvation Army whenever she could, and who doted on her daughter. There were no initial indications that either Walter or Audrey had been unfaithful to each other or of anybody having any motive to kill them.

Paul had been in contact with the Force Intelligence Bureau and glumly informed everybody that within the last year there had been 6968 house burglaries in the Nottingham area involving an attack to the rear kitchen window. He was trying to get hold of any burglars who used the same MO and who also had convictions for sexual offences and/or violence. This, however,

was extremely time-consuming and nothing particularly constructive had been collated. He had issued a teleprinter with
the relevant details on it to all forces and had prepared the basis
of a press release, which Superintendent Wagstaff had given on
the lunchtime radio news. There had been twenty-eight similar
murders in the country in the previous year, but none that
seemed related as yet.

Jim complained that he was getting swamped with his action
sheets and information returns. There was nothing of any great
importance from him that hadn't already been said and he
couldn't 'bloody wait' for the HOLMES computer to be set up
tomorrow.

Stark gave the group the information that he and Nobby had
gathered, then instructed Charlie and Steve to find out if there
were any relations living in the area who could be seen, or any
friends of Walter and Audrey. Stephanie and Ashley were to go
to see Faye's bank manager and, once they'd done that, to visit
as many as they could of those left unseen from the list in
Faye's diary. Paul and Jim were to carry on as before, with Jim
to type a list of all the names in the diary and make photocopies
of the list.

'Would you like me to ride a unicycle at the same time?' asked
Jim, as ever happy with his life.

They were to reassemble at 10.30 p.m.

Stark was itching to talk to Chantelle Naylor. She was in the
diary, and as the detectives got up from the tables Stark began
to tap out the digits on the phone.

A female voice answered. 'Hello?'

'Is Chantelle there, please?' asked Stark.

The woman's voice was coarse. 'Hold on a minute, duck . . .
Chantelle!' she screeched.

A distant voice could be heard. 'What's up? I'm watching
telly. Can't it wait, Mum?'

Her mother was insistent. 'Telephone call – come on, it's a
man.'

Stark heard Chantelle walk heavily to the phone.

'Yes, who is it?' He could hear the sound of chewing gum.

'Hello, Chantelle. It's Detective Inspector David Stark from
Nottingham CID. How are you?'

'All right. Why? What's up?'

48

'Nothing's up, but I would like to come and have a word with you if I can. It's nothing to worry about.'

'Yeah, all right. When are you coming?'

'Now, if I can. It is rather important.'

'Yeah, all right then.'

Stark didn't have her address and did not have time to make enquiries from Telecom.

'I'm just trying to read my mate's handwriting. What street is it again?'

'Damian Villas, Farm Estate.'

'That's it. Number fifty-two,' he guessed.

The girl tutted. 'Number twenty-eight. God, your mate's handwriting must be terrible!'

'Yes, it is.' Stark smiled. 'See you in about twenty minutes then. Put the kettle on, love, won't you?'

'OK? Bye.'

Stark didn't let go of the handset, despite having replaced it on the telephone itself. He thought aloud. 'Damian Villas. That's a bit of a contrast.' He turned to his colleague, sitting to his left. 'Come on, Nobby. I want to introduce you to a nice young lady.'

The concrete block of flats stood six storeys high. At first glance it looked incomplete, due in part to vandals' handiwork during the last riot and in part to a disgruntled architect. Not the sort of place one would choose to live – but, then, the occupants had no choice in the matter.

The metal outer security-door had long since ceased to secure anything. The smell of urine in the corridor was dissipated as the nostrils became accustomed to it. Stark had learned as a young PC many years ago not to hold on to the handrail of steps as one walked up, because of the human excrement smeared on it by people with a sense of humour alien to his own understanding. As the two detectives weaved their way up the steps, Stark asked Nobby what motivated people to draw penises all over the walls. Nobby couldn't answer.

Number 28 Damian Villas had a yellow-coloured door with two glass panels, one upper and one lower. Stark noticed that the lower panel had been replaced by chipboard, as had many others in the block. The problem was that it was too easy for the local tow-rags to kick in the lower panel and take whatever they could get their grubby little hands on. These weren't homes: they were just places where people lived.

Chantelle was twenty years old. Her natural blonde hair was permed and fluffed out, away from her head; her blue eyes could melt ice and tug at the heartstrings of any red-blooded male. Her skin had never felt the heat of a tropical sun, but it was tanned, and played its part in emphasising her pearly-white teeth. Her pert, nubile young body fought to get out of the skimpy, one-piece mini-dress that she wore most days. Nobby's mouth dropped open as the goddess greeted the two startled detectives. Stark wondered how such beauty could emanate from such a shit hole.

Chantelle had a lot going for her in life, appearance-wise, but elocution wasn't her strong point. 'Eh-up. You're the coppers, aren't you? You'd better come in.'

Stark wanted to know how nature, after creating such beauty, could drop it into this environment and allow her to be dragged up in such deprivation. Nobby's eyebrows were raised; his practised eye noticed that Chantelle didn't have any knickers on under the skimpy dress. Her perfectly formed buttocks displayed not a hint of a line or indentation. That indescribable chemical reaction that has ruined many a happily married man began to stir deep down within Nobby's loins.

Chantelle ruined the moment. She spoke. 'First of all there's no bent gear here, so you've shit out!'

Stark laughed. 'You don't think we'd ring up and make an appointment if we wanted bent gear do you? It's about Faye Marriott. Do you mind if we sit down?'

Chantelle extended an arm. 'No, suit yourselves. Mum's out at Bingo. You didn't want her as well, did you?'

Stark and Nobby sat on the worn furniture, the cigarette burns all too apparent. The carpet had a sticky feel to it.

'No, love, we don't want to speak to your mum.'

Stark didn't know which family the coat-of-arms portrayed, but it was plastic and it had two swords sticking out of it. Every other flat in the block displayed one on its wall, along with the cheap picture of a boy crying and the overfilled ashtrays.

He went on: 'Chantelle, I've got some bad news for you. It's Faye . . .' His voice trailed off.

'Why, what's she done?' asked Chantelle.

'Nothing, but I'm afraid she's been attacked. It's bad, Chantelle – it's very bad. I'm afraid she's dead.'

Stark just caught it. A fraction of a second of grief and pain appeared on her face before the years of accepting adversity slammed shut the doors of real emotion.

'I'll go and put the kettle on.' Chantelle left the room wearing the vacant stare that Stark had seen too many times. He could hear the muffled crying in the kitchen.

Nobby's insensitivity rose to the surface. 'You know she hasn't got any knickers on, don't you?'

Stark shook his head. 'For Christ's sake, Nobby!'

Nobby protested. 'Oh, come on, boss, she's gorgeous. I'd bet a month's pay that she's got no knickers on and no bra on either!'

'All right, I'm not blind, you know!'

The two men watched the end of *Wogan* on the large, rather ancient television set in the corner of the room. Chantelle returned with two white mugs; they had that unmistakable dried tea-stain on the side that hadn't been caused by this pouring. Stark explained the sorry tale to a now more sullen Chantelle. She had got over the initial shock and was starting to come to terms with everything; she was starting to get her brief relationship with Faye into perspective. She had only really known Faye as a drinking partner rather than as a close friend.

Chantelle spared an occasional glance at Stark's well-built colleague. She knew he was staring at her breasts and instinctively her nipples grew erect. Stark was attempting to be the soul of tact, but the size of her nipples diverted his gaze and he began to get lost in mid-sentence. Chantelle began to feel hot.

Stark had enquired how she and Faye had met; they didn't seem to have a lot in common. How wrong he was.

'I met her at Penny's Night Club. It was quite funny, really, because my mate had gone off with somebody and her mate had as well, so we got talking.'

'Did you arrange to see her again or what?'

Chantelle crossed her legs slowly as she sat on the settee,

facing the two men. 'No. We were talking and these two black guys came up and asked if we wanted to dance, so we did. Before we knew it we were back at a flat at Hyson Green.'

'Then what?' Stark enquired.

'They screwed us, of course. In fact both of them screwed me. Faye just had one of them.'

Nobby coughed into his tea, spilling some of it.

Chantelle smirked, savouring her audience's reaction. 'Are you all right, duck, or do you want me to get you a cloth?'

'No, I'm fine.' Nobby's face rapidly reddened.

The Inspector continued his questioning. 'Was Faye into that sort of thing then, Chantelle?'

'I don't know. But if she wasn't then, she certainly was from that moment on.'

'How do you mean?'

'Well, she couldn't get enough of it. She's like me.' Chantelle glanced at Nobby, who smiled at her but then looked away as she met his gaze full on.

'So she used to go out shagging regularly then?' asked Stark, adapting to his common surroundings.

Chantelle laughed. She lit up a half-smoked cigarette that she had fished out of the full ashtray on the settee arm. 'Not half! She used to give her phone number out like confetti. She used to get more blokes than me, for some reason. We joked once that if I could talk all posh like her, I could become Miss World, but she said I'd be Miss Turkey 'cos I'm the best gobbler!' Chantelle imitated all the best pantomime witches as she threw her head back and shrieked out a raucous cackle of a laugh, which drowned Stark's and Nobby's embarrassed attempts.

'So how long have you known Faye?' Stark went on, amazed at the honesty of the conversation.

'About six months.' Chantelle coughed throatily into her mug.

'How many times have you been out with her, Chantelle?'

'We used to go out two or three times a week. Sometimes I couldn't afford it, but she would help me out. Apparently one of her boyfriends was loaded, so she had it made.'

'Was she on the game, Chantelle?'

Her pretty mouth opened, aghast. 'You cheeky bleeder! No, she wasn't and before you ask, neither am I.'

'How many boyfriends did Faye have?'

Chantelle screwed the cigarette butt into the others in the ashtray. 'Oh Christ. Let me think . . . She used to score most nights. She never took them home, though – I think her dad used to give her some grief about going home so late. I don't think her mum even knew she went home late. Faye once told me that her mother still thought she was a virgin. I ask you!' Chantelle's eyeballs rolled upwards to emphasise her apparent incredulity.

Stark's mind was quick. 'So if she scored twice a week for six months, that's forty-eight men. Did she keep any names or phone numbers, other than in her diary?'

Chantelle shrugged her shoulders. 'I don't know, to be honest.'

'Did she used to confide in you at all?'

Chantelle nodded. 'A fair bit, but I've told you all there is to know really. There's no secret or owt like that.'

Stark was persistent. 'Did she have any arguments or any enemies?'

'I don't think so. Although she was forever complaining about someone at work, but I didn't pay any attention to her so I can't tell you any more than that.'

'Did you go out with her last night?' asked Stark.

'Yes, we went out about eight o'clock and ended up at Blitz's Night Club.'

Stark took the obligatory written statement. Chantelle explained how the two had gone out together; they had been to the Star and Garter, the Princess, the Sentinel, and had completed the evening's festivities at Blitz's at about eleven o'clock. They had become split up at around midnight. She had seen Faye smooching with a guy about ten minutes later and then she didn't see her again. This, however, was not particularly unusual. Chantelle had not seen the man Faye was dancing with before; all she could say was that he was a white man, mid-twenties, brown hair, quite attractive, wearing a white shirt and grey trousers. She had then seen Faye talking to Winston Kelly, a black guy whom Faye knew quite well. That was about it.

Chantelle signed the declaration at the top of the first page and at the foot of each subsequent page.

The two men left the flat, their footsteps reverberating, hollow, as they walked down the corridor and on to the steps. Chantelle's door slammed shut behind them.

'Still want to screw her then, Nobby?' asked Stark, smiling.

'What a waste, though, isn't it?'

Stark nodded. 'It sure is.'

Nobby stopped in his tracks. 'Flaming hell – just look at that!'

Hatred is expessed in many ways, and on this particular occasion it took the form of human excrement neatly placed on the bonnet of the red Ford Escort CID car.

'I'll go and get some paper,' said Nobby.

Stark shook his head and smiled to himself. He shouted after Nobby: 'Don't bother – he'll be miles away by now!'

The group of detectives had decided to discuss the day's events in the public house that had been so conveniently built next door to the police station. After Nobby had got the drinks in, he told the others about Chantelle and her 'chapel hat pegs'. The conversation then took a more constructive turn and the subject of murder had priority. Jim explained that SOU had finally finished the fingertip search and had seized three miscellaneous pieces of paper, two bottle tops, a used condom, six cigarette ends and a plastic loop thing.

'What's a plastic loop thing?' enquired Stark, understandably.

Jim attempted to describe the object more eloquently. 'Well, if you look at your shoelaces, the ends of them have got a plastic loop thing on them, to stop them fraying. It's one of those.'

'Is it traceable?' asked Stark.

'I don't know yet. I'll check in the morning if people stop giving me mountains of jobs to do.'

'What about the condom?'

'That's nothing. It was half buried, and perished. It's been there ages.'

'And these are all out of the back garden?'

'Yes.'

Nobody else had a great deal to say to each other about murder. Nobby crudely began comparing Stephanie with Chantelle. Steph joined in the tease and stuck out her chest, which pleasantly surprised Nobby, as there was little difference in the women's proportions. Stark decided it was time to leave and head towards home; tomorrow was going to be another long day and all the unanswered questions were dancing around his head to the accompaniment of the loud pop music blaring from the jukebox.

'Aren't you stopping behind, boss?' asked Steph.

'No, I'm going to be boring and get off home. See you all.'

The River Trent is the pride of the Nottingham Tourist Board. It sweeps majestically through the south side of the city, dividing the two famous football clubs, which dwarf the occasional passing barge or river-boat. Despite the lateness of the hour, the faithful anglers were there on the bank. Staring meditatively at the bobbing floats, they failed to see a shadowy figure creep down the worn track across on the far side of the river.

The killer had had a nightmare of a day, wanting to speak about it, tell someone, anyone, but not daring to. The clothes had been burnt; the remnants were now in a large metal tin, which in turn had been placed in a dustbin-liner along with the video and the screwdriver; the bag had been sealed tight.

The splash it made as it hit the water was heard by several anglers. A couple of them craned their necks in an attempt to ascertain the cause; the rest didn't bother. None of them had seen the bag hit the water, nor the person scrambling, somewhat clumsily, up the banking in the darkness.

It was a relief. Surely now the killer was safe? Surely it could now all be forgotten? Surely the police could never find out?

Dave Stark pulled into his drive. He couldn't remember a lot about the journey home; the unanswered questions wouldn't go away. It looked as though Carol had waited up. He tried to close the door quietly, and he removed his shoes in the hallway. It was after midnight and he would at last see his wife; his children would be asleep in their beds.

He was proud of his family and of what he had built up. Fleetingly, his mind returned to the first day he saw Carol, seventeen years ago. He was a young Detective Constable, investigating a series of thefts in a large office block. He had to spend a lot of time there in an attempt to catch the offender. The management had given them full co-operation and access to all personal files. A young woman in the Personnel Department was most helpful. Her name – Carol Needham. She was a pretty little thing, who gave out a warmth and genuine kindness; her smile would light up the office. Her naïvety and vulnerability drew Dave to her. He envied her innocence, wanting to protect it for her, wanting to taste it, wishing he still had some left. She wasn't a tall girl – five foot three. She was slim and always dressed immaculately. She had short, light-brown hair and wide, sparkling eyes, like the eyes of a child on Christmas morning. When Carol laughed, nothing else mattered.

Dave first saw her as he sat scrutinising some documents; she spilled some coffee on his trousers – she was most apologetic and embarrassed. Dave reminded her of the accident the following week when he asked her out to dinner. She couldn't refuse. Dave arrested the office thief – a cleaner – and his job there finished, but he knew the love that had grown for Carol would never diminish.

After their marriage Carol had settled into her role well, but the obverse of her innocence was her continual need to be held and caressed. Dave, playing the role of hard man at work, struggled with the sometimes sapping business of continually showing his love to Carol at home. He refused to tell her about the horrific incidents at work; it was bad enough that he had to go through them, without subjecting Carol to them. It was often hard when, after spending all day with a four-year-old who had been perverted, who thought the most bizarre sexual acts were a normal occurrence for a boy, Stark then had to be friendly with the offender, almost condone his acts, so that he could feel at ease to admit them. To come home and then discuss the shopping or some ridiculous soap opera was rather odd. Dave took comfort in the feeling that Carol *almost* fully understood the predicament; she could now read his moods and she very rarely queried the late nights, the special occasions ruined, or the rest days cancelled. And here they were, seventeen years later, still together and, more importantly, still happy.

Today had been a strain for Dave. He stretched and loosened his tie before entering the living-room. Carol was wearing a pair of his pyjamas, the sleeves a foot too long. She got off the settee, standing to greet her husband; her eyes looked tired as they blinked to focus on the tall man in the white shirt. She put her arms round him and kissed him.

'You look as if you were fast asleep, love,' said Dave, happy to be home.

'I was. How are you?' She rested her head on his chest and closed her eyes. Her impish features smiled; she was happy to be reunited with him.

Stark squeezed her lovingly. 'OK. Are you?'

'Yes, apart from Christopher and Laura messing about all night. They're in bed now.'

'What have they been doing?' asked the vaguely concerned father, with more burning questions on his mind.

Carol said, 'I don't know what's the matter with them . . .'

Dave released his grip on his wife and collapsed into the soft armchair. Carol continued talking to herself: '. . . they've been at each other's throats all day long. I'll be glad when the six weeks' holidays are over and they get back to school. Are you taking Christopher to the football match tomorrow?'

'Sorry, love – what did you say?' Stark rubbed his eyes.

'You're not listening, are you? I said, are you taking Christopher to the football match tomorrow?'

'No. I'm sorry, love, I'm going to be tied up at work tomorrow. I did tell you that on the telephone.'

'Oh yes, of course, those murders . . . You're not even safe in your own home, are you? That Mr Wagstaff's dealing with it, isn't he?'

'Well, sort of, but in truth – ' He was interrupted.

'It's terrible, isn't it? I saw it on television. Does he know who's done it yet?'

'No, not yet. It's going to be an awkward one, I think. Still, it's early days. I'm hoping that by the end of tomorrow we'll know exactly where we stand.'

'Are you going to be late again tomorrow, then?'

'It certainly looks that way, love, yes.'

Carol dropped down on to her husband's knee. He let out an exaggerated gasp. She was sarcastic. 'Oh sorry, I'll go and sit in the corner of the room, shall I?'

Stark was too tired to argue. 'Don't be like that, love. I just want some breathing space, that's all.'

There was a pause. Dave put on a silly voice, as if he had a sore throat. 'Do you love me, Carol?'

'What do you want?'

'Charming! Just a little whisky would be nice.'

Carol screwed her face up. 'Ah, can't we go to bed? I'm tired. I haven't stopped all day, you know.'

'Well, you go up. My mind's still going round. I'll be up in a couple of minutes.'

'Well, don't be too long. I want that cuddle you promised me on the phone.'

Carol poured him a whisky and kissed him before going upstairs to bed. Dave clung on to his crystal glass and closed his eyes. His body had stopped moving but his mind raced, darting and dancing around in a whirlpool of ideas and images, occasionally stopping at incidents that had scarred the tissue: a naked girl brutally murdered; the post-mortem; Paul Fisher's lunch; Bernie Squires; Charles 'Fop' Lyon; Chantelle's breasts; Winston Kelly . . . That name rang a bell . . .

Eventually tiredness battered down the jack-in-a-box images and Stark struggled upstairs to bed. An hour passed. He snuggled up to his now sleeping wife. He thought of his daughter Laura, sixteen next birthday, a young woman now; his son young Christopher, a rumbustious thirteen. He smiled. The image of last Saturday's football together in the park healed the scars in his mind. He had never had that: his father was a bully of a man who had chosen drink and left when Dave was a mere boy. He stroked his wife's slim stomach and thought of Chantelle in that dingy flat, striving to get some cheap bit of attention. He thanked God he was who he was.

As Stark eased into a restless sleep, the end of the first day of a murder enquiry drew to a close.

4

'The biggest sin is sitting on your ass.'
Florynce Kennedy

A hundred years ago, if there had been a murder in Nottinghamshire, the local constabulary would have sent for Scotland Yard to investigate it. This would have involved one or two detectives travelling from London to the area of the murder, at the expense of the local police. Eventually the provincial forces began to question this policy, and the whole process of major investigations was examined at great length. It transpired that there was no mystical secret to Scotland Yard's success. Their investigation revolved around a card-index system which they would initiate immediately upon their arrival. This index would incorporate the details of every person who could possibly have any connection with the murder or any other single aspect of its circumstances. Then, by a process of elimination, a short-list would be produced and, with the aid of other detective skills, the offender would be brought to the surface. The provincial forces decided that they were capable of doing this for themselves, and until the recent advent of the computer age, the process remained unchanged.

It is generally well known that most murders are of a domestic nature. These are obviously relatively easy to detect, as they are usually committed in the heat of the moment, and heat cools down bringing remorse and guilt. If, nevertheless, no husband or wife or lover gives themselves up and confesses, then the murderer has usually in any case made so many mistakes that a probationary PC can detect them.

The sort of murder that faced Detective Inspector Stark, however, is far more problematic. Where there is nothing in particular staring the police in the face, no set motive, no common link, where the murder appears to be a quirk, a one-off – that's when heels have to be dug in and all available resources deployed, including the old process of elimination techniques. These, however, are now made considerably less wearisome by the use of the HOLMES computer. It was this wonder of modern technology that was available to Stark as he sat in Detective Superintendent Wagstaff's office. Wagstaff had obviously tried to personalise his working environment. A large trout hung in a glass case on the wall above the surprisingly modern grey desk with green trim; an array of group photographs was company for the trout. The papers on his desk were all very neatly placed in three piles. A green flexible lamp and matching telephone stood symmetrically on the desk.

Wagstaff, wearing a blazer, twisted round in his chair; he held on to his lapels, thumbs sticking up, as he concentrated on the rudiments of Stark's account of the investigation.

'. . . so that's how the enquiry stands at the moment, sir,' finished Stark.

'Mmmm – we need an inroad, a break,' Wagstaff said to the wall.

Stark moved his head closer in an attempt to get within the field of Wagstaff's vision. 'That's right, sir, we'll just have to make our own luck.'

'So what's your plan of attack for today then, David?' Wagstaff enquired.

Stark was ready for the question. 'Well, the first thing is the setting up of the HOLMES computer.'

'Yes. I'll come to headquarters to do that with you. There's another press conference at midday.'

Stark thanked God that most Superintendents weren't like the ageing Wagstaff. He continued relating his plan for the day. 'There's plenty the lads can be doing from yesterday's activities. SOU can carry on house-to-house enquiries: the people that weren't in yesterday should be today, with it being a Saturday. I've got to decide what manpower I will need from sub-divisions and in what way I will deploy them. I'm going to use my lads for the main body of the investigations; SOU and staff from other divisions can do the slogging.'

Wagstaff made his comment. 'Right, David, it looks as though you've got your finger on the pulse. I'll see you in about half an hour. If you sort your men out with their various jobs, then we'll travel over to headquarters at Sherwood Lodge.'

'There is just one other thing, sir.'

'What's that, David?'

'I'd like to lead from the front of this one. I don't want to become part of the furniture at Sherwood Lodge.'

'That's understandable, David. I'll co-ordinate things from the Incident Room for you, once the wheels are in motion. You've got a free rein.'

'Great. See you in a bit then.' The excited Detective Inspector left the office.

Wagstaff allowed himself a wry smile as he leaned back in his chair.

Stark was in an ebullient mood as he entered the packed CID office. 'Morning, team. Right – where's my tea? Come on, Steve, get your act together! You know the aide to CID always makes the tea for the boss!'

The timid Steve went red. He mumbled, 'Sorry, sir.'

Stark addressed the portly figure in tweed. 'Now, Charlie, what's this about some witness?'

'Well, there's only three basic witnesses at the moment. There's the milkman that found the bodies, somebody called Ernest Gray, and – would you believe it? – an ex-copper, Peter Glover.'

Paul sat to Charlie's left in his one ill-fitting light-blue suit. 'He should be a hell of a good witness,' he said. 'What did he see?'

'His Ford Sierra had broken down nearby and as he was looking under the bonnet, apparently he saw somebody running away from the direction of the murder,' Charlie replied.

'Great stuff. He and I joined the force together,' Paul said.

'He'll be a fine one then if he's joined with you!' mocked Stark.

Paul defended himself. 'We had some good men join us that year.'

'That's what Hitler said in 1939!' retorted Charlie.

'Who asked you, you old fart?'

'Now girls, no bickering,' said Stark.

61

Steve Aston returned with the cup of tea. His brown Hush Puppies made no sound and Stark gave an exaggerated jump as Steve suddenly appeared at his side. 'You must stop doing that,' he said, laughing. Steve lowered his head and gave a sickly grin as he turned away; he wanted to reply, but couldn't think of anything.

Stark spoke to the group. 'Listen, I'm going to have to go and set up the HOLMES computer this morning with old Wagstaff. Jim, you'd better come with me and bring all the returns you've got so far.' Jim tutted. Stark continued: 'Paul, if you know this Peter Glover you might as well take the statement off him. Ashley, if you take a statement off Ernest Gray, and Charlie, you do the milkman. The rest of you get a couple of actions off Jim and carry on. I want you to put the word out on the street, use your own informants and keep me posted. From this morning the enquiry will be based in the Incident Room at Sherwood Lodge, so we can get out of the way of the lads who are holding the fort. There's a main briefing at 2.30 p.m. in the Parade Room, which is next door to the Incident Room: make sure you're there. Good luck, and I'll see you later.'

'Cheers, boss. See you, sir,' came the various replies, as Stark disappeared out of the room.

Jim spoke: 'So it looks like I've got the short straw again. I do all the work while the gaffers sit on their arses all day – typical.'

'Privilege of rank, Jim,' Steph commented philosophically.

The phone rang. Paul's suit jacket stretched as he reached to pick it up. 'CID, DC Fisher.'

The lady caller spoke from the downstairs counter. 'Paul, I've got a Peter Glover at the counter asking for CID.'

'Bring him up, love, will you?'

Six years before, Pete Glover had looked as though he had a very bright career in the police service ahead of him until he fell foul of the Police Complaints and Discipline Procedure. He had been in the force only ten months and was still a probationary PC when it all went wrong. A young black woman had been caught glue-sniffing at the back of a deserted warehouse by Pete and Paul Fisher. Paul had gone to radio in; on his return he found the black woman had a broken jaw and a bruised eye. She complained and produced a mystery witness, a supposed passer-by. They believed her, and Glover was persuaded to resign. Paul Fisher remained adamant to the present day that Peter was innocent and that, as he said, she injured herself whilst wild and strong in a drug-crazed outburst.

Glover's short-lived police career might have been a blessing in disguise: he was now a manager of an insurance company; he had a company car, a fat salary, perks and was doing very well for himself. He certainly wasn't bitter about what had happened, and he was public-spirited enough to attend Nottingham Police Station, of his own volition, to make a written statement. Paul Fisher was sure of one thing: that if Pete Glover had any information it would be completely accurate.

As Pete stood in the doorway of the CID office he grinned cheekily, a sparkle in his eye. His curly brown hair was longer than Paul had remembered.

'Bloody hell – Paul Fisher!'

Paul smiled at his old friend. 'Charming! What a greeting!'

'I didn't know you were on CID, Paul,' said Pete.

'It's been a while since I've seen you.' Paul stood up and shook the hand of his former colleague. It was good to see him again. 'You must be doing very well for yourself – double-breasted suits and a Pierre Cardin tie, unless I'm very much mistaken.'

'You always did have an eye for fashion, Paul.'

The two reminisced. 'Is her with the exceedingly large breasts still on the job?' They talked freely with each other about old times, they insisted that they keep in touch, and eventually Paul took his statement.

It transpired that Pete in fact had no knowledge of the Marriott family at all; he could only give an account of what he had seen that night. He had been driving back from Traditions Night Club and was about half a mile from home when his car began juddering and he had to pull in. This was at about a quarter to one in the morning. Whilst Pete was looking at the engine he heard a scream; he didn't bother investigating it as he was slightly pissed and it was probably a 'domestic'. A minute or so later he saw a man run down the opposite side of the street, towards Hucknall. The man was carrying something, but he was unsure what. Peter had run a few steps but didn't have much chance of catching him, so he left it. After a while he walked to the all-night petrol station and filled his portable petrol can with a gallon of petrol. This did the trick and he was able to drive home. It was only this morning that he heard about the murders on the radio and wondered if the incident could be connected. Pete hadn't had a good look at the man running in the dimly lit street: the description was basic – about six feet tall, slim build, wearing dark clothing. It was a start if nothing else.

Glover signed the statement. Despite the promises to keep in touch, Paul didn't expect to see him again. Peter had moved up a notch in the social bracket, and anyway, Traditions was for yuppies.

In the room adjacent to Paul's sat Ashley Stevens and Ernest Gray. Two more different men you couldn't imagine.

Ashley was probably the most handsome and best-dressed CID officer on the division. His hair gelled and quiffed, he wore a double-breasted suit, a white silk shirt and a Paisley tie. A gold watch and signet ring set off the package perfectly.

Sitting opposite him across the wooden desk was a man about forty years old. He needed a shave – in fact both of his chins needed a shave. His unkempt, straggly hair hung limply over his long-out-of-date 'Elvis' sideburns. The oily stains visible on his stubby fingers had not been acquired that day, but served to disguise the nicotine stains which were being reinforced by a Park Drive cigarette, spewing out smoke that irritated Ashley's eyes. Ernest Gray's boiler-suit displayed his one virtue: he worked very hard. He had worked as an odd-job man at the colliery for eighteen years, 'man and boy', and he had only had four days off sick in all that time.

He explained his story to the man who would never have oily hands. He had finished work early for once on the night in question; at about twenty-five to one in the morning he started the trek home, through Maple Close and up to the council estate perched at the top of the hill, where he lived. As he turned into Maple Close he heard a scream: 'Don't, please, I beg you, please, no!' He, like Glover, had assumed that it was a couple arguing and paid it no heed. A minute or so later he saw a man running full pelt along the back of Maple Close, away from Hucknall, towards Bulwell. He had only seen him from behind, but he appeared to be carrying something as he ran. The man was about six feet tall with a slim build. He couldn't give a better description because Maple Close was a dimly lit street. Ashley asked him if he had seen a man under the bonnet of a car and Ernie said he had.

Ashley finished off the self-description with great relief and opened the door to let some oxygen into the by now smoke-filled room. He bade farewell to the dirty man and watched him as he coughed his way out of the main door of the police station.

Paul and Ashley compared notes and passed the information through to the Incident Room at Sherwood Lodge.

'At least it looks as if we've got some people who have actually seen the killer,' said Paul.

Ashley replied thoughtfully. 'Yes. The problem is, Pete Glover and Ernest Gray say that the man was running in two different directions.'

'That's for Stark to sort out. Anyway, I know who my money's on,' said Paul.

'Hello, here's happy Charlie,' said Ashley. Paul turned to see the dishevelled detective shuffle in with a long face.

'Piss off about happy. I've just spent over an hour with that prat of a milkman. What a miserable bleeder he is!'

'What did he have to say?' asked Paul. 'Anything sparkling?'

'No. He found the bodies and phoned the police. He reckons he might have touched some of the things inside, but he's not sure.' Charlie dropped into a chair and lit a cigar. He wasn't getting any younger.

Paul laughed. 'I take it you cancelled the Marriotts' milk then?'

'Ha bloody ha!' A spent match bounced off Paul's head.

Ernest Gray felt quite pleased with himself as he walked home. Who would have thought that one day he would be the police's star witness in a murder case? He couldn't wait to tell the lads in the Ginders' Arms about his little adventure. His wife, Violet, was in the kitchen when he arrived home. Violet was a buxom woman; she wore a small apron and screwed her mascara'd eyes up at Ernest as he came in, any love long since gone; her

65

contempt for the fat, dirty man festered away inside her. She greeted him with more than a hint of acid in her voice: 'And where the hell have you been?'

'Here we go! Do you mind if I get in first, before you start?'

Violet over-emphasised her banging around of pots and pans and cupboard doors. She scowled out another sentence. 'I'm asking you a question, Ernest Gray, and I expect an answer!'

Ernie was still flushed with excitement. 'As a matter of fact, it's got absolutely nothing to do with you and I'm not sure I should tell you with a gob like yours!'

Violet was annoyed. She stood in the doorway which separated the kitchen from the living-room. 'Do you know, in eighteen years of marriage you've never once volunteered to tell me where you're going? Do you think that's normal, do you, eh?'

'I shouldn't have to report to you every verse end – I'm a grown man, for Christ's sake!' Ernie wanted to hurt her; he was glad he had come home early that night, despite everything.

'A man, are you? So why do you behave like an insignificant nobody?'

'Oh, hark at the long words! Well this nobody has been to see the CID.'

Violet's pursed lips opened in complete surprise. 'You've done what!'

Ernie felt a little intimidated as Violet came and stood immediately in front of her seated antagonist.

'I've been to the police station and given a written statement to the CID.' Ernie picked up the tabloid newspaper from the side of the armchair.

'What about?' Violet stood firm, her concern rapidly increasing.

Ernie spoke into the now opened newspaper. 'About the murders on Maple.' He was smiling, pleased with himself. Violet sat down in the other chair. Ernie was loving every minute of it.

'Well, what can you possibly know about the murders, Ernie?'

He glanced at his wife. 'Oh, it's Ernie now, is it?'

She was losing. She barked at him, 'Stop being so bloody stupid. I'm being serious!'

Ernie leaned back into his armchair, before the revelation. 'I've seen the killer!'

Violet screwed her face up again. 'You've done what?'

Ernie put the paper on his lap and looked her in the face. 'I've seen the killer. I didn't know it was him at the time, but it's him all right.'

'Well, where did you see him?'

'The CID treated me like royalty, they did. "Anything we can do for you, Ernie," they said, "just let us know."' Ernie clasped his hands behind his head and stuck his chest out proudly.

Violet persisted. 'I said where did you see him, Ernie?'

'That night, of course, just as I was coming home. I saw him run off towards Bulwell town centre, down Maple Close. Carrying something he was, too.'

'Which way was he running?' she asked, her face puzzled.

'I've told you, towards Bulwell. Why?' He released his hands and let them rest on the paper in his lap.

Violet rose from the chair and shouted at her bemused husband. 'You never get anything right, do you? You are the most stupid, ridiculous person I have ever met!'

Ernie raised his hands and shrugged his shoulders. 'What have I said now?'

Violet picked her thin jacket up off the chair back. 'I'm going to my mother's. You can get your own bleeding dinner!' She stormed out of the room and slammed the door shut behind her.

Ernie tutted. 'Women! I don't believe them – they're bloody mental!' He reopened the paper and marvelled at the young strumpet displaying her assets for people just like Ernie.

5

'Forgive your enemies, but never forget their names!'
John F. Kennedy (1917–1963)

Steven Aston was excited. Two weeks ago he had been patrolling the streets of Nottingham, sorting out domestic disputes, fighting the elements. He had loved the job, the variety and everything about it, but he wanted more. Steve hadn't joined the police to report motorists for having a light out; there was a place for that, but he had joined to catch criminals. A lot of policemen looked down on him for his eccentric ways, but his heart was in the right place and he would always give one hundred per cent. It was the rewarding feeling of putting a real criminal behind bars, of protecting the public so that they could live their lives without encountering that nasty side of life, that had prompted him to apply to be a member of the Criminal Investigation Department. To be a detective. He still had a hell of a way to go, but this was his chance. He wasn't certain that he would get into the department, but nothing ventured, nothing gained; and after his interviews with Detective Superintendent Wagstaff and Detective Chief Superintendent Davies he was told that his application had been accepted and he would start shortly as aide to CID, with his mentor David Stark as his Detective Inspector. Now here he was, acting Detective Constable Aston, on a three-month trial.

Steve's stomach churned as he sat in the Parade Room at headquarters, next to the Incident Room. Here he was, just two weeks into his aideship, part of a murder investigation. He couldn't help but feel slightly uncomfortable as he looked around the crowded briefing room. He sat plumb in the centre of the room, surrounded by a wealth of experienced officers; he was conscious of his bright ginger hair, making him stand out from the rest. There were more than twenty detectives, two units of SOU, and two Detective Sergeants hovering near the front. There were no tables in the room, which had a glass ceiling, the pastel décor adding to the brightness of the sunlight that streamed through the panes of glass. Everybody was chatting excitedly and sporadic bursts of laughter would erupt from time to time. Steve hadn't had time to forge any friendships within the department, and if it hadn't been for Paul Fisher, sitting to his left, who had taken him under his wing, he would have felt even more uncomfortable.

Paul sensed his uneasiness. 'What's the matter with you, Steve?'

His neighbour replied, 'Sorry, Paul – I was miles away. How do you think it's going so far?'

'OK, but I can see it dragging out at this rate.'

Steve laughed quietly. He gave the response he thought he should give. 'There'll be a lot of overtime going, though, if it does.'

Paul felt protective towards Steve; he was a nice lad, but Paul thought he might struggle on the department. He said, 'You've done well getting involved in a murder on your aide, haven't you?'

Steve shrugged. He never quite knew what to say for fear of saying the wrong thing. 'I suppose so. There's nothing like being thrown in at the deep end, is there?'

The two men's conversation was interrupted by a loud, deep voice. It was Wagstaff. 'Right, gentlemen, can I have your attention, please?'

'*Quiet!*' shouted Nobby. The men got the message and silence prevailed. Wagstaff continued his address, with Inspector Stark looking on. 'Thank you, Sergeant Clarke.' Nobby acknowledged the thanks with a nod. Wagstaff, in blazer and razor-sharp grey flannels, only needed a yardstick and a drill square and he was away. He settled for 'his' men's full attention.

'For those of you that don't know me, you should. I'm Detective Superintendent Wagstaff.' The moustache twitched. 'I'm heading this murder enquiry, but in my wisdom I've decided to allow Detective Inspector Stark a free run at cracking it, under my discerning eye of course. I'm going to be in or around the Incident Room while Mr Stark gets involved in the exciting bits. Now because of this it will be Mr Stark who gives you the briefing proper this morning. All I will say is this: in an investigation of this sort, any one small piece of information could be crucial once it's married up to the full facts of the case. It only takes one irresponsible copper to overlook it and we're in shit street. Make sure you're not that copper!' Steve swallowed hard. 'Now I'll pass you over to Mr Stark. Happy hunting.'

Stark stood six foot one in his stocking soles; his broad shoulders were tight in his grey pin-striped suit. A small bead of sweat trickled down the side of his face from underneath his brown hair, which was smart, cropped short. He replaced Wagstaff at centre stage and took a deep breath before commencing his monologue. He held a briefing sheet in his right hand.

'Good morning, gentlemen, I'm Detective Inspector Stark. Remember my name, because if any of you are unsure about something or have a suggestion about the case, I urge you to discuss it with me. It might be important, and I will never criticise anyone for trying to do what we are being paid for, and at this precise moment it's to catch a killer! You should all be in possession of a typed briefing sheet and some photographs. These will give you the whole scenario of events in its entirety, so I want you to read it and soak it all in. I'm going to highlight the salient points and tell you about some recent developments; these may well be of use to you as the investigation continues.' He paused for a sip of the water he had placed on a chair to his right.

'At approximately 1 a.m. on Friday 24 August 1990, Walter and Audrey Marriott and their nineteen-year-old daughter Faye were brutally murdered. If you glance at the photos they will show you the position of the bodies and the state of the room when it was discovered.' It was an unusual step by Stark to have so many photographs printed and distributed to the men on the ground, but he felt that each one had to feel as important as the next during the investigation, and when things got rough, or even boring, a look at the photographs might just revive any temporarily lapsed motivation.

He continued. 'The Marriotts lived at 43 Maple Close, Nottingham, a nice, quiet residential area. Walter and Audrey went out that night for a meal and dance at the Queen's Hotel in the city centre, while daughter Faye went out on the town. At some

70

time before 1 a.m. the house appears to have been broken into, the rear kitchen window having been forced with a blunt instrument approximately half an inch wide. Faye Marriott has come into contact with the burglar at some stage; whether she was in when he entered or whether she disturbed him, we don't know yet.'

Paul Fisher asked, 'Is there definitely only one burglar, sir?'

'Yes, only one man at the scene, forensic are certain of that. As you can see . . .' All heads bowed to look at the photographs on their laps. '. . . Faye was semi-naked when she was found and she'd had sexual intercourse. We can only assume that the burglar raped her, or there was a third person present when the burglar struck. Whoever had sex with her didn't ejaculate.' Stark paced slowly from one side of the room to the other as he spoke, his hands animated in a subconscious attempt to express himself more articulately.

'At some stage Faye was asphyxiated to death. Audrey and Walter Marriott had bad timing: they returned home and disturbed the burglar-turned-killer. He appears to have heard their imminent arrival and he lay in wait behind the front door. He killed Walter with a single blow to the back of the head with a fourteen-inch-long ornamental brass clown. He then chased the screaming Audrey, who had walked in first, around the house, culminating at the top of the stairs, on the landing. Audrey was then strangled to death manually; no ligature was used. It was at this point that the killer began acting irrationally. He went to the foot of the stairs, retrieved the clown ornament and proceeded to club the already dead Faye and Audrey, in an obvious, if naïve, attempt to disguise the cause of their death. He then unplugged the video-cassette recorder and left. At some stage he wiped the clown on Audrey's dress, presumably to remove his fingerprints. Two witnesses have seen the man running off along Maple Close, carrying the video, but no definite direction of travel is known. He is described as six foot tall, slim build and dark clothing.'

'That's a big help!' muttered Jim, loud enough for Stark to hear. Stark ignored the comment, not wanting to disrupt the men's concentration any more than it had been. He would let Jim have the wrath of his tongue later. He sneered at Jim, who instantly got the message and wished he'd kept quiet.

71

Stark went on: 'There are no alien fingerprints in the house
. . .' Jim immediately thought of a quip, but bit his tongue. '. . .
The house was kept very clean, apart from Faye's room, which
was like any other young girl's – untidy. There was no sign of a
struggle, apart from Audrey's chase around the house. The hi-
fi was still switched on upon our arrival, which tends to indicate
that Faye was at home prior to the burglary taking place. This,
of course, could be another ploy by our killer, who is obviously
trying to throw us off the scent. Scenes of Crime have detected
some red woollen fibres on Faye's clothing; these are almost
certainly the killer's or third person's. The video recorder is still
missing. We have found the manual for it in a cupboard at the
house: it's a Matsui VHS; the serial number is on your sheet.
There were no other burglaries that night. It is more than
feasible that there was a third party at the house that night,
who escaped the killer. If that is the case he must be traced
urgently, for our benefit and his! Incidentally, Faye's handbag
contained the usual make-up, purse and several small sheets of
paper with "Squires Turf Accountants" on them. The money –
£12.64 – was still intact. We have found a personal diary on
Faye's dressing table containing a whole host of names of men,
who will be seen and interviewed. We don't think she was a
"totty" but she certainly enjoyed male company, if you know
what I mean.'

Stark paused for another sip of water, before continuing his
address. 'Faye Marriott had been to several pubs that night and
finished up at Blitz's Night Club, where she was seen smooching with an as yet unidentified white male and talking to one of
our ethnic cousins, somebody called Winston Kelly.'

Charlie couldn't help his reaction. 'Not that evil bleeder! I
take it you know he's a pimp, boss?'

Stark nodded. 'That's right, Charlie. For those of you that
don't know this man, I'll give you a potted history. Winston
Samuel Courtney Kelly is a West Indian male. His previous
convictions are numerous.' He glanced down at the briefing
sheet. 'They include wounding, supplying controlled drugs,
living off immoral earnings, possession of firearms and police
assault. He's a bad bastard! He's thirty-three years old and
drives a red BMW motor car, C489 FTO. Now at some stage
he's going to be arrested: it's the only way we have a chance

72

with him. I'd like a bit more, but he will come. When he does, I want it doing right because this man enjoys hurting people, including policemen. His arrest will be organised at the right time, properly.'

Paul again asked a question – Steve marvelled at his confidence. 'Has he got any form for burglary, sir?'

Stark pointed the now rolled-up briefing sheet at the young man. 'Good question, Paul. Only as a fourteen-year-old; nothing for burglary since then. He doesn't need to – he's earning enough as it is!

'Faye worked for a betting shop called Squires Turf Accountants. Hence the headed notepaper in her handbag. It's run by one Bernard Squires. I'm convinced that both he and his whole set-up are bent, but whether he would stretch to murder I don't know. There's a stack of intelligence for this guy, but he has no previous convictions at all; he pays others to do his dirty work for him. Bernie is a clever, cunning criminal. He worries me, so I'm setting up a small team to have a close look at him and his cronies. That'll be you, Dave Smith, Tom Jardine and Cheryl Spencer.' Stark looked over to the three sitting in the corner; Tom waved acknowledgement. 'Keep me posted with anything relevant, won't you Tom?' He nodded.

Stark continued. 'The next man who is up with the front-runners is Faye's main boyfriend-cum-sugar daddy – Charles Edward Lyon. This man is a major wimp. He owns his own business, called Foibles; it's a clothes shop on Maid Marion Way in the city. I don't know how to start describing the prat to you.' He laughed and looked at the ceiling for inspiration. 'He's twenty-three years old and a mummy's boy. He hasn't got any form for criminal activities and he was born with a silver spoon in his mouth. He has been seeing Faye for about three months and claims he didn't see her the night she was murdered; he has an alibi, but he will be spoken to again in the near future.'

Stark threw the briefing sheet on to the floor and put both his hands in his pockets, speaking off the cuff. 'I've only just found out, before the briefing, that on the night of the murders, at about midnight, one of the uniformed lads stopped a gentleman who was walking home along Firs Avenue at the back of the public house the Laughing Scotsman. This is about four streets away from Maple Close. The man stopped by the young policeman was Stanley George Tindle, nicknamed "Jobber" Tindle. This man is a burglar and always will be. For those of you who don't know Jobber, he earned his name because he would do any job, and for his rather distasteful habit of doing "jobbies" – i.e. defecating on people's carpets whilst burgling their house. Jobber isn't a particularly violent man, but there were no other burglaries last night apart from Maple Close, and he was clocked close by. He lives at the other end of the city! He will be coming in for a chat later. The young copper is adamant that there wasn't any blood on him, but he isn't sure whether he was wearing a jumper or not.

'I want DCs to pair up with uniformed lads wherever possible. For those of you doing house-to-house, make sure that you see every member of the household and complete the proformas accurately. The killer may well live in the locality, so be careful. If you're not happy about a person, let us know and we'll have a look at them. Your own Sergeants will debrief you. Any questions?' There was a pause. 'Right, see your Sergeants and get your actions. Good luck!'

Stark turned away from his audience and the chatter quickly resumed. Paul stretched and said to Steve, 'I suppose we had better see Nobby and get our actions.'

Steve stood up. 'Yes, we'll find out who our partners are.'

The two young men joined the short queue that led to DS Clarke. Paul was handed his action. 'House-to-house enquiries, Torkard Terrace, rear of Maple Close.' He wasn't particularly happy with it. 'Bloody hell, I bet most of these have been done already. I'm with a PC 2407 Jones. What's your action, Steve?'

Steve read the action from the sheet for the first time, out loud: 'General enquiries at Blitz's Night Club.'

'Shit!' Paul cursed. 'You don't want to swap, do you?'

Steve looked worried. 'I don't think we ought to, Paul. I'm sorry, but we don't want to get into trouble, do we?'

Paul tutted and walked away in search of his partner, shaking his head.

The civilian clerk entered the room. He shouted: 'DI Stark?'

Stark craned his neck to see who was calling him; he was in deep conversation with Mr Wagstaff. 'Yes?'

'Telephone call for you, sir.'

Stark excused himself and followed the callow youth into the HOLMES room. He picked up the phone. 'DI Stark.'

He recognised the voice immediately. 'Hello, Detective Inspector Stark. It's your beloved wife here. Do I qualify for an audience with you, oh great one?'

Stark glanced at his watch. 'Of course you do. What's the matter?'

'Does there have to be anything the matter before I speak to my husband?'

Stark sighed inwardly; this he didn't need. 'No . . . so how are you?'

She was smiling. 'I'm fine. Missing you.'

He sat down and his body became tense. 'I'm missing you too. Are you on your own?'

Carol sighed. 'Yes, the kids are out. I'm going to go and see Mum later.'

Stark tapped at the desk. 'Good. Give her my regards, won't you?'

Carol was smiling again. 'I might do. What do you want for dinner?'

He couldn't hold back any longer. 'Look, Carol, I'm not being funny, but it is slightly awkward to talk to you at the moment. You know I won't be home for dinner. I did tell you!'

The smile in her voice had gone, she was feeling sorry for herself. 'All right, grumpy, I know I shouldn't have called you. I'm sorry.'

'Don't worry about it. Listen, I'm going to have to get back now. I'll see you later then.'

Carol was bored. 'How much later?' He again looked at his watch before he replied. 'I've no idea. Probably the same as yesterday. It might be later. You don't have to wait up, you know.' Inwardly he cursed her selfishness at ringing when she knew he was dealing with a multiple murder, for Christ's sake!

'I am tired. I think I will go to bed tonight, if you don't mind.'

Wagstaff came into the HOLMES room. Stark turned away from him and spoke more quietly into the phone. 'Of course I don't mind. You go to your mum's and have a good time. I'll be thinking about you, OK?'

Carol felt a bit better. 'OK, I'm sorry for ringing again. I love you. Bye.'

Stark glanced around the room. His eyes met Wagstaff's, a few feet behind him. He spoke to Stark with a smile, twitching his moustache: 'Tell her you love her, then.'

Stark whispered into the phone. 'And you too. Bye.' He quickly replaced the receiver. 'I'm sorry about that, sir,' he said apologetically.

Wagstaff looked stern; he appeared annoyed. 'Don't you ever aplogise to anyone again for caring about your family! Understand?' Wagstaff's face resumed its smile and he smacked Stark's back with a strength that surprised the big Inspector.

'Thank you, sir. I won't.'

Stark had obtained most of his information about Stanley George Tindle from Charlie, who had known Stan for years. Tindle hadn't made much of himself. He was a scruffy forty-three-year-old and he was knackered. He sat in the dimly lit vaults of the Pig and Whistle; his head was balding and he had a walrus moustache, the remnants of his breakfast clinging to it for dear life, in fear that they might have to journey past the yellowing teeth and into the pit of stale ale that was his bulbous belly. He wore a tatty grey jumper underneath the thin blue anorak that served as both winter and summer wear. He coughed into his pint of mild as he contemplated his life. The ash from his Park Drive had fallen on to the table; he had made no effort to guide it into the brewery's ashtray.

From the age of twelve Stan had been breaking into houses. He always did it the same way – nothing sophisticated: he would just force open the rear kitchen window and he was in. He would only ever steal three things: cash, jewellery and video recorders, these being the items that were easily saleable in the pubs and clubs in the city centre. Unfortunately, Stan was the nervous type; whenever he burgled a place, nine times out of ten he would have to empty his bowels. He didn't like doing it – he just couldn't help it. He never allowed himself to think about the disgusting sight that would greet the householders upon their return. He didn't try to justify the rights and wrongs of his actions; if he needed money he would get it the only way he knew how – burglary. He always blew the money on fags, booze and the odd bet on the horses.

Stan wasn't a particularly good burglar, despite the years of practice; but like most, he got away with it for so long and then he would get arrested. That's when the problems started, because after a long enough period he would admit all the previous indiscretions he had perpetrated. Stan had been in Her Majesty's Prisons on seven occasions. His last stretch had been his longest: five years – two and a half, with remission. He didn't fancy a return visit and he was nervous. Why had that bloody copper stopped him? It could ruin everything. No way was he doing time again, he couldn't hack it. His paranoia rose.

Stan was so engrossed in his own thoughts that he didn't notice the two tall men standing at the bar drinking half-pints. They had noticed him, however, and Charlie Carter and Nobby Clarke walked towards him. Stan was oblivious to them until they sat down next to him, one on each side.

Charlie spoke. 'Hello, Stan. How are you, mate?'

Stan jumped, spilling some of the mild on to the round wooden table. His eyes were wide, afraid. 'Bloody hell! Charlie Carter! I've done nowt, Charlie, honest, mate. I've done sod all!' His hands were raised as if in surrender.

Charlie reassured him. 'Nobody said you had, Stan. We just want a cosy chat, that's all.'

Stan was literally in a corner. He bit back. 'Don't talk stupid. I know your lot, you can't trust any of you, so why don't you just piss off!'

Nobby heard his cue. 'Listen, prat, your attitude could cause you very serious problems. Listen to what nice Mr Carter has to say to you. All we want to do is talk to you.'

Stan remained unconvinced. 'Well, I don't want to talk to you, so bollocks!'

'What were you doing when you were pulled by that young copper?' asked Charlie.

Stan was frightened. 'I haven't been stopped by no coppers.'

Charlie remained patient. 'We're talking about last Thursday around midnight, Stan.'

'Well, I was in all last Thursday. Ask our Marj.'

Charlie endeavoured to explain. 'Look, Stan, we're not talking about burglary – we're talking about something a lot more serious.'

Stan didn't listen. He folded his arms. 'Talk about what you like. I'm not coming with you, I've told you once!'

Nobby had heard enough. 'We're not pissing about, Stan. You're under arrest!'

'What for?' Stan protested.

'Try: on suspicion of murder!' said Charlie. Nobby told him his rights.

'You what? Here, hold on a minute – I was only joking! Of course I'll talk to you.'

Nobby smiled. 'Too late, Stan. Drink up – we're going.'

Stan knew it was pointless arguing; he fell quiet, drank up, and the three men left. Charlie tried to strike up some conversation with Stan on the way back, but Stan just stared into space with a vacant look on his face.

Charlie and Nobby led him through a maze of corridors into the cell complex. The Custody Sergeant was just placing the set of large cell keys on the desk as the three men arrived. The cell complex consisted of a high counter, behind which the Sergeant stood on an elevated platform; behind him was a wall of clipboards with various 'custody records' on them. To the Sergeant's right was a perspex board with the names of the prisoners listed against a cell number. To the Sergeant's left was a corridor which led through two thick-barred steel gates to another corridor of individual cells.

Tom had been Custody Sergeant for a number of years. He had brown hair, thinning slightly; his blue shirt-sleeves were rolled up to the elbows, displaying his veined forearms. He wore thin, gold-rimmed spectacles and had rather over-bushy eyebrows. He was a quiet, serious man who didn't suffer fools gladly; he had seen a lot of criminals walk through that door, and he wasn't impressed with Stanley Tindle. He sounded depressed at the arrival of the men. 'Not another one!' he sighed.

'I'm afraid so, Tom,' Nobby replied.

Tom leaned underneath the desk and produced various sheets of paper. He began filling out the custody record. His voice was a monotone. 'Name?'

The prisoner knew the position and answered quietly: 'Stanley George Tindle.'

'Date of birth?'

78

'8.6.47.'

Tom glanced over the top of his glasses at the spectacle before him. He muttered to himself: 'Male, white, five foot six inches tall. What's your address?'

Stan's throat was dry. He croaked out a reply: 'Number 28 Billington Mews, Trent Bridge, Nottingham.'

'Reason for arrest?'

It was Nobby's turn. 'Suspicion of murder.'

Nobby thought Tom would miss the correct space on the form, because as he wrote it his eyes looked at Nobby through-out. He looked down at the form again. 'Officer arresting?'

'Me, Detective Sergeant 1312 Clarke.'

'Time and place of arrest?'

'4.12 p.m. The Pig and Whistle pub.'

Tom looked at Nobby. 'Don't disappear, Nobby. I'll have a word with you in a minute. Is the officer in the case DI Stark?'

'Yes.'

Tom began the spiel that he must have said a thousand times; he was on autopilot. 'Right, Mr Tindle, I'm the Custody Sergeant. I'm here for your benefit. Whilst you are detained here you are entitled to certain rights. These are: the right to have someone informed of your arrest; the right to consult with a solicitor of your choice; and the right to consult a copy of the Codes of Practice relating to your treatment whilst you are detained. You may do any of these things now or at any subsequent time while you are being detained. Do you under-stand all that?'

'I should do – I've heard it enough times.' He was beginning to adjust to his environment. Tom gave him the piece of paper that spelled out his rights. 'I don't want you to tell anybody I'm here and I certainly don't want a brief. Give us your pen and I'll sign your bit of paper.'

Tom continued. 'Right then, Stan, empty your pockets. You know the routine.' Stan placed his wooden tobacco box, which he had made in prison, on the desk. This was joined by a box of matches, cigarette papers, a comb and £7.48 in cash. Tom returned the tobacco box and cigarette papers to him.

'Don't forget your shoelaces and belt, Stan,' Tom reminded him. Stan dutifully removed them.

'Just check him over, will you?' asked Tom.

Charlie searched him. 'He's clean. Eh-up, what's this?' Charlie retrieved a screwdriver from the lining of Stan's coat. 'Oh dear,' said Charlie.

'Oh dear,' said Stan.

He was taken down into the cells and the door slammed shut behind him. Nobby explained the circumstances to Tom and told him that if Stan suddenly decided to contact anybody, they would make application to delay such a process, at least until Stan's house had been searched. Tom agreed and asked to be kept informed.

Stark was busy at the computer terminal, tapping away at the keys. .

'DI Stark?' came the shout from a PC clinging on to a telephone.

'Hello?' he replied.

'They've got Tindle, sir. He's being held at Nottingham nick.'

Stark jumped up from his seat. 'Right, I'm going straight over. I don't want any interruptions unless absolutely necessary.'

'I'll cover for you at this end, David. Good luck!' cheered Wagstaff.

Eventually Stark reached his Cavalier. He turned the ignition, paused for a moment and took a deep breath. 'Right then, Stanley George Tindle, let's see what you've got!'

6

'A kleptomaniac is a person who helps himself,
because he can't help himself.'

Henry Morgan

Stan Tindle sat on the wooden bench that just passed for a bed, his beer-belly straining at his tight-fitting jumper. The room measured eight feet by six; it had a concrete floor and a small area with a toilet in it, which was not obscured from the watchful eye of the 'cell man'. Stan clung to the only blanket in the cell. Throughout his criminal career he had been in this position many times. It didn't get any easier. His fellow criminals often bragged that being locked up did not affect them; in fact Stan had said it himself, but they all knew it wasn't true. He sat staring at the floor, his mind churning over the wrong things he had done. He promised himself that he wasn't going to admit anything. He failed to reassure himself, and he paced the floor. He wondered how long he had been there – an hour? Two hours? He pressed the buzzer and waited for the approach of the heavy footsteps behind the thick metal door.

Tom slid open the square metal spy-hole to cell Number 9. 'What's up, Stan?'

Stan stood up and approached the door. 'Give us summat to read, boss.' Tom didn't speak; his leather boots clamped out the journey to the counter and back to the cell. A paperback book flew through the spy-hole and landed on the floor at Stan's feet. The spy-hole slammed shut.

'Cheers, boss,' Stan shouted gratefully. He picked up the book and read the title: *Love's Lost Dream*. Stan frowned and thought momentarily of his haggard wife, Marj, then quickly shut the image out. He pressed the little metal buzzer button near the door again.

Tom slid open the spy-hole. He was not pleased. 'You know

if you keep pressing that buzzer you'll get sod all!' His patience was wearing thin.

Stan was apologetic. 'Sorry, boss. Can I go into the exercise yard, please?'

'I've just given you a bleeding book!' exclaimed Tom.

Stan tried to look sheepish. 'Yes, and I'm looking forward to reading it, but I would love a roll-up.'

Tom sighed. 'Come on then.' He led Stan to the exercise yard, bundled him in and gave him a light, before slamming shut the large metal door.

Stan examined the exercise yard. It was about twenty feet long and eight feet wide, enclosed by high walls that reached up to a metal grille which only partially obscured the sky above. Stan sucked on his rolled-up cigarette, and a quarter of its length turned to ash; he had learned to use his baccy sparingly. He busied himself reading the graffiti scratched on the wall by previous occupants.

Stan began to think out loud. 'Murder! They're bleeding mental! They're not pinning this on me. I'll just deny it outright. I wonder if I should have a brief? What for, though? They never do bugger all. "Say nothing." Brilliant! What are the coppers playing at? I bet I've been here two bleeding hours now. I mean, what can they be doing? I hope they haven't got Sammy Morris in – he'll tell every bleeding thing, that prat will.'

He was getting nervous; he wanted to go to the toilet and pressed the buzzer. Tom escorted him back to his temporary abode. Stan couldn't resist it: the Sergeant seemed a reasonable bloke and Stan needed a friend to comfort him.

'Eh, boss . . .'

'Now what?'

'What are they playing at? I mean, what's taking them all this time?'

Tom smiled: the age-old question, the need for reassurance. 'You know better than to ask me that, Stan. Just try to get your head down. They'll be with you soon enough, then you'll probably wish they weren't.'

Stan was alone again. He went to the toilet, then lay on the hard wooden bench and covered himself with the thin grey blanket. He closed his eyes.

He heard a young voice from the next cell shout to another invisible colleague: 'What have you told them, Billy?'

He got a reply. 'I've told them nowt, mate. They're trying to say we've nicked a car, an XR2, but I've told them that we were in the Wagon until about ten, and then we went . . .'

The shouting between the two lads prevented Stan from getting his beauty sleep. He stared out into the semi-darkness and swore under his breath at his own carelessness. 'That flaming screwdriver!'

'A flaming screwdriver!' said Charlie excitedly. 'It would be great if it matches up forensically with the marks at the murder scene.'

'Yes,' Nobby replied, 'but you know how long forensic takes. It'll be two or three days, if we hurry them up, and we've only got thirty-six hours at the most before we've got to charge him with something.'

Charlie put a question to his younger Sergeant: 'Do you think Stark's jumped in a bit with getting us to nick Stan?'

Nobby protruded his bottom lip in thought. 'No, not really. He's out of the way for the search; he can't contact anyone and if we find nothing at the house it's got to be done through interviewing anyway.'

'Yes, you're probably right. What time does the chinky open?'

Nobby looked at his watch. 'About six o'clock I think. I must admit I am hungry – I think I shall have to sample some chicken fried rice.'

Stark arrived at the station and Nobby explained the situation to him. Stark decided that he and Nobby would interview Stan, while Charlie and Ashley would search his house. Stark and Nobby began the pre-interview analysis. They contacted officers who had interviewed Stan on previous occasions to ascertain what his strengths and weaknesses were, what strategy they would implement and any particular plan of attack they might try. Stark studied Stan's previous convictions: he was particularly interested in an ABH three years ago. They decided on the usual strategy, then to play it by ear as things developed.

*

Charlie and Ashley stood in front of the green door to 28 Billington Mews. The door of the terraced council house was opened by Marj, a middle-aged woman with badly highlighted hair, heavy make-up and a cigarette hanging from her mouth. The cigarette looked in jeopardy as she spoke.

'Eh-up, Charlie! Come in, duck. What's he been up to now?'

Charlie was honest in his reply. 'To be fair, Marj, I can't really say.' His feet were sticking to the well-worn carpet in the hallway.

Marj cackled. 'Top secret is it? He's never started working for MI5, has he?'

Charlie joined in her laughter. 'No, it's nothing like that.' Ashley was still behind Charlie, partly hidden, as the three stood in the narrow hallway.

Marj enjoyed the company. 'I'll put the kettle on. Aren't you going to introduce me to your mate?' She flashed her eyes at the man in the expensive-looking suit.

Charlie apologised. 'Sorry, duck – this is Ashley Stevens, my partner in crime for today.' He put his back against the wall so that she could have a better view of the dashing young man. Ashley smiled coyly at the narrowing eyes of Marj Tindle.

She looked him up and down. 'I don't know – they get younger, Charlie! Do you take sugar . . . Ashley, is it? Oh, that's a posh name.' She nudged Charlie and tittered.

'One, please, Marj,' said Ashley, slightly embarrassed.

Both Charlie and Ashley followed Marj into the kitchen-cum-bombsite. Ashley looked around: there were pots all over the place and nobody could ever clean the oven rings, which had long been suffocated by the overflow of Marjorie's culinary delights. The chip pan that took pride of place was covered in fat, and mould had formed on two plates on the cheap wooden table. Ashley regretted agreeing to the cup of tea.

Marj spoke with her back to the two men, while she rinsed some mugs under the sink tap. 'So you can't tell me what it's about then, Charlie?'

'No. It'll be nothing, I bet – don't worry about it.'

Marj laughed. 'Worry? I've long since stopped worrying about Stanley Tindle. What have you come for? To search the place?'

Charlie smiled. 'You've got it right in one, Marj. Is there anything here?'

'No. Bloody hell, Charlie, he might be thick but he's not that thick!' Marj reached for the teapot and Ashley spotted the torn, off-white underskirt beneath her flowered polyester dress.

Charlie tried to pump her again. 'Has he brought any gear back lately, Marj? It's important that we know from the start if he has, to keep you out of trouble, duck.'

Marj turned around from the worktop and looked Charlie in the eye. 'Eh, Charlie, how long have you known me – ten years? I wouldn't have it in the house, duck, and I'll tell you something else: I don't want to know where he is, where he's been or what he's done! I am not interested in the man.' She continued preparing the tea. Ashley noticed the pile of potato peelings that lay rotting in the sink.

The three eventually adjourned to the sparsely furnished living-room and made small-talk. Charlie reminisced with Marj about the time that Stan had hidden in his attic and they had sent a police dog in after him. She laughed, 'Soft old bugger – he should have come down.'

After Marj had enquired after Stark's health, the two detectives finished their tea and commenced a search of the Tindle household. Marj knew the routine: she'd been done a dozen times or more. She didn't protest – what was the point? Anyway, she was positive the place was clean.

Ashley had, of course, drawn the short straw; the attic. He pulled himself up into the darkness, with Charlie shouting encouragement from below and Marj puffing on her cigarette, dropping ash on to the floor as second nature.

'Shit!' came the cry.

'What's up?' asked Charlie.

Ashley's muffled voice came out of the darkness: 'I've caught my trousers on a bleeding nail! Bloody hell!' His troubled face peered down on Charlie and Marj who were shaking with silent mirth. 'Thanks very much for the sympathy!'

The search eventually drew to a close. They had seized a chisel, a pair of gloves, two red jumpers, three necklaces and a gold bracelet.

'Thanks a lot then, Marj,' said Charlie as they left the house. He appreciated a good working relationship.

85

'Don't forget, I want that bloody jewellery back!'

'You'll get it back if it isn't nicked,' Charlie assured her.

She waved. 'I believe you, thousands wouldn't!'

Ashley was still cursing at the two-inch slit at the side of his trouser leg as the two men loaded the property into the car.

'Oh, to be young again,' smiled Charlie.

Most interviews of prisoners in custody for criminal offences are now recorded on audio tapes. The system works as follows. Sealed tapes are handed to the interviewing officer in sets of two. They are unsealed in the presence of the accused and both tapes are placed into the tape recorder. The interview is recorded simultaneously on both the tapes, which are removed at the end of the interview. One tape is then sealed in a tamper-proof seal with information written on it and signed by all parties present. The second tape is marked with a label but not sealed. It is from this second tape that written statements are prepared by the officers present at the interview. It is only the first, sealed tape that is designed to be opened in a court of law.

DI Stark asked Tom for four sets of tapes, as he stood in the cell complex. Tom handed him the tapes and recorded them in his log.

Stark gave his instructions. 'Fetch him up, Tom, please. Let's have a word with him.'

Tom disappeared down the corridor, returning a short time later with Stan Tindle, whose shoulders were hunched. 'What took you so bloody long?' he asked Stark and Nobby.

Stark beat Nobby to the reply. 'It's taken us this long to sort out everything we're going to talk to you about.'

The three men went into the interview room, off a corridor adjacent to the cell complex. The room contained a grey table, which was screwed to the floor, and four chairs; on top of the desk stood a large tape recorder.

Nobby sat opposite Stan, with Stark at Stan's side, at an angle to him.

'Have you got an ashtray?' Stan enquired, already starting to shake.

'You'll have to use this bin.' Stark placed the metal waste-paper bin on the floor next to Stan. He touched the prisoner's arm. 'Have you been interviewed on this new tape system before, Stan?' He shook his head and Stark explained. 'Well, it's very simple: as soon as we press "record" there will be a loud bleep. Then I will introduce myself and ask you your name and stuff, then we can talk properly and forget all about the tape recorder. OK?'

Stan still hadn't looked at the detectives; he appeared moody. 'OK, but I'll tell you now I've done nowt.'

Nobby undid the transparent seal on the tapes, inserted them in the recorder and pressed the 'record' button. The bleep lasted only twelve seconds, but it seemed a lot longer as Stark and Nobby sat looking at their dishevelled quarry.

The bleep came to an end and Stark commenced: 'This interview is being tape recorded. I am Detective Inspector David Stark of the Nottinghamshire Constabulary, presently stationed at Nottingham Police Station. The other officer is . . .' He paused; Nobby was ready for his cue.

'John Clarke, Detective Sergeant 1312, of the Nottinghamshire Constabulary, stationed at Nottingham Police Station.'

Stark continued. 'Can I have your name and date of birth, please?'

Stan muttered into his walrus moustache. 'Stanley George Tindle, 8.6.47.'

'And your address?'

'28 Billington Mews, Trent Bridge, Nottingham.'

Stark smiled inwardly at himself. It was always at this stage that he felt like Magnus Magnusson on *Mastermind* and he had to refrain from saying, 'And your chosen subject is . . . burglary. You have sixty seconds on burglary starting . . . now.' Instead he kept rigidly to the codes of practice.

'We are at Nottingham Police Station. It is Saturday, 25 August 1990, and the time is now 6.14 p.m. I will remind you, Stan, that you do not have to say anything unless you wish to do so, but anything you do say may be given in evidence. Do you understand that?'

Stan nodded; he felt sorry for himself.

'I'll have to ask you to speak up, Stan, because the tape can't hear you nod.' Stark smiled.

'Oh, sorry – yes, I understand that, yes.'

'At the end of the interview I'll give you a notice which will tell you what happens to the tapes, OK?'

'OK.' Stan still avoided Stark's gaze.

Stark leaned back in his chair. He sat with his arms and legs apart, his palms always open when gesticulating; he wanted the friendly stance to be conveyed to Stan's subconscious so that he would relax. If he was relaxed he was more likely to make a verbal mistake; in addition, Stark would be able to observe his body language and note what made him tense up during the interview.

Stark began the interview proper. 'Now then, Stan, I've not met you before. I'm the Detective Inspector at this police station. Did you kill the Marriott family?'

'Bloody hell no!' said Stan. This outright question was asked to see if he would justify his denials without prompting.

'I like to know who I'm talking to, Stan, so tell me a bit about yourself. Do you come from this area?'

'Yes, I was born and bred in Nottingham.' He stared at the table.

'Do you work at all, Stan?' asked Stark, lighting up his pipe.

'No. I've been in and out of work all my life. I've done the odd job here and there, you know.'

Stark lit Stan's excuse for a cigarette. 'The odd job?' he repeated.

'Yes – a bit of bricklaying, a bit of turfing, that sort of thing, you know.' He glanced at Stark.

'Doesn't bring much money in, though,' the DI observed.

'You're bloody right it doesn't. It's a struggle to survive at times.' He raised his eyebrows thoughtfully.

'I bet it's a struggle.' Stark nodded.

'That's what sent me out thieving in the first place. We never had a penny when I was a kid. My mum was always trying to make ends meet.'

'I don't suppose it's been easy for you then, Stan,' Stark said sympathetically.

'You can say that again. I mean, them youngsters in the pub, you try and tell them what it was like but they don't believe you. They don't know they're born, half of them.' His glances at Stark were becoming longer.

'I'm just trying to work it out, Stan: you weren't a war baby, were you?'

'No, my dad was in the army, though – Sherwood Foresters.'

'Sherwood Foresters, eh?' Stark sounded impressed.

'Yes. He got the rank of corporal until he came out in 1948.'

'What did he do when he came out then, Stan?' asked Stark, interested.

'He went down the pit – Babbington. That's when it was rough down the pit.'

'I bet it was. Didn't you ever think of following in your dad's footsteps?'

Stan's arms unfolded as he leaned back in his chair. 'No way. You wouldn't get me working down that bloody great hole!'

There was no light shining in Stan's face, there were no detectives leaning over him menacingly; it didn't work like that. Stan was loosening up: he was doing what everybody likes doing – he was talking about himself. Stark was just fuelling the fire. There was plenty of time to put him under pressure.

Ashley was annoyed with Stark and Nobby as he walked into the CID office. 'You'd have thought they'd have waited,' he said, as he dumped Stan's belongings on the desk. 'How are we going to tell them about the jumpers and jewellery that we found at the house? They've started interviewing and they don't even have the full facts. We can't interrupt them while they're interviewing, can we?'

'No.' Charlie pulled at his chin as he thought. He picked up the phone and dialled four digits.

'Cell block, Sergeant Jade.' It was Tom.

'It's Charlie upstairs. How long has Stark been interviewing Tindle?'

'About twenty minutes,' came the sullen reply.

'How many sets of tapes has he taken in?'

'Four.'

'Oh shit! OK, mate, cheers.' Charlie replaced the receiver.

It was Nobby rather than Stark who noticed the 'enquiry' light come in in the interview room.

'DS Clarke leaving the interview room. The time now is 6.37 p.m.,' he announced to the tape recorder. Nobby closed the door behind him and appeared a trifle annoyed at the interruption as he met Ashley in the corridor.

'Sorry to disturb you, Sarge, but we thought that you should know what we seized from Stan's house.' Ashley spoke in a whisper and passed Nobby a piece of paper with the details of the search written on it.

'Has he said anything yet?' asked Ashley inquisitively.

'We've only just started. Stark's into this psychology bit, so we could be here till next bloody week!'

'You don't want anything from the Chinese takeaway, then?' asked Ashley.

'Yes, get us something and get something for Stark, will you? We'll warm it up in the microwave later. I'll give you the money in a bit. What have you done to your trousers?' Nobby asked, puzzled at the untidiness of the usually immaculate DC.

Ashley shook his head. 'Don't ask. It's a long story.'

Nobby looked at the piece of paper supplied by Ashley as he walked into the kitchenette to prepare plastic cups of coffee before returning to the interview room.

Stark glanced at the piece of paper that Nobby handed to him. He supped at his plastic coffee; he had created an air of affability in the room. He continued the interview.

'It's fair to say you're a burglar, isn't it, Stan?'

'It's fair to say that, I suppose, but it's only 'cos I'm skint half the time.' There was a pause. 'Here, can I ask you a question, Mr Stark?'

'Yes, of course you can. I can't guarantee an answer though.' He smiled.

Stan asked, 'Why the hell have I been nicked for murder? It's a joke, isn't it? You know full well that I'm just a run-of-the-mill burglar. I wouldn't hurt no one – honest.'

'Well, your name hasn't been picked out of a hat. We've got our reasons for believing you could be involved,' Stark replied honestly, his palms once again displayed to his prisoner. 'So you accept that you're a burglar then, Stan?'

'Yes, but that doesn't mean that I've done any burgling jobs lately though.' Stan grinned uncontrollably, for the first time.

'How would you describe the way you do your jobs, Stan?' asked Stark, leaning back in his chair.

'Always the same way: back kitchen window, with a big screwdriver.'

'Do you do it that way every time without fail?' Stark lined up his quarry.

'Without fail,' Stan confirmed, with a definite nod of his head.

'Well, what sort of stuff do you take? Do you nick to order or what?'

'I sometimes get people asking me to get them certain stuff, otherwise I nick owt that I can get rid of quickly, like.'

'So what sort of stuff is that then, Stan?' Stark again asked, the net drawing in.

'Videos, cash, sometimes a bit of Tom – that's it. I wouldn't nick owt else – it's too risky.'

'Who are you knocking the gear out to, Stan?' Stark raised his eyebrows disarmingly.

'Come off it, Mr Stark, I'm not that daft, and anyway it's to a lot of different people. But as I've told you, I've done nowt lately.'

'Well, how are you living then?' asked Stark.

'How does anybody live nowadays?' Stan replied vaguely.

'Have you been doing any bricklaying lately?' Stark puffed out another cloud of smoke from his pipe.

'No, there's plenty of casual work about but I've been having difficulty with my back,' said Stan.

'Yes, you can't get it off the bed!' said Nobby, unable to resist it. He instantly regretted the unprofessional interruption.

'What's this on your form sheet, Stan? ABH? What was that all about?' Stark ignored Nobby's quip.

'Oh, that was over three years ago. Some stupid tart caught me in her kitchen, so I just gave her a back-hander, that's all. She reckoned I'd knocked a tooth out, the lying cow.'

Stark allowed himself a glance at Nobby, who met the stare.

The telephone in the CID office was answered in mid-ring.

'CID, DC Stevens,' Ashley's well-spoken voice greeted the caller.

'Hello, mate. Is Nobby Clarke there?' said the gruff unannounced voice.

91

'Well, he's here, but he's interviewing at the moment.'

'Is he likely to be long?'

'Probably quite a while yet. Can I take a message?'

'No, leave it. I tell you what, you might be able to help me. You've got Stan Tindle locked up, haven't you?'

'Can I ask who's calling?' Ashley didn't like giving information to just anybody.

'Sorry, mate. It's Dave Saunders from Regional Crime Squad speaking. Can I ask you what Stan's in for?'

'Yes: murder.'

'Murder! You're joking!' The voice laughed.

'That's funny – that's just what he said,' Ashley retorted.

'It's not that triple killing on Maple Close, is it?'

'You've got it in one.' Ashley toyed with the pliable telephone cord as he sat at his desk.

'Bloody hell! Look Stan's been doing a bit for us lately and there's an armed robbery that's due to go down next week and we could do with him being out. He's not seriously in the frame for this, is he?'

'He's in the top three or four at the moment.' There was a slight pause.

'Listen – do us a favour. If you kick him out, tell him it's because I gave you a ring, will you?'

'Yes, of course we will. Consider it done.'

'Cheers.'

'Cheers.'

Stan was sweating profusely in the interview room and the questions kept coming. He felt trapped; he was incredibly uncomfortable. The build-up of the interview had thrown him into turmoil and the pressure was getting too much for him.

Stark continued the barrage. 'If you haven't done any jobs lately, what were you doing with the screwdriver in the lining of your jacket?' His voice had become considerably harsher.

'I always carry it,' answered Stan, wiping his forehead with his sleeve. The sweat left a wet mark on it.

'Bullshit, Stan! Now I want some pissing answers. What's all this crap about you being with Marj the night you were stopped?' Stark leaned forward, resting his elbows on the desk.

'I didn't know what to say to you.' He looked at Nobby. 'So I was stopped – so what? I was clean.'

'Yes, but why lie to Charlie and this officer about it, Stan?'

'I don't know, I just did. I'm telling the truth now, aren't I?' He raised his eyebrows.

'I don't know, Stan – are you? What were you doing in Firs Close?'

'Nothing.'

'Nothing! You're just bloody lucky that it was a young copper that stopped you, otherwise you'd have been searched properly and you'd have been nicked, Stan, wouldn't you?'

Stan had his answer. 'I didn't have the screwdriver on me, did I?'

'More bullshit! You're lying, Stan!' Stan folded his arms; his fists had become clenched tightly. Stark went on: 'Because a couple of streets away a whole family were wiped out, Stan, murdered by a burglar who'd been disturbed!'

'Bloody hell! Honest – listen . . .'

'Guess how the burglar got in, Stan? Through the back pissing window, Stan. It was forced with a screwdriver!'

'I wouldn't do that.' Stan was fidgeting on his seat, his eyes wide and darting between Nobby and Stark, looking for a friendly response. He didn't find any.

'But you've just told us you hit a tart that disturbed you last time!'

'Yes, but that was on the spur of the moment.'

'Who said these murders weren't? Do you know something we don't, eh?'

'I've told you, I didn't do any jobs that night. That young copper scared me off!'

'Guess what was nicked, Stan.'

'How should I know?'

'A video was nicked. What another amazing coincidence! Get it off your chest, Stan – it's not worth all this aggro, is it?'

Stan didn't answer.

'That screwdriver's going to match up with the marks on that window, Stan, and you know it,' said Stark, leaning back into his chair again confidently.

'I know it won't.' Stan shook his head and rubbed the palms of his hands together firmly.

'Stan, nobody's saying you meant to do it. It was probably all an accident – a spur-of-the-moment job, like you say. You were there, Stan. We've got a policeman who can put you there an hour before it happened. The same MO, the same stuff nicked – it's too much of a coincidence: it's got your name written all over it, Stan. It's down to you. We've even got your jumper you were wearing that night, Stan, and the gloves and the jewellery from your house. Give it up, Stan – we all make mistakes. I know you're not vicious, you're not a killer. It might have been an accident – I don't know until you tell me, do I? I can't say it was an accident for you, can I? It's down to you. You're making yourself out to be worse than you are. What's the court going to think, Stan? Was it an accident or did you go in there intending to kill them? You were there, weren't you . . . weren't you, Stan?'

The onslaught continued for a quarter of an hour. Before Stark went into an interview he tried to get his mind right; he would tell himself that the person he was about to interview had done it, there was no doubt about it – he'd done it and that was it. He had learned the hard way; he had sympathised with suspects in the past, when he was a young copper. He had been conned into believing these people and regretted his good nature when that vital bit of evidence came to light weeks later, proving positively that they had in fact committed the crime. If it transpired that the man he had interviewed was innocent afterwards, then so be it. He would never apologise for doing his job to the best of his ability, because if that person had done it, he wasn't going to admit it in a nicely worded letter to the Chief Constable, was he? The CID deal with the most evil people in society: burglars, rapists, armed robbers, child molesters, murderers. The mothers of children who have been sexually abused, elderly ladies who have been brutally raped are hardly going to thank you if you have a cosy, comfortable chat with the perpetrator and, if he says he hasn't done it, let him go! Stark was paid to do a job; he wasn't paid to make friends. He was paid in this instance to find a murderer and that's just what he intended to do.

Stark and Nobby took Stan back to the cell block and the loving arms of the Custody Sergeant. Stan had his hands in his pockets and his head was bowed. He didn't speak; his face was flushed and his palms sweaty. His ordeal was over, for now.

'Just have a think about what's been said,' Stark shouted to Stan as he was led down the corridor. 'We'll speak to you again later.'

The cell door slammed shut behind Stan. He turned and pounded the wall repeatedly with the side of his clenched fist. 'Bastards . . . Bastards . . . Bastards . . .' with every strike.

Nobby placed the chicken fried rice in the microwave in the brightly lit kitchen. 'What do you reckon then, boss?' he asked, pressing out the digits on the control panel.

'No idea, Nobby. What about you?' Stark had sat down at the white table.

'I don't know. It could be him, but I tend to think it isn't.'

'Could be isn't good enough. We need a lever on him, Nobby. We've got him overnight at least.'

The kitchen door opened and a man asked for Detective Inspector Stark.

'That's me.'

A callow-looking youth of about twenty-one in a summery shirt introduced himself. 'I'm Pete Bloomfield from Scenes of Crime. Do you want the good news or the bad news?'

'Give me the good news,' said Stark.

'Your man Tindle isn't the murderer!' He looked almost apologetic as he broke the news.

'You what? And how do you know that, might I ask?' said the DI.

'The report from forensic – it's categoric. There was no break-in at the house. The murderer had chipped away at the window while it was open! It was a set-up! Forensic have studied the plaster cast and photos of the marks. It's definite.'

'Well, bloody hell,' said Stark.

Bloomfield continued his information. 'So the murderer was either invited in or he conned his way in; he certainly didn't open any windows or doors!'

'That doesn't mean Tindle hasn't done it!' Stark's determined interviewing state of mind still hadn't fully returned to normality.

'Come on, boss,' said Nobby. 'Tindle didn't even know the Marriotts. It's not his way. It can't be him – he's just a piss-pot burglar!'

Stark conceded. 'All right, but bail him to come back to the nick in a couple of months' time. I still want his gear forensically checked against those marks. And get the jewellery checked out – it's bound to be nicked.'

Nobby went out to give his instructions; he certainly wasn't going to do it – he hadn't had his Chinese meal yet.

Stark muttered under his breath. 'Right, Winston Kelly, you've got some questions to answer.'

Nobby returned to the kitchen and joined him at the table. The two men ate in silence, their eating habits indicative of their personalities. Stark toyed with the contents of the tinfoil tray, deciding which morsels he wanted on his fork, teasing the food with his knife before carefully and steadfastly placing it in his mouth. Nobby, however, used only a fork, shovelling large quantities in as if there were no tomorrow, the occasional pea or piece of rice falling on to the table or floor.

Violet Gray hadn't gone to her mother's. She had told another lie to Ernie; for the last week she had seemed constantly to be covering her tracks.

She deposited ten pence in the slot of the call-box and dialled a number. A man's voice answered. 'Hello?'

'It's me.'

'What the hell are you doing ringing me here?' the man whispered in a panic.

'Can you talk?' she asked, the adrenalin pumping.

'No, not really. You never know who might be listening, for Christ's sake!' The man's voice was raised.

'Well, don't talk, just listen,' said Violet. 'Ernie's been to the police and given a statement about the murders. He's seen you running away!'

'Jesus Christ!'

She continued. 'Don't worry – he's not named you, but it could mean trouble. Try and get an alibi for that time and if anybody asks about it just deny all knowledge, no matter what they say.' She waited for a response.

'Thanks for ringing. I'll be in touch when things calm down.'

The man put the receiver down and Violet hurried out of the telephone kiosk, beginning to regret ever having got involved in the web of deceit.

7

'The only normal people are the ones you don't know
very well . . .'

Joe Ancis

Paul Fisher knocked on the door of Number 6 Torkard Terrace,
one of a row of two-bedroomed terraced council houses. He
already had his warrant card in his hand as the elderly lady
partially opened the door, her wrinkled face staring out suspiciously. A friendly expression met her doubting glare.

'Hello, love. I'm from the CID. I'm making some enquiries
about the murders across the road the other night. Have you
heard about them?' The lady opened the door wider.

'Yes, I have. It's awful, isn't it?' she replied.

Paul agreed. 'Yes. Has a policeman spoken to you about it at
all?'

'No.'

'Do you mind if I come in then and have a chat?'

The lady pulled Paul's hand towards her and scrutinised his
warrant card. 'It doesn't look like you,' she said, her deep-set
eyes examining the young detective's face.

'It was a long time ago,' Paul smiled.

The woman relented. 'All right, you'd better come in.'

It wasn't long before it became apparent to Paul that the lady,
Mrs Charles, had some information that could be of great use
to the enquiry. She gave an account of her activities on the
night of the murders.

'You see, I can never get to sleep, so I usually don't bother
going to bed until one or two in the morning.'

'Yes, but would you just explain to me what you saw again?'
Paul asked.

'Well, I was putting the milk bottle out and that's when I saw
him whizz past me.' The woman backed up her description by

moving her loose-skinned arm quickly across the front of her body.

'Who was it? Do you know him?' Paul enquired.

'Of course I know him. It's Elsie Markwell's eldest lad, Colin.'

'Are you sure?' asked Paul excitedly.

The woman was adamant. 'Of course I'm sure. He's at church most Sundays with his wife and those two brats. Oh, what's his wife's name?'

'Do you know where he lives, Mrs Charles?'

She screwed her eyes shut to concentrate. 'Somewhere on that new estate – it's the corner house. It's either Charnwood Grove or Ellis Avenue. It's the corner house, anyway.'

'Did you notice if he was carrying anything?'

'Well, I only saw his face as he ran at me. He was running really fast and in a real panic. By the look on his face he looked as if he'd seen a ghost!'

'So you didn't see him holding anything, then?'

'I didn't say that. From behind, I would say that he was carrying something, yes.'

Paul asked the obvious: 'Did you see what it was he was carrying?'

'No, I didn't. Aren't you listening, young man? I've just told you that.'

Mrs Charles couldn't give any further information, but it was a red-hot lead and it didn't take long for Colin Markwell to be located at 23 Charnwood Grove. Stark had instructed Charlie and Ashley to bring him in to the station to help with their enquiries.

Stark had told them that he would speak to Markwell later, but they were to start things off and if it looked promising they were to contact him immediately. Stark and Nobby were in the process of drawing up plans to arrest and interview Winston Kelly and they only had two pairs of hands.

Charlie and Ashley heard the strains of a James Bond film issuing from the family focal point as a young girl with a bow in her black hair opened the red-painted door and greeted them. They explained who they were and expressed their wish to speak to Mr Markwell. The girl cocked her head back and shouted: 'Dad? . . . Dad!'

'What? Who is it?' came the irritated reply.

'It's the police.'

'The what?' Colin decided to get off his backside and came to the door, passing his daughter as she returned to the living-room. He was a man of about forty; his black sideburns were turning grey, he had a tanned face and wore a smart, casual beige shirt with white trousers. He tried to look puzzled; his heart was pounding and he became short of breath. 'What can I do for you, gentlemen?'

Ashley produced his warrant card. 'We are police officers. Are you Colin Markwell?'

'Yes. There's nothing wrong, is there?' Colin asked as he pushed his hands deep into his white trousers.

'No, there's nothing wrong, but we'd like to have a chat with you at the station, if you don't mind.' Colin surreptitiously closed the interior living-room door and Roger Moore's rhetoric faded.

Colin protested mildly. 'Well, it is slightly awkward . . . I mean what do you want to talk to me about, for heaven's sake?'

Ashley cautiously explained. 'I'd rather not discuss it on the doorstep, but it involves your being seen in very suspicious circumstances at the rear of Maple Close the other night.'

Colin grimaced momentarily and his lips tightened. 'Oh God, I've been dreading this. I'll get my coat.'

He closed the living-room door behind him as he re-entered the room; it didn't, however, completely disguise the conversation which took place behind it.

'What do you mean, you're going to the police station?' asked a concerned Mrs Markwell as she rose from her seat, her portly body clad in a green leisure suit.

'They want someone to help them with an identity parade and I said I'd help. I shouldn't be more than a couple of hours.'

She was not amused. 'Whatever possessed you to agree to that? Tell them to go away. It's Saturday night, for Christ's sake!' Her voice displayed her consternation.

Colin passed over the remark and struggled with himself to remain calm. 'I've told them I'd do it now; they're waiting outside. Do you want some chips bringing back?'

'No – er, yes, OK, just bring me a bag of chips. Don't be too long, will you?'

Colin kissed his wife, attempting a smile that wrinkled into a frown. He really didn't want to leave his family to go with the two strangers outside. Why did he have to do it? Why had he ever set foot in Maple Close?

He took a deep breath and addressed the two solemn men on his doorstep. 'Sorry about that, gents. Right – shall I follow you in my car?'

'Do you know where Nottingham Police Station is?' Ashley asked.

'Well, yes, of course?' A hint of question was in his voice.

'In that case, we'll follow you then,' said Ashley with a wry smile.

'Fine . . . fine . . .' Colin's voice trailed off as he trudged to his car.

The operator answered the police-station switchboard. The female caller's voice was low and sensual, despite the distortion of the telephone.

'Can I speak to Detective Sergeant Clarke, please?'

There was a pause and some clicks before the deep voice answered, 'CID DS Clarke.' Nobby and Stark had been busy discussing Winston Kelly and his voice betrayed slight irritation at the interruption.

'Hello, it's Sally.'

'Hello, Sally?' Nobby tried to mouth to Stark: 'Who's Sally?'

The lady was a trifle embarrassed. 'You don't remember me, do you?'

Nobby hastily searched his memory. 'Of course I do . . . hold on, I'll come clean; it's slipped my mind, I'm sorry.'

'That's OK. I'm the girl from Bernie Squires' betting shop, remember?'

Nobby remembered. 'Oh *that* Sally. How could I ever forget? How are you? Hey, I'm going to send you the bill for my jacket – your mascara wouldn't come off!' he joked.

Stark scribbled on a piece of paper and held it up for Nobby to read: 'You dirty bastard'. Nobby smiled and displayed his middle finger to Stark, in best American tradition.

Sally was oblivious to the malarky. 'I'm fine. I'd like to apologise for breaking down and crying like that – you must have been really embarrassed. I feel extremely silly now.'

101

Nobby put on his best sympathetic voice. 'Don't feel silly – it's completely understandable. Have you got over it a bit now?'

'Yes, there's no point in worrying about things that we can't change. I would like to thank you for being so kind, if you'd let me?'

Nobby smiled and looked over at Stark before giving his reply. 'That's nice. What did you have in mind? How are you going to thank me?'

Stark screwed up his face and groaned. 'It's pathetic!'

Sally continued with her rehearsed conversation; things were going well. 'I thought you might like to come over to my flat and I'll cook you a nice dinner.'

'It sounds absolutely terrific, but it would have to be quite late?'

Her sensuality travelled through the telephone into Nobby's loins. 'Sounds interesting.' A little giggle followed her observation.

'What – about ten o'clockish?' asked Nobby.

'Great. How does Chicken Tikka grab you?' The excitement in Sally's voice was apparent.

'That sounds absolutely delicious. I can hardly wait.'

'I'll see you then: ten o'clock.'

'*Wait!*' shouted Nobby.

'What's the matter?' asked Sally, concerned.

'I don't know where you live!' The two laughed.

'Oops, sorry! Number 12 Sunderland Court. It's off Mapperley Plains – do you know it?'

'I know it very well. It's quite a select area: I'm impressed!'

Sally offered a word of caution. 'Don't build your hopes up too high. Have you ever been in a student's flat?'

'Would I admit to that if I had?' asked Nobby, smiling.

'It's a date then.'

Nobby agreed. 'Yes, I'll be there. I take it you're on the phone?'

'Yes, it's 309569.'

'Got it. I look forward to seeing you. Take care.'

They said their farewells, and Nobby spoke aloud as he replaced the receiver: 'Well, Clarkey old son, you've done it again.'

Stark spoke. 'I think it's pathetic, a man of your age taking advantage of a poor defenceless girl. I think I should go in your place for the sake of the reputation of the force.'

Nobby laughed. 'Defenceless young girl! Anyway, you're only jealous, boss, and it is an inroad into Bernie Squires' activities.'

Stark shook his head. 'You are so full of sh – '

Nobby raised a warning finger. 'Now, sir, don't be like that.'

Ashley explained Colin Markwell's rights to him as he and Charlie prepared to 'chat' with him in the interview room.

'You are not under arrest, Colin. You are free to leave the police station at any time, and you can consult with a solicitor at any time.' Ashley then cautioned him, but it was Charlie, standing near the door, who started the questioning.

'Right, what were you doing at the back of Maple Close the other night?'

Colin sat on the black plastic chair, staring at the floor. 'I can't remember being at the back of Maple Close,' he said.

'I take it you've heard all about the murders on the news?' asked Ashley.

'Yes, but what's all that got to do with me?'

Ashley continued. 'You were seen running down the back of Maple Close in the early hours of Friday morning. All we want to know is why, Colin?'

Markwell appeared very uncomfortable; he was lying and Ashley and Charlie knew it, but he continued the charade. 'To be honest with you, I don't even know myself what I would want to be doing at the back of Maple Close!'

There wasn't a tape recorder on and Colin wasn't under arrest, but Charlie endeavoured to explain. 'Well, you'd better think and think quickly, because you may not be under arrest at the moment but you're a gnat's bollock away from it!'

'Who says I was there?' Colin enquired with a quick glance at Charlie.

Ashley, however, replied: 'A witness.'

'Yes, but who though?' Colin asked again, his confidence growing.

Charlie interrupted. 'Look, pillock! We ask the bloody questions! Just take it from me that somebody who knows you has seen you running along Maple Close, all right?'

Ashley felt that they had jumped in too aggressively too quickly, but there was no going back. He tried to offer an olive branch. 'Colin, nobody is saying you've done anything wrong. We just want to know why you were there?'

Colin was adamant. 'I'm sorry, but I refuse to answer that question!'

DPW Stephanie Dawson walked into the Oak Tree public house alone, her long flowing hair cascading over the purple, clingy dress that emphasised the curves of her figure. It wasn't personal, but she had been 'paired up' with a young copper and she didn't want her 'snout' scaring off by some spotty-faced youth straight out of training school. Similarly she didn't want the youth's confidence shattered by some embarrassingly accurate insults from the tactless petty criminal she had arranged to meet.

Benny Willows was in his late thirties and scruffy. He stood at the bar of the seedy joint, where sticky bare floorboards welcomed all visitors and ancient pictures of trains hung on the walls in a vain attempt at decoration by the shabby alcoholic landlord. The pub was almost empty. The closest Benny had ever come to the big time was agreeing to drive for an armed robbery a couple of years ago. He'd bottled out at the last minute and had contacted Steph. All his mates had been charged with 'conspiracy to rob' and received five years at the Crown Court. Steph had used her sensuality to cultivate Benny; she knew he fantasised about 'having' her and she just kept him hanging on a thread, with a hint that she would one day let him. She always paid Benny in cash for any good information he gave her; she was running him, not the other way round.

'How much if this comes off, Steph?' Benny was quick to enquire; his toothless grin supported the question.

'If it's any good and we get him charged, you've got to be looking at five hundred, something like that.' Steph knew she could probably get more, but £500 to Benny was a fortune in his current financial state.

Benny asked another question: 'Do I get a thank-you kiss if it pans out OK?'

Steph shuddered at the thought. 'Of course you will. You'll get me into trouble, you will, Benny.' The two laughed.

'Chance would be a fine thing,' he said.

Steph made sure that her ample breasts brushed against him as he leaned over to pay the barman. 'It'd better be good, Benny. How do you know about the murders?' she asked.

He was honest in his reply. 'I don't know about the murders, but I know about her.'

'Who?'

'That tart Faye. She's been about a bit, she has, Steph.'

'What about her?' she asked, sipping at her gin and tonic.

'Five hundred?' Benny smiled.

'Well, I'll put in for six hundred, so I should get five. You know I can't be precise about figures.'

'I'll take you out for a candlelit dinner when I get it,' said Benny, as he wiped his nose on the sleeve of his jacket.

'I'll look forward to that,' said Steph with a straight face.

'Does the name Winston Kelly mean anything to you?' asked Benny with a sideways glance.

'It might do.' The verbal fencing had begun in earnest.

'He was trying to get her on the game, you know.' Benny's mouth widened to give her yet another view of his three stubby teeth, joined together by a chain of thick, clear saliva.

'How do you know that?' asked Steph, closing her eyes momentarily to shut out the ghastly image.

'I've been out with them loads of times. She didn't want to know, though, so he beat her up!'

'When was this, Benny?'

'About a month ago in the Florin pub. He punched her full on, right in the stomach, he did. He's a mental bleeder, you know.'

Steph nodded solemnly. 'I know he is, Benny. What else?'

'He threatened to kill her, Steph. He told her straight out that if she wouldn't go on the game, he'd kill her. Now here she is, dead. He's capable of it too, Steph, believe me.'

Steph was cautious. 'People are threatening to kill each other all the time, Benny.'

'Not people like Winston Kelly. When he says it, he means it!'

105

'Who else witnessed the fight and the threats?' asked Steph, seeking corroboration.

'Everyone. Billy the landlord threatened to throw him out, but he daren't. If it had been me causing the aggro, I'd have been out on my arse.'

'Thanks, Benny.' Steph grabbed at his dirty hand and squeezed it, before hurriedly leaving. Benny felt as if he had been paid already.

Steph quickly checked the information out with Billy the landlord, who was going to tell her about it, 'honest', but he'd been too busy! She told Stark about the information, who laid down plans to contact a magistrate to swear out a warrant to 'do the business' on Winston Kelly.

The interview of Markwell continued.

'What were you carrying that night, Colin?' Ashley asked, hopefully.

'I've told you, I wasn't necessarily there that night,' Colin persisted, his confidence waning.

'In that case, where were you?'

'In town, in the pubs.'

'Which pubs?' asked Charlie.

He moved the plastic chair towards the desk. 'I don't know. I can't remember. The Sentinel, I think.'

'Who with?'

'I was on my own . . . was I? Yes, I was, that's right.'

There was a pause. Charlie 'laid it on the line'. 'Colin, we talk to dozens upon dozens of people a year like this. Do you honestly expect us to believe this bullshit? My grandmother wouldn't believe it!'

'Well, it's all you're getting!' He crossed his legs; his arms were already folded adamantly.

Ashley pleaded with him. 'What are you hiding, Colin?'

'Nothing, honestly. I just can't tell you, that's all.'

Charlie was becoming impatient. 'Have we got to arrest you, Colin? Have we got to burst into your home and search it? Have we got to do it the hard way? Are we being too reasonable with you, eh?'

'There's no need for that.' Colin squirmed in his chair,

106

thinking of the reaction of his wife and children to any such action.

'Why did you say you'd been dreading us coming?' asked Ashley.

'I never said that!' said Colin, not quite as confident as before.

Ashley was certain. 'Yes, you did, Colin, you said it to us as we spoke to you at the door.'

'I didn't!' He turned in the chair to face away from the officers so that he was sideways on to them.

Ashley sighed. 'Look, we're going round in circles here. Do you accept that you were at the back of Maple Close?'

'No!'

'Jesus Christ!' Charlie was becoming rather annoyed.

Ashley continued. 'What were you carrying, Colin?'

He stared blankly at the wall. 'I don't know what you mean.'

Charlie clenched his fists menacingly. He spoke to Ashley. 'Are you going to or am I?'

Colin put his hands up, ready to protect his face, his actions full of melodrama. 'I hope you're not threatening me. I can leave, you know.'

'Of course you can,' said Charlie, his mood apparently changing. 'But get one thing straight: if your arse leaves that chair, it ends up in a cell!'

Nobby had set off dutifully for his rendezvous with Sally. Stark had traced his 'magistrate on call', and Cyril Forsythe was the Justice of the Peace who welcomed the Inspector into his large, detached house. Forsythe was a man in his late forties; he wore well-pressed trousers, a shirt and tie, and a fawn cardigan. He was well groomed and spoke with an authoritative air.

Stark was on his best behaviour. 'I'm sorry to disturb you at the weekend, sir, but I'm sure you'll understand the urgency once I explain.'

'The clerk who rang me informed me that it's regarding the Marriott murders. A ghastly affair,' observed the JP.

Forsythe led Stark into his old-fashioned study and handed him a small black Bible from his large oak bookcase. 'I suppose we ought to get the formalities over with,' he said.

Stark hated this part of the proceedings. It was all right in court, but it felt so silly when there were just two people present. He looked past his attentive host as he gave the slightly different oath: 'I swear by almighty God that the information that I lay before the magistrate is the truth, to the best of my knowledge and belief.'

Forsythe retrieved the Bible from the embarrassed Inspector. 'Thank you, Mr Stark. Now perhaps you will relate to me the basis of the application?'

Stark explained the details over a cup of coffee brought in by Forsythe's lady 'helper'. He explained why he suspected Winston Kelly: the sighting of him with Faye that night; the assault and threats to kill in the Florin public house; his previous convictions; and the general background to the relationship between the two. Stark added that he would like the warrant to arrest Kelly to incorporate the searching of his flat as he suspected that entry would be refused if asked, and that the mere request to enter without the relevant back-up would jeopardise the investigation, resulting in loss of evidence or injury.

Forsythe asked a few token questions before signing the already prepared warrant and the written information that accompanied it. Stark thanked him and said farewell. As he stepped on to the magistrate's drive, Forsythe said, 'Oh, just one other thing, Mr Stark.'

Stark groaned inwardly. 'What's that, sir?'

'Good luck!'

Ernie Gray was out when the knock on the door came. It was expected. Grudgingly, Violet forced herself to answer it.

'Is it Mrs Gray?' Paul Fisher enquired, his warrant card displayed readily at the end of his outstretched arm.

'Yes,' she croaked. Her dry lips bit at her already chipped varnished nails.

'I thought so. I'm DC Fisher from Nottingham CID. Your Ernie's been up to the station earlier, hasn't he?'

Violet nodded. 'Yes, so he tells me, but he's out at the moment.' She swallowed hard.

'That's OK. I'm doing house-to-house enquiries and I notice that you haven't been seen yet.'

Violet bit her bottom lip and said, 'That's OK. I was going to come and see you anyway. You'd better come in.' She couldn't carry the secret any more.

Violet Gray revealed all to young Paul Fisher: her involvement in the activities of the fateful night and how it had all started. Tears were shed and explanations given. At the end of it all, Paul stood on the doorstep of the Gray household and put his hand on her shoulder.

'Don't worry, Mrs Gray. Your secret is safe with me. My Inspector will be more than interested in what you've told me.'

Violet summoned up a tired smile for Paul. 'I'm glad it's over, in a way. Thank you . . . thank you very much.'

Charlie was pacing the interview room floor impatiently. 'What were you doing running around Maple Close like a headless chicken in the early hours of the morning?' he asked for the fifth time.

Colin was getting tedious. 'I've told you all I can tell you.'

Charlie sighed. 'What were you carrying?'

Colin made his declaration. 'Look, I'm getting just a little pissed off with this. OK, I was in Maple Close, but I honestly cannot tell you any more. I am a Christian man. If I could tell you, I would. I know you're getting mad with me, but I don't know what the answer is.'

The door to the interview room opened and a beaming Paul Fisher stood on the threshold. 'Can I have a word with you, Ashley?'

'Yes, sure.' The two men went out, leaving a bemused Charlie alone with Colin Markwell. Charlie could see Paul and Ashley in hysterics outside, through the glass door-panel. He wondered what was the matter with the pair of idiots. Ashley returned to the room alone and spoke to Colin.

'The game's up, mate. We know all about what happened last night. I think you'd better confess all to DC Carter.'

'What do you mean?' Colin asked nervously.

'Well, it's not difficult. I mean, it's time you told DC Carter the whole story about you and Violet Gray!' Ashley spoke confidently.

Colin's head fell into his hands. 'Oh God! How do you know?'

'Violet's told us everything,' Ashley assured him.

And so Colin explained how he had met his unlikely consort at church. He had admired her honesty and strength of character, and they had fallen in love. The affair had been going on for two years now, and he had thought that each of their spouses was oblivious to it. On the night of the murders Colin had been in bed with Violet when they heard a spine-tingling scream. They had both rushed to the window and looked out. Violet had to stop herself from screaming when she saw Ernie staggering towards home. Unbeknownst to the two adulterers, Ernie had suspected the long-standing affair and, in a fit of self-pity, had gone to the pub instead of to work. With the bravado that ten pints of ale bring, Ernie had set off home from his after-hours' session to confront his wife and her lover. He had subsequently been surprised to find her alone in the house. In the panic that ensued, on seeing Ernie returning home, Colin hadn't had time to put on his jacket or shoes and it had been these that he was carrying as he sped down the road, almost knocking the elderly Mrs Charles over as he hared along, not daring to look back.

Charlie refrained from laughing until the story drew to a conclusion. It was at that point that he exploded into a huge guffaw. 'Why didn't you tell us?' he laughed.

Colin stared at the floor. 'I swore on the Bible never to tell a soul!'

'You bloody idiot!'

Charlie showed Markwell to the door, assuring him that they were not at liberty to tell his wife. He returned to the general office. Paul was pleased with himself. 'I told you Pete Glover was right. That was why there was the mistake with his and Ernie's observations that night, why they said that the man they saw was running in different directions. Ernie was pissed and got it around his neck. Ernie was wrong, not Pete.'

Ashley agreed. 'Yes, Markwell said that he was running in the same direction that Glover said, towards Hucknall.'

There was a momentary silence, before the three men simultaneously burst into laughter. 'Poor old Ernie,' Charlie guffawed.

*

Ashley, Paul and Stark met in the pub next door to the station. Charlie had declined the offer to join them, having made prior arrangements to meet an ex-DC he knew from way back in the Miners' Welfare. As always, the three stood at the bar, the odd men out, in their suits and ties; like creatures in the zoo, their every move was assessed by their uninvited audience. The three men were in a jovial mood after the Colin Markwell interview, and they laughed and joked. The pub was thronged. Stark noticed a bronzed, blonde-haired beauty, wearing a tiger-skin summer dress, at the other end of the bar. Unfortunately she appeared to be in male company. He pointed her out to Ashley and Paul, who studied the girl and then her man friend.

'Eh, that's Pete Glover!' Paul declared.

Glover, wearing a rather loud, summery shirt, had noticed the detectives; he waved and started over. Paul introduced Stark to Peter, who ordered a round of drinks.

'What brings you in here, then?' Paul asked his friend.

'I thought I'd try it for a change. I didn't think I'd see you reprobates here.'

'Well, it is next door to the nick, Pete,' Stark observed.

'True, true. So what's happening? How's the investigation going? Obviously very well if you're in here boozing!'

Paul laughed. 'Sort of OK. We've had no confessions yet. How are you fixed?'

Pete put his hands out, wrists together. 'OK, I'll come clean. Take me away, officer!' The men laughed.

Ashley was interested in other things. 'Here, who's the dolly bird, if you don't mind me asking?'

Paul beat him to the answer. 'He probably doesn't even know her name, the amount of women this guy gets through!'

Pete smiled, proudly. 'Now don't be like that – you'll get me a reputation.'

'You've already got a reputation,' Paul commented.

Stark joined in the banter. 'I tell you what, Pete, she can give me a bad reputation any day of the week!'

There was pause. Stark's attention was drawn to the door-way. 'Eh, look who's here!' He nudged Ashley.

The heavily muscled body weaved through the crowds towards the bar. The man, with his broken nose and short-cropped hair, towered well above everybody else. Thirty years

111

old, wearing jeans and a tight-fitting, light-blue collared T-shirt, the well-known criminal was smiling as he made a wake through the sea of people.

'Isn't that Terry Banner?' asked Paul, butterflies starting in his stomach.

Stark was ready with the reply. 'Yes. I'm surprised to see him: the last intelligence on him said he was down the smoke.'

Pete Glover turned around to see and promptly trod on Banner's soft grey shoes. The hardnut's smiling face turned serious and his eyes flashed wide.

'What do you think you're fucking doing?' he barked at Pete, who had turned white. Banner's fists clenched, but relaxed when he saw Stark.

'All right, Terry. No problem, I take it?' said the DI. There was a challenge in his facial expression.

Banner thought better of a confrontation and turned away. 'Hello,' was all he could muster.

On hearing the reluctant greeting, a memory came searing through from Stark's subconscious: the voice on the telephone in Bernie Squires' office!

Nobby's red BMW pulled into the kerb adjacent to Sunderland Court. He peered through his car window at the ageing house. It was three storeys high, with a dirty-grey, pebble-dashed façade. The large oak front door was barely visible in the darkness of the shadow cast by the stone archway which surrounded it. Nobby alighted from the car and his hard leather heels clicked on the large paving slabs, which had become uneven through the ravages of time. The slabbed path to the house dissected a garden of overgrown shrubs. He pushed open the exterior door, which led into a somewhat dingy and dusty entrance hall. A corridor peeled off to the left, revealing four bare wooden doors, even-numbered; generous wooden stairs faced him. He began to climb, disturbing a ginger tom-cat who leapt on to the banister and eyed the stranger suspiciously.

The effort of climbing the stairs added to Nobby's sticky feeling in the mugginess of the late-summer evening. It was a quiet building, too quiet, and Nobby began to feel strangely uneasy as he found Number 12 in the far corner of the landing to his left. Perhaps he should have brought Stark after all.

He tapped on the blue-painted door, not wanting to disturb the quietness of the sleepy building. There was no reply. He knocked again, only harder, straining to hear any noises from behind the door. There were none. The silence was becoming unbearable. He checked his watch: he was on time. His heart began to beat faster; he was becoming slightly concerned. He banged on the door a third time with the side of his powerful fist. Still nothing. He tried the door handle: it was locked, a Yale lock. He placed his ear to the door: still nothing. He banged again: quiet.

He had a choice: either he walked away, or he put the door in. He shouted 'Sally' loudly, his voice reverberating around the rafters in the eerie silence.

He thought aloud. 'She knew I was coming . . . Oh, stuff it!' He stepped back three yards to get a good kick at it, leaning his large frame back to gather momentum for the kick. It was at this point that the door opened. Nobby became unbalanced as he stopped the kick in its infancy. He stumbled to his right, having to steady himself on the banister.

Sally's happy face suddenly became troubled. 'You're not drunk, are you?' she asked, removing her stereo earphones.

Nobby was embarrassed. 'No, no . . . sorry . . . er, how are you? I've been knocking ages.' He quickly regained his composure.

Sally was wearing tight-fitting jeans and a loose white T-shirt; her young breasts moved independently, without the support of a bra. Her jet-black hair shone in the new brightness emanating from her room.

'You've been knocking ages? Oh, I never thought – sorry.' She threw the earphones on to the floor just inside the doorway and continued with the explanation: 'It's old grumpy next door. She's about ninety, so I have to resort to those.'

Nobby stepped into the flat at Sally's invitation. The open-plan kitchenette was to his right, its lino floor stopping to allow an old carpet to lead into the living area. There was a large, soft brown settee and two armchairs, both of which looked as though they were straight out of an old people's home, with high backs and wooden arm-rests. A rectangular glass coffee-table, dead centre, strained under the weight of numerous books. A small portable television rested on a shelf in the corner, next to a storage heater, which lay redundant on the warm summer night. A shelf ran along one wall, supporting family pictures and some cheap ornaments. Black-and-white framed pictures of moody coastal scenes adorned the white woodchip wallpaper.

Nobby, feeling slightly awkward, stood on the lino as Sally closed the door behind him. She asked, 'What do I call you? Sergeant, Mr Clarke or what?'

'Everybody calls me Nobby.'

'Oh, right. I'd better not ask why.' The two laughed nervously. Nobby could smell the aroma of the Indian dish coming from the second-hand gas cooker.

'Smells lovely. What is it, did you say? Chicken Tikka?'

Sally nodded, her hands behind her back. Her breasts stood out proudly.

'Yes. I hope you like it?'

Nobby smiled. 'I love it.'

They sat down on the chairs, and made small-talk for around half an hour, before Sally served up the meal. She apologised for their having to eat it off a tray. Nobby shook his head and waved a dismissive hand. 'Don't be silly – it's the only way to eat.' He was glad he hadn't brought Stark after all.

At the end of the meal they sipped at their coffee. The conversation had relaxed, and Nobby asked her about her Uncle Bernie.

'You don't think I like him, do you?' She sounded surprised that he would.

Nobby shrugged his shoulders. 'Well, I don't know what I thought. I . . .'

Sally continued. 'I know what he is, you know. I won't have anything to do with his underhand dealings. I only work there for the money. He pays well for people who work hard and don't ask questions.'

'And that's what you do, is it?' Nobby asked, seriously.

'Yes.' There was a momentary pause. Sally swirled the dregs of her coffee around the base of the plain white mug.

'Is something the matter, Sally?' Nobby enquired.

'Well, it's probably nothing, and I wouldn't accuse anybody . . . I mean, much as I dislike the man, he is my uncle,' Sally thought out loud.

Nobby's experience had taught him that often the best way to get information was not to ask for it. 'Listen, you don't have to tell me anything. I've just come around as your guest . . .'

Sally plucked up the necessary courage. 'No, I will tell you, Nobby – you seem a nice man.' She stared at the coffee mug. 'You see, Faye and Uncle Bernie had a love-hate relationship. He more or less ignored me, but he was all over Faye. He fancied her something rotten. Obviously she didn't fancy him.'

'Hence the groping sessions I've heard about?'

'You've got it. She suffered those, but I walked in on them once, in his office.' Nobby sipped his coffee, listening intently. Sally looked sad and lonely as she related her story. 'Faye was in the corner of the room and Uncle Bernie stood in front of her with his arm resting on the wall, as if blocking her path. They looked startled as I came in. I apologised and left, but not before noticing the fear in Faye's eyes. She was scared, Nobby, really scared! When I got outside, I listened at the door. I could hardly hear, but I could tell Uncle Bernie was angry.'

Nobby's face remained serious, his eyebrows raised. 'What were they talking about, Sally?'

She shook her head. 'I'm afraid I don't know. I'm sorry.'

'When was this?' he asked.

'About a week ago. We'd just closed. I think it was a week last Thursday.'

Nobby persisted. 'Did you hear anything at all of the conversation, Sally?'

'I'm sorry – that's all I can tell you.'

Nobby felt sorry for Sally; she was a lonely kid, and as he left she grabbed his arm and asked him to stay 'a little longer'. He was tempted, but even he didn't have it in him to hurt such a vulnerable girl, so he made his excuses and left.

He called Stark at home from a nearby telephone kiosk. Stark was obviously very interested and immediately notified the detectives who were targeting Bernie Squires.

8

'If called by a panther, don't anther.'
Ogden Nash (1902–1971)

Carol turned over, the bed her cocoon of warmth. She reached for her husband: he was gone. He stood at the bedroom door, sounding like a music-hall ventriloquist as he tried in vain to make Carol understand him from behind the froth that he'd created as he brushed his teeth.

Carol struggled out her instructions in a sleepy daze. 'Rinse your mouth out, Dave, and I might be able to understand you.'

Dave rinsed his mouth out and returned to the bedroom to kiss his wife. 'Morning, darling.'

'Good morning, hunky.' The two hugged each other.

'You don't have to get up, you know,' Dave assured his wife.

'I know, but I'll probably go back to bed when you've gone,' mused Carol. She wrenched her body out of the quilt and off the white ruffled sheet. She stretched. 'Most normal people are in bed at this time on a Sunday.' Her eyes sagged.

'So who wants to be normal?' Stark replied.

'I do. I'll go and put your breakfast on.'

Carol put her robe on and flounced downstairs. Dave stepped into the shower cubicle and relaxed as the powerful jets of water cascaded on to his aching body. This life cannot be good for you, he thought.

A banging on the bathroom door jarred into his privacy. 'What's the matter?' he shouted, trying to sound interested, but only succeeding in sounding irritated.

Christopher's young voice sounded desperate. 'Come on, Dad, I want to go to the toilet!'

'Bloody marvellous!' Dave quickly rinsed himself down and stepped out of the cubicle. He threw a towel around himself and opened the door. The blond-haired, blue-eyed boy was a comical sight as he stood with his hands squeezing into his privates, his pyjama'd legs crossed.

'About blooming time, Dad,' Christopher said, as he ran in and shut the door behind him. Dave heard the bolts slide across on the inside. He dried his hair, put his robe on and ventured downstairs.

As he entered the living-room, he pressed the button that created images of annoying people talking heatedly. The television couldn't be heard upstairs, where Laura continued the dreams that her parents wouldn't let her watch if they were a movie.

Dave was sitting in the armchair as Carol walked in with the food. 'Here you are, love. I've done you some bacon sandwiches.'

He ate the sandwiches heartily, pausing only to thank Carol for the effort she had put into making them. He stared at the television, but the images he saw were those created in his own mind. He pondered the forthcoming day's events. He knew that Kelly had access to firearms; in fact, word had it that he might have one in his flat. Unfortunately, however, rumour didn't qualify one to draw on the glorious resource of the armed-response teams. The best he could do was arrange for an armed-response traffic car to be in the area at the time of the raid, and take a dog-handler in with him. One of these days, the rumours were going to be justified, and another needless police widow would receive the knock on the door. Stark hoped it wouldn't be today, and that it wouldn't be Carol receiving the sycophantic condolences of a senior officer who had ignored him in the corridor the day before.

'Have you got a shirt ironed?' Carol asked hopefully.

Stark glanced at the clock on his brick fireplace. 'I don't know. Have a look, will you, Carol?'

Carol reappeared with a clean but unironed white shirt. Stark's response was spontaneous. 'Bloody hell, Carol, I've got to be going in ten minutes! I was just coming up to get dressed!'

Carol tried to remain unflustered. 'It won't take a minute!'

Dave could feel himself becoming more and more tense as the 'minute' turned into five. Carol followed him upstairs and watched him get dressed. He was a big man and he had kept his strong muscular body hard despite the onslaught of approaching middle age.

'What are you doing today, Dave?' asked his wife.

'We're going to try and nick a black guy and see what he's got to say to us,' Stark replied, sparing his wife the doubts and fears that such an action can bring with it.

'Oh. I thought I might take the kids to Wollaton Hall, if Laura hasn't planned on seeing that boyfriend of hers. Have you had that talk with her about going on the pill?'

'But I don't want to go on the pill,' said Stark, as he hurriedly buttoned up his shirt.

Carol threw a pillow at him. 'You know what I mean. She's fifteen, you know. Think what you were doing at that age!'

Stark threw the pillow back. 'I daren't – it frightens me to death! I'll have a word with her when I get time, which is precisely what I don't have at the moment!'

Carol sat on the pillow Stark had thrown back at her, one leg dangling over the side of the bed. 'What time will you be back tonight, Dave?'

'I don't know.' Dave kissed her, then held her tightly. He squeezed hard, closing his eyes and caressing her hair. The danger of the day ahead flashed across his mind. He spoke softly to her: 'I love you, darling. You know that, don't you?'

Carol was oblivious to his private fears. 'Of course I do. What's the matter with you?'

'Nothing, love.' Dave took a deep breath and released his grip. 'Listen, I'll try to be home as soon as I can.' He walked down the stairs to the door.

'See you, love,' shouted Carol. 'Time's running out for our Laura, you know.' The door slammed shut. She jumped back into bed and became lost in the literary wonders of Jackie Collins.

Time was also running out for Winston Kelly. Those officers present in the room were after him and they were determined to get him. Stark had explained the plan of attack. He and Nobby would go to the front door accompanied by a dog man, Steph and two SOU men with a sledgehammer and crowbar to effect a forced entry, if required. There were no back doors in the flat complex. They didn't know how many men would be in the flat; there could be just Kelly, or there could be half a dozen – there was no way of knowing. The armed-response traffic car was only allowed to tour the area, low-key. They would use a separate radio channel to ensure that there would be no routine transmissions at the crucial time of the mini-operation. Everybody was to bring their truncheons and hand-cuffs. If there were any females on the premises, they were Steph's business. Once captured, Kelly would be handcuffed and searched immediately. SOU would remain behind whilst Kelly was taken away, and they were to search the flat, outhouses downstairs, garage and car. Stark gave them a potted history of Kelly and his capabilities, and warned them about his extremely violent nature. The interminable rumours that circu-lated about his behaviour indicated that he had 'disposed' of a 'Yardie', a fellow West Indian, in Birmingham three years ago.

'Right,' said Stark, 'let's go. Pull into position out of sight first, then I'll give you the word to strike over the radio.'

The small bedroom was dirty. It was furnished by a solitary item: a bed. The bed was surrounded by a pile of clothes, strewn around by their unfastidious owners. The ashtray on the floor at the side of the bed was overflowing with roll-ups and reefers. The sweet, pungent smell of marijuana hung in the atmosphere. The sheets were soiled and displayed a cigarette burn towards the foot of the bed.

The quilt had been thrown off as the two people became active on the sheets, which were covered in dry semen stains. Kelly made the skinny young blonde squeal as he entered her from behind, as she positioned herself on all fours on the bed. She thought her insides were going to burst as she arched her back and let out a cry that was a mixture of both pain and ecstasy. She had been hoping that the two sessions they had in the night had satisfied him; but no, he wanted more. She threw her head back as he thrust into her; she clawed at the sheets; his Rastafarian dreadlocks tickled the side of her face whenever he lowered his head to bite at her neck. He pummelled into her with great force and speed. She turned her head in an attempt to seek moderation, but she didn't dare speak to the eyes that stared at her so wildly. Kelly took pleasure in hurting people.

The pain grew as the relentless onslaught continued, and she groaned out loud. Her strength fading, she grew courageous. 'Stop! Stop! Please!' she begged, her speech distorted by the pounding of bone into bone, racking her entire body. Still he continued, until her pleadings turned into sobs. The crying seemed to stimulate Kelly, and the rush of orgasm forced his long length of penis into her, up to the hilt. The arms that had been supporting the girl collapsed and her face crashed into the headboard. Kelly thrust into her, harder but more slowly, his throbbing penis emptying into her. A smile touched her face as it was rhythmically forced between the base of the headboard and the mattress. Kelly had finished. The girl was in a sexual whirlwind, confused about her emotions. They lay together for a while, before he withdrew and reached for a cigarette.

Kelly claimed to be a Rastafarian. True Rastafarians are mellow, peace-loving people. Kelly was a violent, hardened criminal. He ran prostitutes and dealt in drugs; he was interested only in money and power. He was a big man, six foot three inches tall and powerfully built. He tied his long dreadlocks back over his shoulders and strode around the Hyson Green area of Nottingham as if he owned it. He was a bully; he gesticulated aggressively and spoke in a loud, challenging voice. If it suited him, he could use a normal, reasonably educated voice; but to keep his street credibility on a high, a strong patois, such as many young Rastafarians speak, was his usual tongue.

Despite his aggressive appearance, Kelly was quite intelligent, and it was his clever manipulation of people that had gained him his false standing among his 'brothers' in the community. He had been arrested by the 'Babylon' several times and charged with only one offence on each occasion. Kelly didn't talk to 'filth'. He claimed to be oppressed by authority, but he wasn't a tenth as oppressed as the young girls he had taken advantage of, the girls who in their innocence became enslaved by the ingenuity of sheer evil cunning. Once he had put the girls on the street as prostitutes, he would ensure that he had complete control over them. If there was a hint or suggestion that they had cheated him, or if they tried to return whence they came, he was not averse to forcing them to sit naked in a bath of bleach, until their private parts became swollen and sore, causing agonising pain.

Kelly abused women's vulnerability; he abused the children he had spawned around the place; he was all-powerful. That was about to change. It was soon to be his turn to be bullied, his turn to know what fear is, his turn to do what he was told.

Stark had seen Kelly's BMW car parked in its usual place in the street, outside his two-storey flat, with its entrance at ground level. The four cars and a transit van pulled slowly into the kerb, out of site of Kelly's flat.

Stark spoke into his radio: 'Is everybody fully clear about their jobs? If not, speak now.' There was a silence, followed by his command: '*Strike! Strike! Strike!*'

The vehicles sped around the corner and screeched to a halt. Their occupants jumped out and raced to their positions. The adrenalin was pumping, hearts were beating fast and senses strained to the limit.

Stark arrived at the dirty grey door and hammered on it. '*Police – open up!*' He could only guess at the pandemonium inside. He hammered on the door a second time. '*Open up! Police!*' Neighbouring dogs began to bark and curtains twitched; the police dog, Goliath, joined in the canine chorus as he strained at his leash, his large fangs exposed and dripping saliva.

Stark stepped aside. 'Right, I'm not waiting all bleeding morning – hit it!' Keeping his distance from the dog, he shouted at the door: '*Keep away from the door: we're breaking it down!*'

It took one well-practised blow from the sledgehammer to split the door almost in two as it crashed off its hinges. Stark ran in first, followed by the rest.

'*Police!*' Stark shouted as they quickly checked the downstairs rooms, which were empty. The group ran upstairs, Stark leading from the front. He and Nobby together attempted to open the door ahead of them. It moved a few inches, then slammed shut again. Obviously the occupant didn't want to let the nice policemen in.

121

Stark shouted through the wooden barrier: *'Don't make it harder than it's got to be!'* The platitude was ignored.

Nobby was on an adrenalin high. He succinctly explained the position to the occupant: *'Move out the way of the door, Kelly, or the sledgehammer's going to smash it down and you with the fucker!'* Nobby had a very persuasive way with words, and his impassioned plea obviously had a good effect: the door opened. The group burst in.

The skinny white tart lay curled up on the bed, the quilt pulled over her, only partly concealing her naked body. Kelly stood in the far corner of the room in his baggy brown underpants. The knife he was holding was a large one – the blade itself was four inches long, and all eyes focused on it.

Stark spoke, an immediate conciliatory response. 'Now don't be stupid – just drop the knife, Winston, and we'll say no more about it!'

The dog man had subconsciously unclipped the lead and held the heaving mound of teeth and muscle back with great effort by the collar. Kelly didn't drop the knife; he began walking towards the group with his arms outstretched. He waved the knife from left to right. He was smiling and his eyes were wide and dispassionate.

On police open days the public applauds with great enthusiasm the way in which police dogs majestically attach themselves to the outstretched padded arm of the fleeing 'villain'. That's not what generally happens in real life. A police dog bites the first thing on the aggressor that it happens to focus on, as soon as it is released by the handler. Police dogs can be evil. Goliath was the most evil! The first thing Goliath focused on as he was released were Kelly's testicles.

Even Nobby winced. The knife went flying, and there was an indescribable scream of pain from Kelly. The tart's hand went to her mouth and her eyes widened. Kelly's eyes widened too.

The dog-handler bellowed: *'Leave!'* Goliath's ears went down; he released his grip and returned to his handler with his head down and the whites of his eyes displayed sheepishly as he glanced up at his master. Nobby looked at the dog with pride; he felt sure – no, surely not: dogs can't smile. Kelly rolled on the floor screaming and crying, clutching between his legs.

Nobby thought he could see blood. He patted the dog: 'Good boy.'

Kelly was handcuffed. He had been lucky. Later that day the police surgeon noted bruising to the testicles and blood emanating from small cuts on his lower abdomen, just above the pubis.

SOU stayed at the flat and searched it. They seized two Bowie knives; one flick knife: a woolly red, yellow and green 'Rasta' hat; four reefers; and some plastic 'dealer bags', some of which contained a vegetable matter that was undoubtedly cannabis.

Stark ascertained that the tart was only fifteen years old and had been reported missing from one of the local children's homes. She was returned, quite the worse for wear, and not on the pill. Stark thought of Laura.

Kelly, of course, had asked to see a solicitor, a Mr Bard from Kirkham, Turner and Ross. The better criminals usually asked for him. Stark had attempted to delay access to a solicitor but Chief Inspector Turley had insisted that they play safe.

Stark entered the interview room with Nobby. Kelly sat next to his solicitor. Mr Bard was good. He was a small man with a thin face and wispy moustache; he wore the almost obligatory pin-striped suit and carried a black briefcase that appeared to be a little too heavy for him. Stark and Nobby sat down on the other side of the table. Three suits and a black shiny tracksuit manoeuvred for positions. Stark turned on the tape and went through the routine. At first Kelly refused to give his name on tape, but Mr Bard assured him that, although he had the right to remain silent, he could give the officers his name and personal details to speed things up a little, for identification purposes only.

Stark began the interview proper. 'Have we met before, Winston?'

Kelly leaned on the desk with his arms folded and stared at Stark unflinchingly, his dreadlocks hanging limply on his shoulders. Stark had encountered this manner with other West Indians he had interviewed; he wasn't sure what it was supposed to do – it just meant that everybody became slightly embarrassed. Perhaps that was the reason behind it, who knows? Stark was not going to be intimidated, nor was he going to go away.

'What were you doing in the early hours of 24 August, a couple of days ago, Winston?'

Silence, just staring.

Stark continued. 'I see, it's going to be one of those jobs, is it? Well, I've got plenty of time.' He leaned back in his chair and put his feet on the spare chair that he had brought in from the other room. He went on: 'What were you doing the other night, Winston? You might be an innocent man for all I know. Oh, by the way, I almost forgot, consider yourself under arrest for possession of cannabis, resisting arrest and unlawful sexual intercourse with a girl under the age of sixteen years – in addition to murder, of course.'

Kelly began to shake his head. He tutted and began to chant: 'Babylon burn . . . Babylon burn . . . Babylon burn . . .'

Well, if nothing else, it was a reaction. Stark pondered. He raised his voice over the chanting. 'So are you a true Rastafarian or what?'

Kelly stopped his chanting and just said 'Whiteboy!' in heavy patois. He continued his staring.

It was apparent that Stark had a big communication problem. 'That's very observant, Winston, but not particularly relevant. You see, if you give us proof that you didn't kill the Marriott family, I'll be happy to drop the murder tag.' Stark smiled at the staring face and received silence in return. He continued: 'Did you know a girl called Faye Marriott, Winston?'

Silence.

'Were you with Faye Marriott the other night, Winston?'

Silence.

'We're trying to get the truth, Winston. If you haven't done it, fine. Prove it to us and we'll go and find the bloke that has.'

Silence.

Mr Bard piped up. 'I'm sure it's apparent even to you, Mr Stark, that my client doesn't wish to answer any of your questions, so I can hardly see the point in continuing.'

Nobby clenched his fists under the table.

Stark smiled. He had been underestimated. 'I'm surprised you didn't know that I also have the right to ask him questions. I'm sorry if this makes you uncomfortable, but ask them I will,

Mr Bard.' He looked into the staring eyes of Kelly and smiled. 'All right, Winston?'

Kelly laughed. 'Checkout, bigshot.'

It's going to be a long day, thought Stark.

Charlie watched Ashley scribbling on a piece of paper at his desk in the CID general office. It was the result of a telephone call that Ashley had just brought to an end, and Charlie was curious. 'Who was that, Ashley?'

He didn't look up; he carried on scribbling as he spoke. 'The Forensic Science Lab at Huntingdon, giving us an update on their work so far.'

'So what did they say?'

Ashley stopped writing and swivelled his chair to face his cigar-smoking friend. 'Well, the plastic shoelace loop in the back garden comes from shoes made by Clarks. It's used only in their grey-coloured ones and there's eight different styles of shoes that they used the loop on.'

Charlie looked thoughtful. 'Well, it's a start,' he said optimistically.

Ashley raised an eyebrow. 'Apparently there are three hundred and fifty thousand such shoes on the market!'

Charlie exhaled some smoke. 'Oh,' was all he could muster.

Ashley continued with the good news. 'Yes. The red fibres are from a crimson-red jumper or cardigan which is approximately eight months old.'

'Brilliant! What would we do without them?' Charlie's momentary optimism had gone.

Ashley was philosophical. 'Come on, be fair. It's not one piece that completes the jigsaw, it's the whole lot put together.'

Stark had never agreed with the ethic employed by some detectives, that if a suspect remains silent all you can do is ask him the relevant standard questions, return him to his cell and try to prove it some other way. He felt that it was not only defeatist, but it was also the easy way out. He would talk to Kelly and he would ask him questions; he didn't need a reply to motivate him, because he knew that no matter what Kelly did, he couldn't help but listen. Kelly couldn't escape and, if nothing else, it put him under that bit more pressure – which, despite his image, he was undoubtedly under. Stranger things had happened; who knew, he might give up and admit it, or at least make a mistake.

'How long have you known Faye, Winston?'

Silence.

'Months, years, or what?'

Silence.

'Have you had sex with her?'

Silence.

The pause after each question would always be around five seconds, but no more, because after that length of time human nature, even if one is aware of what is happening, dictates an overwhelming subconscious urge to say something, especially if the question is directed at one. Stark knew that Kelly was under pressure because a couple of seconds after each question he would shift his position in his seat.

'Tell us you haven't done it, Winston. We might believe you.'

Silence.

'We know you've punched her, Winston.'

Kelly glared at the tape recorder and began rocking his upper body backwards and forwards.

'Don't you like the tape recorder, Winston? Are you afraid of its honesty? Are you scared?'

Kelly gave Stark a mock smile and began drumming the table with the flats of his hands. Another reaction; things were looking up.

'What are you scared of, Winston?'

Kelly continued his drumming and resumed his chant. 'Babylon burn . . . Babylon burn . . .'

Stark continued, his voice raised. 'I'm not asking for an admission, Winston, just where you were, stuff like that.'

Mr Bard butted in. 'My client doesn't want to tell you, Mr Stark!'

Stark ignored him. He took his feet down and leaned on the table, close to Kelly's face. 'Yes, you do, Winston. You don't want to be in the frame for murder if you haven't done it, do you?'

Silence. Kelly looked down at his shiny tracksuit trousers and

126

brushed some imaginary dust off them. He was feeling the pressure.

Paul Fisher had completed the witness checks that the HOLMES computer had, as a matter of course, given him.

Obviously Ernie Gray had been telling the truth, as his wife and Colin Markwell could testify all too painfully. So had Pete Glover; in addition to the Markwell episode he had, as Paul diligently checked, been to the nearby garage and bought a gallon of petrol; he had collected the till receipt as instructed by the computer.

The milkman too was telling the truth, which also came as no surprise to Paul. The milkman had continued his round and accepted payment from several customers before and after the Marriott household, and he was not dripping with blood as he collected the money.

It was getting on towards lunchtime and Stark knew only too well that the Police and Criminal Evidence Act dictated that Mr Kelly must have his refreshment at the appropriate hour. He decided that at the end of the tape he would adjourn proceedings.

'You were trying to get her on the game, Winston. She didn't want to know, so you punished her, Winston, but you went too far. You killed her, didn't you?'

Silence.

'But unfortunately her mum and dad came home and caught you, didn't they?'

Silence.

'So you killed them and pretended it was a burglary, didn't you?'

Kelly shook his head and stared down at the desk in front of him.

Stark continued. 'You've even been seen running away from the scene, Winston. You see, it's got to be you, 'cos you've done it, haven't you?'

Silence.

The interview went on along much the same lines until the end of the tape.

'Do you wish to clarify anything you've said, or do you wish to add anything?' Stark was compelled by law to ask.

Silence.

'The time now is 12.40 p.m. and we'll stop the tape.'

Stark and Nobby sat at the table in the station kitchen. Nobby tucked into his fish, chips and peas, but he didn't refrain from talking simply because his mouth was full. 'I tell you what I think . . . his big black arse wants kicking all round the station!'

Stark nodded. 'I couldn't agree more, but that isn't going to help us prove murder, is it?'

They discussed the options open to them. Stark decided that if the stalemate continued, they would charge him with unlawful sexual intercourse, resisting arrest and possession of cannabis, and apply to the Magistrates' Court for him to be detained in police custody for a further three days, or to be remanded in prison. They would seek further evidence and apply for three days' interviewing at a police station at a subsequent remand hearing, when they should have more evidence to put to him.

In the mean time, Stark ordered his men to go out on the streets and get some evidence on Kelly. They were to shake the bag and see what fell out.

9

'All truths are half-truths.'
Alfred North Whitehead (1861–1947)

The woman on the street corner displayed the tattoos – almost immediately regretted – on her wrists and an artistic but common swallow flitting across her exposed shoulder blades. At thirty, she knew the ropes. She had remained rather trim through the exercise her employment gave her; her bleached blonde hair was offset by heavy mascara, recklessly smeared around her eyes. She didn't like working on a Sunday afternoon, but times had been hard. Kelly hadn't had sex with her for a couple of weeks and she felt that she was falling out of favour. She wanted to impress him with a higher income this week and so avoid the beating that she felt was only a wrong word away.

She was growing disgruntled; business had been slow, all her regular punters were obviously mowing their lawns or washing their cars. She noticed a blue Vauxhall Senator drive slowly past her; she wasn't sure if he was interested or just a 'gawker'. She smiled at the driver, who seemed a little tense. Things were looking up. There was only one other girl on the street and she appeared to be new to the game. Maureen had her usual working clothes on: tight-fitting top, no bra and a black PVC mini-skirt which was so short it revealed the darker part of her black stocking tops. She tottered on four-inch stiletto heels. She was not an unattractive woman, but her attempts to look more so had spoiled the original specimen and she was beginning to look old beyond her years.

The Vauxhall Senator reappeared and drew up alongside where Maureen stood. The man looked apprehensive and offered a nervous smile. He was middle-aged, balding, chubby and sweating. Maureen confirmed that she was doing 'business' and informed the prospective purchaser of the rates: fifteen pounds for straight sex, twenty pounds for nude sex, and anything – and she meant anything – was negotiable. The man nodded and opened his passenger door to allow the tart access. Maureen made small-talk with the punter as she directed him to her flat. His eyes kept flicking to his rear-view mirror; Maureen reassured him in her broad Geordie accent: 'Don't worry, love, I've not seen no vice squad all day.'

The man glanced down at Maureen's firm, tanned thighs, the tops of which were exposed above her stockings as her mini-skirt rode up towards her crotch. He was beginning to enjoy his little adventure. Maureen rubbed his inner thigh and told him to pull in at the tower block of flats in front of them. Hers was the ground-floor flat at the end. It was on two levels.

The man could hear a television on in a downstairs room as he was ushered immediately upstairs; he heard a child's voice as he pushed open the thin, hollow door. The room was unkempt and tawdry. The wattage of the unshaded bulb was inadequate, but the punter seemed comforted by this as he undressed and revealed his plump white body. Maureen, as always, had taken the twenty pounds first and hidden it in an adjacent room. The two lay on the bed. The man attempted to kiss Maureen, but she pushed him away, explaining the rules: 'No kissing.' She massaged his genitals methodically and mechanically, without interest or emotion. She was confident that it would all soon be over and she could return to her 'beat'. His penis was large, and when it grew erect she masturbated it with two hands, one on top of the other. The man began to groan; if she timed it right, he wouldn't be inside her for long. She was slightly bored and wondered how many of her sex had missed out on the excitement such a large weapon could bring them, simply because of the man's outward appearance. The act would hold no excitement for Maureen; she was simply interested in performing a physical act, completely aloof from what she classed as sex, for the purpose of obtaining money. The sooner it was over the better.

She reached over to the bedside table and lubricated herself as a precaution. She then rolled the customary sheath on to the man's penis and he rolled on to her. He had to raise his backside high in the air to give him room to manoeuvre his long, thick shaft into a position to enter her. This he did slowly

130

and deliberately. He puffed and panted away; Maureen felt obliged to let out a few moans and groans, as this usually hurried a punter up. She was wrong. Ten minutes became fifteen, and she was starting to feel slightly uncomfortable as there appeared to be no sign of the man ejaculating. Maureen reached down and toyed with his testicles, squeezing them gently. This did the trick; he groaned aloud and pumped his seed into the prophylactic. He withdrew quickly and rolled off, much to the relief of Maureen, who this time let out a genuine groan. The man's pink face betrayed the fact that it had all been rather a strenuous physical effort for him.

Maureen got off the bed to put her knickers on, while the punter sat on the edge of the bed holding the used sheath, not knowing quite what to do with it. The two glanced at each other; they could hear raised voices downstairs.

DPW Stephanie Dawson knocked on the double-glazed windows of the UPVC door. He was the last on her list. After a short time a well-built man of around thirty answered it.

'Yes, my love, what can I do for you?' He smiled a toothy grin.

'I'm Detective Policewoman Dawson from Nottingham CID. May I speak to you in private, please?'

The smile faded. 'Well, what is it about?'

'Your name has been found in the diary of a young woman – Faye Marriott.'

The man didn't have time to reply before his two-year-old boy appeared between his legs and a woman's voice could be heard in the background. 'Who is it, darling?'

The man called over his shoulder, 'It's OK, love, I've got it.' Stephanie could see the panic in his eyes. She shook her head.

The man spoke to her in a whisper. 'Come and see me at work, McInley's Engineering, 210 Mapperley Plains.' He shut the door in her face.

She had a problem: did she ruin a marriage or not? Is he being discreet to save his marriage, or is there something in the house or that his wife knows that he doesn't want the police to find out? Stephanie shrugged her shoulders and muttered to herself: 'You made the choice, pal, when you got your cock out. It's you who took the risk!'

DPW Stephanie Dawson again knocked on the double-glazed window of the UPVC door.

Charlie had known Maureen for the three years she had been on the streets in Nottingham. She could be a wildcat at times and her faggot brother was just as bad. Now as the young gay, Reginald, opened the door, in his off-white, baggy silk shirt and floral neck-scarf, Ashley asked, 'Is Maureen here?'

'No!'

It was only Charlie's size elevens that prevented the door being slammed in their faces, and it was his shoulder that caused it to be slammed into Reginald's face. The wiry youth camped up his protest. 'Oh, how dare you!'

'Thanks for inviting us in, Reggie. You don't mind if we check, do you?'

Charlie's question didn't beg an answer. It was as he and Ashley entered the house that Reggie started the shouting; he effed and blinded as Charlie and his companion checked the downstairs rooms. Reggie had hoped the furore would alert his sister, busy upstairs. It did. Pandemonium broke out in Maureen's bedroom. She hastily fastened her stockings, her bare nipples becoming erect for the first time in the panic. The rotund punter, his dream turned nightmare, struggled to his feet and hopped around the bedroom with new-found energy in an attempt to put a sock on.

Charlie told Reggie to put a sock in it, as he threw open the bedroom door. The comical pair inside froze, momentarily, in their states of undress. Maureen was the first to move. She flew at Charlie with fingers outstretched and nails exposed, like a cat landing from a very high jump. Charlie caught her wrists and threw her on to the bed.

'Now don't be naughty, Maureen. Sunday is supposed to be a day of rest, you know!'

Maureen was breathing heavily and quickly as she lay on the bed, her rather splendid bare breasts rising and falling, attempting to keep pace with her diaphragm. The punter, meanwhile, had escaped under Ashley's arm, as the detective leaned against the door. Ashley turned his head to see the man's large pink bottom wobble downstairs and away out of the front door. Reggie raised an eyebrow as he craned his neck to follow the fleeing punter's naked form, disappearing out on to the street.

'What the pissing hell do you want, Charlie Carter?' Maureen said eloquently. She reached for her cigarettes on the bedside table, lit one up and exaggerated her exhale. She made no attempt to cover her heaving breasts.

Charlie explained the reason for his impromptu visit. 'Sorry to burst in like this, Maureen, but the shit's hit the fan!' He went on to explain that Kelly was locked up and that they needed to find out all about him and his sordid lifestyle, specifically anything he had told her about Faye or the Marriott family.

Maureen wanted to help Charlie; secretly she quite fancied him – strong, father-type figure. The problem was that Maureen also wanted to stay alive. OK, she had a crappy existence, but it was an existence. Charlie had to understand that Kelly would have her killed if she talked. He'd probably do it himself; he had beaten her before now and had pulled a knife on her on a couple of occasions. She had seen his brutality in action. On one occasion she could only watch as he sadistically carved his initials into her friend's buttocks to brand her. While the girl sobbed and pleaded for mercy, he just laughed.

Charlie asked if she could just tell them off the record about Kelly's activities; he would get the proof elsewhere. Maureen was too scared, too sensible. Charlie was disappointed but not surprised. He had seen the fear too many times before – a sheer terror that easily whipped morality into a poor second place.

Maureen tried a smile as Charlie and Ashley left her flat. She stood at the top of the stairs looking down. Charlie stopped at the door and shouted up to her. 'Oh, by the way, Maureen.'

'What?'

'I love the tattoos!'

Steve Aston returned from his enquiries at Blitz's Night Club. It had been closed to the public as it was Sunday, but he had caught the manager there, a clean-cut, mid-thirties man, without an education but with an entrepreneurial streak of genius.

The manager had known Faye Marriott and remembered having seen her dancing with a man at around midnight on the night of the murders. He described this man as white, 5 feet 9 inches tall, slim, wearing a white shirt and grey tie, expensive-looking trousers and brown collar-length hair. He could remember the man, because he had spoken to him earlier as he stood next to him in the toilet. He had a local accent. He hadn't seen Faye leave, but he remembered her talking animatedly with Winston Kelly. Did the police know of Kelly's reputation? The manager eyed the sickly-looking ginger-haired detective condescendingly.

Steve had spoken to a few members of staff there and had a drink or two – of fresh orange juice. The information he had gained hadn't particularly helped, but at least it had confirmed Chantelle Naylor's version of events. Other officers had visited the pubs that Chantelle and Faye had been in before going to Blitz's, but had drawn blanks, apart from the landlord of the Sentinel. He was a seasoned publican and he had noticed that Maureen Ross, a 'tottie', had started to make friends with Faye. The landlord offered his opinion that Kelly was using tactics to get Faye on the game and had instructed Maureen to befriend her and tell her what a lovely life it was being a prostitute.

Charles Lyon was a sucker for a sexy voice; that's what he had always liked about Faye. Detective Policewoman Stephanie Dawson sounded incredibly sensual to him as he spoke to her over his marble-and-brass telephone. He had agreed to talk to her regarding Faye. He had felt terribly wicked, and not a little bold, in suggesting that the meeting take place at the Château. He explained that his initial shock on hearing the news about Faye had waned, and anyway he felt more relaxed entertaining over a glass of claret than over a mug of tea. Steph had been reluctant at first, but on reflection she relented and said, 'The Château would be perfect.' They had arranged to meet early, at 6.30 p.m.

*

134

Hundreds of minor, foot-slogging enquiries were continuing in the investigation, as designated by the HOLMES computer, but there was still no sign of a result. The detectives working on Bernie Squires on Stark's instructions had turned up several illegal practices, but had found no connection of any worth regarding the murder investigation. The mysterious telephone call from Terry Banner was so ambiguous that it could have meant anything; it was, however, very coincidental. Stanley Tindle was out of the frame and they were struggling with Winston Kelly. They needed a break, some luck, a new line of enquiry. Stark was hopeful that Steph's meeting with Charles Lyon would throw some light on the current bleak situation.

Charles was most impressed with his first view of Steph as he walked from the car-park towards the red awning which sur-rounded the main entrance and underneath which the attractive policewoman stood. His excitement grew as he approached her; her slender figure and large, firm breasts he considered more than satisfactory. She clutched her plain white handbag, and her long hair waved gently as the slight breeze blew through it.

They greeted each other politely and shook hands, Steph making a point of loosening her grasp of Charles's hand in a slow, deliberate manner. As their hands parted, she noticed a glint of gold cufflink beneath the sleeve of his blue suede sports jacket. The two made their way into the subtly lit entrance hall of the expensive restaurant. Charles was greeted personally by the head waiter and they were shown to a private bay.

After they had sat down, Steph explained that she might have to ask him some awkward, if not embarrassing questions. Charles told her to relax and that he would answer all her questions with the utmost sincerity. He summoned the alert waiter and ordered Camembert Rochelle to start with, and Châteaubriand, for two. Steph met his questioning glance with a nod of her head. Charles was at home in the surroundings. 'A bottle of Moët et Chandon to celebrate being blessed by such charming company.' Steph feigned a blush and lowered her gaze more than adequately.

After ten or fifteen minutes, their slight awkwardness and politeness subsided and the conversation flowed. Charles answered the questions and explained that after meeting Faye on their first night, he took her to the Dans le Club Casino. He took her home in his Daimler and the two of them had become 'amorous'.

Steph asked, 'Did you have sex with her on the first night?'

Charles repeatedly folded and unfolded the immaculate white napkin. 'No, in fact, I didn't. She stopped me at the final hurdle, if you understand me. Infuriating it was – she was a real tease.' He went on to explain that in his lusty daze and partial sexual stupor, she had given him her telephone number on a piece of paper and he had rung her the very next day. She appeared genuinely pleased that he had rung. The romance blossomed and they saw each other two or three times a week.

Steph sipped at her champagne and formed the words of her questions slowly with her blood-red, shiny lipstick. 'Did you meet her parents?'

'No. She didn't speak a lot about them. Thinking back, it was I who did most of the talking about everything; she seemed a little shy.'

'What made her shy, Charles?' Steph asked, lighting a long menthol cigarette, which she held extended at the tips of her painted fingers.

Charles finally placed the napkin on his lap, attempting to smooth out the creases in it as he replied to the question. 'I think the main problem was the difference in our upbringing. My friends are mainly public school, hers were mainly comprehensive school. That's a hell of a chasm.'

'I take it you had a sexual relationship with her, then?' Steph drew at the cigarette, leaned back into her chair and blew the smoke out in rings.

Charles was secretly enjoying the intimate honesty the two relative strangers were sharing. 'Yes. After two or three weeks we stayed at the Major Oak Hotel for a weekend. I think she told her parents she was staying at a friend's house – Chantelle her name was, that's right.'

Charles went on to explain that the sex between them had been good. She had told him that he was her first lover. The sex they had was romantic and not at all debased.

'Didn't you argue at all?' Steph enquired.

Charles began to smile as he toyed with his champagne.

'Only once. It was a dreadful business. She accused me of being useless in bed, so I hit her!'

Steph was taken aback at the revelation. 'You hit her for saying that!'

'No, I hit her for knowing the difference!' Charles began to laugh.

Steph was momentarily puzzled.

'It's a joke! Don't you get it?' laughed Lyon.

Steph's initial shock turned to a smile and the two laughed together. After the laughter had subsided Charles apologised. 'I'm sorry for teasing you, Stephanie. No, we didn't argue at all.' His face suddenly became serious and his lips pursed. He took another sip of champagne and averted his gaze from Steph.

Charlie was struggling; he was getting nowhere fast; he was running out of ideas. Nobody was prepared to talk to him about Winston Kelly. His patience was wearing thin. He and Ashley decided to go and see Kelly's parents.

'If these don't want to play ball, I'm going to nick them!' said Charlie.

'What for?' asked Ashley.

'I don't know. I'll think of something, and if they give me any lip I'll . . .'

Charlie hammered on the varnished wooden door of the ageing town house. It was quickly opened. A middle-aged West Indian man stood in the doorway. 'Good evening, gentlemen.' His voice was soft but assured and he smiled in welcome as he invited the two men in.

They sat down. The living-room was incredibly clean, with everything in its place. The television surround and wall-unit were of dark teak; there was a beige standard lamp and a sheepskin rug in the centre of the room.

The years of bringing up Winston Kelly had left their mark on his father's face. The trauma, the worry and the disappointment had wrought in the man a sad but wise look. His kindly eyes hadn't, after all that, lost the sparkle that had attracted the young beauty to court him in Kingston, Jamaica, in the summer of 1957. Louisa had stayed with Samuel ever since and had been overwhelmed with joy when she gave birth to a boy. Samuel related the story to the two detectives with a distant, faraway look in his eye. The boy had been given a proud name – Winston Samuel Courtney Kelly. The hopes and aspirations that every parent knows had turned sour when the proud, intelligent but misguided boy had kicked back at the racism and underlying pressure that a young black kid suffers. He couldn't cope with it all and had stolen a watch out of the kitchen of an elderly man's house. He had been arrested for burglary and brought shame to his parents' good name. Once word of his arrest filtered back to his 'friends', he had suddenly become a somebody at school. The fights and confrontations stopped; girls became interested; he became the school hard man. He enjoyed the attention and celebrity status, and once there he couldn't back down; he had to live up to his reputation. That was the beginning of it all.

As Samuel related the story to him, Charlie felt a little ashamed of his ignorant comments on the doorstep of the Kelly household. Louisa, in a baggy flowered frock, brought tea in the best cups and saucers and offered biscuits to her guests. The Kellys were a quiet couple who knew how to behave with a polite dignity.

Samuel, in plain white shirt and blue trousers, continued his conversation with the officers. He explained that in between his personal problems and working nine hours a day in the vast chasms of Calverton Colliery, he had taken stock of the boy. He had talked, he had lectured, he had explained, he had shouted, and eventually he had fought with Winston, all to no avail. He explained how it all came to a head one Sunday lunchtime when the boy had grown into a young man. Samuel had been playing dominoes in the Afro-Caribbean Club. One of his friends had passed some comment about seeing Winston showing 'the beat' to a girl in the red-light area of Hyson Green. There had been a fight, and Samuel had fought like a tiger for his son's honour; he had lost and taken a severe beating. Upon his return home, Louisa had bathed his wounds and Samuel confronted the now Rastafarian Winston. The boy didn't admit or deny the accusation; he just said, 'It is time for me to leave.' And with that he left the household for good. Samuel hid his tears, but they silently rolled down his cheeks as he held Louisa in his arms. She was distraught, heaving and sobbing and blaming herself. From that day to this, Samuel had turned his back on his son. Winston occasionally visited the house, but would remain in the kitchen and talk to Louisa; and every time Winston came, twenty-eight years of emotion would well up inside Samuel.

Charlie didn't like asking the questions he had to, regarding the murders, but he phrased them tactfully so that the true inference, he hoped, was disguised sufficiently. Louisa hadn't seen Winston for over a week. He had seemed troubled but he didn't give any reason for his consternation, telling Louisa that it was 'a business matter'.

The two detectives rose from their chair to leave, and Samuel offered his hand. 'Any time you are passing, officer, call by. You are welcome in my house.'

Charlie accepted the hand of friendship, readily and with respect.

Charles Lyon swilled his brandy around the glass, as he puffed away at a large cigar that appeared too big for his little face. The conversation with Stephanie had momentarily ceased. Lyon stared at his drink, then raised his eyes towards Steph.

'I've been lying to you, Stephanie,' he said, with a sullen expression on his face. Steph raised her eyebrows as Charles continued with his truthful confession. 'It wasn't all sweetness and light between Faye and me.'

'Explain yourself, Charles. I'm interested,' she said, trying not to appear too keen.

'I knew what she saw in me, Stephanie: my wallet! I might be a lot of things, but I'm not stupid.' Lyon paused to formulate his words; he didn't know where to start, how to explain. 'I needed her company. Up to meeting Faye, my idea of a good night was a game of bridge or a night on the piano. She gave me a whole new aspect of life. The women I know are all wrinkled or naïve; Faye was different. She was coy, but she gave me everything in bed. It may sound crazy, but she made me feel like a real man at last. So she took me for a few quid, so what? I knew I could never let her go. Then the problems started, the nightmare began. She started to taunt me incessantly, Stephanie.' Lyon lowered his gaze and spoke at the candles, not daring to look Steph in the face. 'She used to tease me and ridicule me, constantly criticising my sexual performance. Even while I was doing it with her she would often laugh out loud.' He dared a quick glance at Steph, examining her reaction meticulously. She smiled sympathetically at him; she looked as if she understood. He continued his story. 'Things deteriorated. I started gambling to take my mind off it, but that just made me more and more depressed. I lost what bit of confidence I had and became almost impotent. She was cruel to me, Steph, hurtful. I wanted to finish with her, but I just couldn't. I didn't kill her, Stephanie. God knows that if I had it would have been a long time ago!'

The two scrutinised each other, one professionally, the other pathetically. Steph thought about his alibi, and the way he had spoken to her. 'Do you know something, Charles?'

'What's that?'

'I tend to believe you.'

Charles sighed. 'Thank you.'

The cell complex was crowded after the interview with Kelly had finished and Mr Bard had departed to his mini-mansion. Stark stood behind the counter, opposite Kelly. The West Indian gesticulated aggressively; Stark had annoyed him with his relentless pressure. Kelly spoke loudly at the Inspector. 'I'm going to track you down, Stark. I'd like to meet your family. Your wife fancy some black meat?'

Stark gave a mock yawn and patted his mouth. 'Sorry, did you say something, Winston?' He despised men like Kelly, who caused fear in people everywhere he went, hurt people and controlled their lives, and gave nothing. He felt like pasting Kelly all over the cell-complex walls. 'Go and have your fingerprints taken, there's a good boy.'

Kelly pointed at Stark. 'Don't you "boy" me, Babylon, 'cos one of these days I'm going to taste me some pig pussy!' He sneered and diverted his gaze towards a uniformed officer.

The officer shook his head before speaking: 'It's nothing to do with me, Winston.'

Typical. Thanks for the moral support, thought Stark.

Kelly was encouraged out of the cell complex by the frightened officer and into the fingerprint room. Stark glared at the PC when he returned and the PC felt he had to make some comment. 'They're all mouth, aren't they, sir?'

Stark smiled at him with tight lips. 'Are they? Thanks for telling me!' The PC's gaze moved downwards and fixed to the floor as the Inspector left the room. Stark muttered to himself, 'Are we on the same job or what?' As he climbed wearily upstairs he felt isolated and alone with his principles. Nobby greeted him on the landing with a cup of tea.

Kelly was charged with unlawful sexual intercourse with a girl under sixteen, resisting arrest, and possession of cannabis. He was not charged with murder.

Both Stark and Nobby were tired as they started to type up the report that would be used in court the next day, in application by the Crown Prosecution Service to remand Kelly in custody. Stark could have applied to have the twenty-four hours extended to thirty-six with a Superintendent's Warrant, but he decided to stick to his original plan – in effect to buy constant access to Kelly if he were remanded.

Stark's mind wandered back to his wife and children: Christopher's and Laura's happy, innocent laughter, his wife's excited, smiling face which always greeted him from work. Then he thought of Kelly and his implied threat. A nightmare mental picture appeared in his head. He wouldn't dare, would he?

10

'If you aren't fired with enthusiasm,
you will be fired with enthusiasm.'
Vincent Lombardi (1913–1970)

Monday mornings are dreaded by people all over the country:
the weekend is over and the drudgery of five days' work looms
over the British work-force. Bedlam reigned in the Stark household as it creaked and groaned with the weight of the family
waking up. Dave Stark liked to start the day gently, building up
to some semblance of normality. Christopher and Laura woke
up at full pelt and wound down from there. Dave could sense
an argument brewing, as he and his family sat at the pine
breakfast table.

'Oh grow up, Christopher!' Laura exclaimed, her fifteen-year-
old body, now almost fully formed, hidden by her long cotton
nightdress.

Christopher responded childishly. 'Hark at Miss Prim and
Proper! Are you seeing that poofy boyfriend of yours today?'
His fringed haircut and Spiderman pyjamas corroborated the
immature display.

Laura was hurt. 'Shut up, little boy. He's more of a man than
you'll ever be!'

Carol thought it was time to interrupt. 'Will the two of you
please eat your breakfast quietly? Your dad's trying to watch
the news!'

Christopher put his tongue out at Laura.

'Pathetic!' she muttered.

Stark drew the pastel-green living-room curtains across to
prevent the sun from shining on the television screen.

Carol shouted from the kitchen: 'Do you want any toast,
David?'

'No thanks, just coffee. Can we have some quiet, please,

142

while I try to watch the news?' He closed the dividing door, diminishing the commotion from the kitchen. He pressed the remote-control button marked 'volume' as he noticed the national weather report draw to a close and the local news begin.

After the lead report on the latest outbreak of Salmonella at a local food chain-store, Stark was surprised to see a story that was certainly not news to him.

'Police are hunting the killer who savagely attacked an entire family in their own home in Nottingham. The Marriott family were brutally murdered in the early hours of Friday, 24 August. A man is said to be "helping the police with their enquiries".'

Stark shook his head. 'What the hell has he released that for without discussing it with me?'

The newscaster continued: '. . . Detective Superintendent Wagstaff, who is leading the hunt, has said that significant inroads are being made in the hunt to find the killer. Our reporter David Smith spoke to Mr Wagstaff at Police Head-quarters last night . . .'

Carol passed her husband a mug. 'Here's your coffee, Dave . . . Oh look! It's old Wagstaff!'

The tuned-in journalist with the garish tie spoke to the one and only Mr Wagstaff, who had been brought up as a police-man, not a television presenter. The smart reporter wore his concerned face as he asked, 'Can you give us any more information on how the investigation is going, Superintendent Wagstaff?'

He stumbled through a robotic reply. 'The investigation is one of a protracted nature and enquiries are continuing as expeditiously as possible.'

He sounded like what he was: a policeman on television, untrained in the subtle art of television communication. Stark laughed. 'He sounds like PC bloody Plod! Why doesn't he talk like he usually does, like a human being! He sounds like somebody from another planet!'

The journalist continued his brief. 'What arrests have been made, Mr Wagstaff?'

'I cannot divulge the full details of the case, but suffice it to say that a gentleman is helping us with our enquiries, as such,

143

in so much that he has been arrested, yes.' The words were a grammatical wasteland.

'Oh, my God!' Stark laughed out loud. Carol put her coffee down on the table; her laughter had almost caused her to spill it.

David Smith went on: 'Is there any sexual motive behind the killings?'

'I would prefer not to be specific in the divulgence of information, otherwise the enquiry could be severely hampered.' Wagstaff tried to look into the lens but couldn't hold the pose, his camera shyness rapidly becoming apparent. He had become red with embarrassment; it seemed that every time he opened his mouth he said something incredibly farcical.

'Are you still appealing for witnesses to come forward?'

Wagstaff pushed his foot further into his mouth. 'Yes. If there is anybody out there who feels that they might have information which may be of direct or in fact indirect use to the enquiry, they should contact us, in confidence. Their call will be treated confidentially . . .' It looked as though he was going to continue.

Smith beat him to it. 'I'm afraid I'm going to have to stop you there, Superintendent Wagstaff. This is David Smith for the East Midland News handing you back to the studio.'

The news continued, highlighting an impending royal visit. Dave smiled and shook his head. 'If ever I start talking like that, I want you to take me outside and shoot me!'

Carol was more benevolent. 'You are rotten! I felt sorry for him. I like him, I do.'

Stark replied honestly. 'I know, I'm only joking. He's a one-off, is old Waggy. The new breed are thoroughly trained in television techniques – they'd leave me standing. I shouldn't criticise him, really. At least he's given me a chance to prove myself with this. I mean, I'm doing more than I would be doing, if it wasn't for him.'

Carol hugged him. 'It's because he knows how wonderful you are.' She kissed his forehead.

'You are so right,' said Stark modestly.

Carol's smile turned to puzzlement. 'Why didn't he mention the sexual side of it?'

'We don't want that released yet. No end of problems arise

144

when you start telling the press things, just to get them off your back. Careless talk costs lives!'

Wagstaff was looking for a scapegoat. His embarrassment during the television interview had fuelled the anger within him. He paced the room as Stark sat looking up at the new television personality, who was now bawling and shouting like a spoilt child.

'I've spoken to the Chief today. He is not a happy man. He wants this detecting like flaming yesterday!'

'I want it detecting too, sir,' said Stark.

'Don't you interrupt me, David. I've given you a chance on this one and yet nothing has happened. Now I thought you were up to this – perhaps you're not. From now on I want to know everything you're planning on doing. I want to know when you intend wiping your bleeding arse!'

Stark protested. 'I can't do an investigation under those terms. I mean – '

Wagstaff cut him short. 'David, all I am saying is get me something tangible, a lead, anything, otherwise I'm not going to be able to keep you on it.'

Stark was beginning to get just a little peeved. 'What's this supposed to mean? Look, sir, I have busted a gut trying to sort this out!'

'Well, you'll just have to bust another bleeder, otherwise I'm going to have to take over the investigation in its entirety.'

There was a pause. Wagstaff felt that he had probably overstepped the mark with his reprimand; he had mistakenly thought that Stark needed a kick in the relevant area. Stark felt that the onslaught had been unwarranted. It was he who broke the pause.

'Can I ask you something, sir?'

Wagstaff sat down in his chair. 'Yes, what is it?'

'Is there anything that I've done that you wouldn't have?'

Wagstaff contemplated the question for a moment. 'I think we're going to have to pressure Lyon a bit more.'

'I'm more interested in Kelly. There's something he knows, but daren't say for some reason, I'm sure of it. I'd like to know what that is.' There was a slight pause, and Stark couldn't resist

145

it. 'I'm glad that Kelly is helping us with our enquiries, in so much as he is arrested.' He was laughing inwardly. Wagstaff's eyes narrowed as he looked for a hint of sarcasm in Stark's face. He found none.

Two other men were in the midst of a heated debate: Simon Derwent and Mr Bard of Kirkham Turner and Ross. Winston Kelly sat impassively in the dock of the Guildhall Magistrates' Court, Number One.

The clean-cut Mr Derwent had completed his rhetoric on behalf of the Crown Prosecution Service. His application to remand the prisoner in custody, with the full reasons, had been based on a quick perusal of the lengthy report forwarded to him via the stubby fingers of Nobby Clarke. Mr Bard, defending Mr Kelly, rose to his feet, full of self-importance, smiling at the three magistrates on the elevated bench in front of him. Bard wore the same pin-stripe suit he had worn to the interview; his hands rested on his lapels, occasionally leaving them to move the array of papers on the desk in front of him. He had a brash, confident air and he spoke very loudly. A pit deputy, a bank official and a high-ranking civil servant, as the three sitting magistrates, attempted to understand what the hell everybody was talking about and look in full control at the same time.

'Your Worships,' began Bard, 'the prosecution has mentioned that my client *may* commit further offences if he were released on bail. I ask the court what further offences? My client has only been charged with three, unconnected, relatively minor offences!'

He paused for an exaggerated cough, before continuing at his own pace. 'Let us deal with the first – unlawful sexual intercourse with a girl under sixteen years. The woman in question gives the appearance of being at least twenty. My client has no previous convictions for any similar offence, and of course it was a one-off incident. My client strongly denies the charge; he is categoric that full sex did not take place at all, despite the girl's advances. The girl is now, thankfully, back in the children's home out of harm's way, and of course now Mr Kelly knows the girl's age he wouldn't dream of violating her. He has been charged with unlawful possession of cannabis. Again, my client vehemently denies this. He has obviously never seen the cannabis and can only assume that it came from that poor misguided child, who he had given shelter to. Finally, he has been charged with resisting arrest. My client has been in fear of his life for a number of months since a threat was made to him. When he heard his front door being smashed to pieces he naturally assumed it was a group of aggressors breaking into the flat to attack him. He went to defend himself and the girl from, as he thought, immediate serious harm, and before he realised that the group of aggressors were in fact policemen, he had become the subject of a rather delicate attack by a vicious police dog! I would suggest to Your Worships that rather than commit any further offences, my client hasn't committed any in the first place!'

Bard paused and sipped at a glass of lukewarm water, allowing his last sentence to sink in. He put the glass down and looked thoughtful in the silence he had created. All eyes were on him. His loud voice was harsh and serious. 'The word murder has been used in this courtroom today. My client has not been charged with any murder or anything closely resembling it!'

Bard waved a dismissive hand and speeded up his next paragraph. 'I'm confident that the magistrates will discount such an allegation, as there isn't any evidence at all substantiating such an outrageous claim. Even if there were an ounce of truth in it, there is no suggestion that there are any co-accused or that he will interfere with "evidence". I use the term lightly, Your Worships. My client has always dutifully attended previous court cases and he wasn't on bail at the time of the alleged offences. There is no outstanding property to be identified, or any specific offences, which are substantiated, about which the police wish to speak to him. Despite my client's previous convictions, he is trying to make a fresh start in life. He has fully co-operated with the police regarding these matters. He tells me that he has the prospect of a labouring job in the very near future. He pays regular visits to his mother, who is not in the best of health, and it is with this in mind that Winston would accept any conditions imposed, should you think that appropriate. Such conditions would enable my client to continue with his recent impeccable record, start a new job, treat his mother's illness and prepare his defence to the grossly inaccurate charges mistakenly laid on him by the police!'

Bard smiled as he sat down.

The magistrates left the courtroom to debate the issue. Those who remained waiting in the court chatted in hushed whispers. Mr Bard and Mr Derwent laughed in a restrained way at an apparently witty comment one of them had made. Then the usher's booming voice barked out the order, 'All stand!'

The magistrates had been deliberating for only nine minutes. The Chairman of the Bench was a man of about forty, sporting a beard and glasses and a suede sports jacket. He said, 'Would you please stand up, Mr Kelly.' The accused obeyed the instruction slowly, beaten to the position by his police escort.

'We have considered the applications made to us this morning, and we are going to bail you to return to this court on 28 September 1990 at 9.15 a.m. We do, however, impose certain conditions, and these are that you reside at your current address at 16 Chard Court, Nottingham, and that you report to Hyson Green Police Station at 4 p.m. every Friday. You are free to leave the court, Mr Kelly, and I hope that your endeavours to find suitable employment are successful.'

Stark received the news of Kelly's release at 11.30 a.m. while he was in the CID office. 'Why do we bother?' were the usual groans in such circumstances. Now Stark spoke above the disgruntled exclamations. 'Nobby, sort the lads out with their actions for today and give me a shout when RCS ring, will you?'

'Why are RCS going to ring us, boss?' asked Nobby.

Stark smiled. 'Because, Nobby, they are following Winston Kelly and are going to contact us regarding any developments.'

Nobby smiled as he shook his head. 'You cunning bleeder . . . sir.'

The team of Regional Crime Squad detectives were busy; they were the best in the force at surveillance operations. They had undertaken such work time after time; only on rare occasions would they ever be compromised by their 'targets' or actually lose a target for any length of time.

148

They had observed Kelly leave the court. He took a taxi to his flat and stayed there for an hour and a half. He then drove his blue BMW car to the red-light area of Hyson Green. He surreptitiously collected some cash from two girls on Southey Street, then went to the Jamaica Club, a well-known haunt for local West Indian youth. It looked as though it was going to be an active surveillance for the Regional Crime Squad.

Stark peered at the piece of paper on his desk. It was a list he had scribbled down in desperation – a compilation of all the relevant features of the case reduced to basics. The top part of the list was headed 'Points of Interest', and the lower part 'People in Direct Contact with the Circumstances'. The lists looked like this:

Points of Interest
1. 3 murders – 2 asphyxiations, 1 head wound – attempts to disguise same.
2. Offender fakes a burglary.
3. Hi-fi still switched on when police arrive.
4. Sex act?
5. Red fibres at the scene.
6. Clown ornament wiped clean of prints.
7. Video removed after murders.
8. Plastic shoelace loop in rear garden.
9. Man seen by Gray and Glover running away.
10. Parents, respectable; Faye a slag.
11. Faye in the Florin pub with Kelly – arguments/assault/ threats to kill.
12. Faye in numerous pubs, before Blitz's, on night of murders, seen with Kelly and mystery man smooching.
13. Lyon ridiculed by Faye.

People in Direct Contact with the Circumstances
Norman Price   (milkman)
Ernest Gray   (saw man running away)
Peter Glover   (saw man running away)
Bernie Squires   (betting shop)
Terry Banner   (voice on phone at betting shop)

149

Chantelle Naylor	(friend of murdered girl – Faye)
Winston Kelly	(seen with Faye shortly before her death; threats to kill)
Charles Lyon	(boyfriend of Faye – taunted by her)
Stan Tindle	(burglar, in the area around time of murders)
Colin Markwell	(ran away from Gray's house)
Violet Gray	(wife of Gray and Markwell's lover)
Maureen Ross	(Kelly's prostitute)
Reginald Ross	(Maureen's gay brother)
Sally Lawrenson	(Bernie Squires' niece; Faye's workmate)
A. N. Other	(involvement of a third party?)

As it stood at the moment, one of these people must be the murderer. What about the diary? All the men had been traced and eliminated from the enquiry. Stark pondered the problem. The only other possibility was a complete stranger. Stark remembered a motto he'd been told as a young DC: 'Go on what you know.' He drew a circle around the name Winston Kelly.

Winston Kelly's bravado was an offshoot of a crash-course in survival on the streets. He might behave like an animal, but he was one worried animal. He had to get out of this mess. He knew Stark wanted him and he had to use every ounce of his intelligence and street know-how to throw him off the scent.

Kelly spoke to an old tramp in the alleyway at the side of the Sentinel public house. The ageing West Indian man had seen better days; his donkey jacket was scruffy, his pork-pie hat stained with years of sweat. The two men spoke with heavy patois accents.

Kelly stood menacingly close to the man and gesticulated in his usual aggressive manner. 'Two G, Pop, cash!'

The old man shook his head. 'Me not know, boy.'

Kelly reached into his tracksuit pocket. 'I have the money in my hand! It's yours!'

The man was in a corner. He stared at the litter-ridden floor. 'Me not know, boy. It's too risky!'

Kelly was insistent. He had thought out the lie. 'Why I was with you all night, checking out the cards, blood.'

The man knocked the leather pork-pie hat to the back of his head, and let out a sigh. 'Me hear about you, boy. Me hear serious shit. Me heard word of murder!'

'Pop check this, or betray me.' Kelly almost pleaded.

The old guy shook his head again, but he was scared. He apologised, in the vain hope that Kelly would understand. 'Me sorry, boy. Me not trust no Babylon. Me smell blood, your blood!'

Kelly punched the old man hard in the face and watched him collapse on to the floor in a heap. He thought about cutting him, but settled for a kick in the ribs instead. Kelly scurried away, leaving the old tramp semi-conscious and whimpering, like a starving puppy, in the deserted alleyway.

RCS dropped a man back to watch the old guy's progress. After a couple of minutes the old man struggled to his now unsteady feet, a cracked rib for his refusal; the injury would never be treated. The tramp had had a lucky escape. RCS had a bigger prize at stake than a cracked rib, so the officer didn't 'show out'; instead he reconnected with the surveillance team. The coded babbling on their radio by each subsequent 'eyeball' told them that Kelly was at Maureen Ross's flat. Shouts could be heard from inside.

Maureen Ross's gay brother, Reginald, stood limply in front of Stark's desk, his hands on his hips. He wore a multi-coloured tank-top and tight-fitting trousers. He was vehement in his protestations.

'It's the truth, Mr Stark. No way could Winston Kelly have killed that family!' Reggie was frightened. No, he was terrified.

Stark zigzagged the smoke issuing from his pipe by the slow shaking of his head. 'I'm sorry, I just don't believe you, Reggie.'

Reggie sighed and transferred the weight from one leg to the other. His hands remained glued to his bony hips. 'I should have told Charlie Carter when he came to see our Maureen.'

Stark laughed. 'Told him what?' he asked, sceptically.

Reggie moved a hand away and karate-chopped thin air, with flicks of his wrist as he explained. He wasn't looking at Stark;

he stared at the ceiling and spoke his lines. 'There was me and Winston at our Maureen's flat all night watching videos. *Predator* was one, and then we played cards for a bit, and then we watched another video, *Running Man* with Arnold Schwarzenegger in it.'

Stark had been informed by RCS that Kelly had holed up at Ross's flat prior to Reggie's crusade to the police station. 'What time did Kelly get to your house that night, then, Reggie?' asked Stark.

Reggie's gaze returned to the ceiling. 'About five past eleven, and he didn't leave until twenty past five in the morning.'

Stark emptied his pipe into the aluminium ashtray, apparently uninterested. 'What was he wearing?'

Reggie counted out the description with his fingers. 'A green shirt, jeans, Adidas trainers and his Rasta hat.'

'What card game did you play?' enquired Stark, as he put his hands behind his head and leaned back in his chair.

Reggie was quick to answer. 'Nine-card brag. He took ten quid off me!'

'How long did you play cards for?'

'An hour and a half.'

'Did anybody see you with Kelly all night?'

Reggie's hands returned to his hips and he stuck his neck out. 'Course not! Maureen was busy, wasn't she?' He was getting agitated.

Stark had heard enough. He leaned forward, his elbows resting on the desk. 'What were you doing two nights before the killings, Reggie?'

Reggie seemed surprised. 'You what?'

'I said, what were you doing two nights before the killings?'

Reggie was confused. 'How the hell do I know? You want to know about this night, don't you?'

Stark wasn't satisfied. 'All right, what were you doing the night after the murders? The Friday night?'

Reggie shrugged his shoulders. 'I went out. No, I didn't . . . Sorry, yes, I did. I went out to the boozer for a bit.'

'How long for?' asked Stark.

Reggie puffed his cheeks out. 'Er, bloody hell, I don't know.'

'Then what?'

'What's this got to do with owt?' asked Reggie, baffled.

Stark ignored the question. 'I said then what?'

'I don't know. I went to our Maureen's, I think . . . No, hold on, I went to the chippy first. Or was that Saturday night?'

'What did you do at Maureen's?' Stark began doodling on his blotting paper.

'I don't know. Watch telly, I suppose. I'm not sure.'

'What was on?'

Reggie put his finger to his mouth and thought hard. 'I don't know – er, a film.'

'What film?'

Reggie was becoming impatient. He thought of his sister. 'Look, what the hell has this got to do with why I'm here?'

'It's got everything to do with why you're here. Goodbye, Reggie!'

Desperation clouded Reggie's eyes. 'Please, Mr Stark, I'm telling the truth!'

Stark explained the position. 'You've got a choice. I can send you back with some of my men to arse Kelly out of Maureen's flat, or you can go back and tell Winston that the nice Mr Stark believed every word and took a statement off you!'

Reggie was puzzled. 'How did you know – ' He didn't bother finishing the question; he didn't want to know. He breathed a sigh of relief. 'Cheers, Mr Stark, I owe you one.'

Stark felt obliged to ask, 'Will you give us a statement about what Winston Kelly is doing at Maureen's flat as we speak?'

Reggie gave a helpless look. 'I'd rather cop for his murder charge than do that, Mr Stark.'

Stark darted his head to one side, towards the door. 'Go on, piss off, and don't say I never do anything for you!' He waved a dismissive hand at the pathetic figure, who scampered away out of the building.

The Regional Crime Squad officers observed Kelly as his large, gangly gait carried him from Maureen's flat to his car. They followed him, using their manoeuvres, the complexity of which would send a mathematician reeling. They were intrigued to watch and log his every move. He went from house to house, flat to flat, person to person. Eventually he finished up at Blitz's at 9 p.m. The club itself was closed, but the adjacent bar, where the regulars converged, was open. Kelly was very active in the bar; he seemed to be asking questions of various people – coaxing further alibis? When sufficient time had elapsed, RCS sent a man in, but to no avail. After half an hour Kelly left, followed by his invisible entourage.

The only light in the corridor emanated from DI Stark's office. He sat at his desk and supped at the glass of whisky he had allowed himself, and stared at his lists. He had told the rest of the gang to finish at 9 p.m. and they had trooped out for a beer. Stark had declined the invitation to join them; he needed some time alone with his thoughts. He began to write another list, entitling it: 'Questions Arising from Facts Known'. On completion the list looked like this:

Questions Arising from Facts Known
1. Why disguise the way they were murdered?
2. Why disguise the entry to look like a burglary?
3. Who had put the hi-fi on, Faye or the killer?
4. What implement was used to cause the marks on the window and where is it?
5. What was the killer's motive?
6. If not burglary, what was he doing at the house?
7. Had he gone there specifically to rape or murder Faye, or her mum or dad?
8. Why no struggle by Faye?
9. Why hadn't the offender ejaculated?
10. Why remove the video after the murders?
11. How did the killer gain access to the house?
12. How did the killer actually get to the house – transport?
13. Is the shoelace loop the killer's?
14. Are the red fibres the killer's, the smooching man's or some other person's from a previous night?
15. Can every person's account of events be taken on face value, and if not, who cannot be trusted?
16. Did the killer know Faye?

Stark was certain that the sum of the answers to these questions added up to the killer's identity. All he had to do was fill in the gaps.

154

11

'Do not insult the mother alligator
until after you have crossed the river.'
Haitian proverb

The Boxer public house derived its name from the fact that it was across the road from the gym used by Nottingham's finest pugilists. It had been quite a sleazy pub at one time, the underworld's connections with the boxing scene dictating that its patrons often consisted of those owing a debt to society for one misdemeanour or another, but it had changed over the decades. Its 'all muck in' atmosphere had been replaced by beautifully decorated walls and sculptures. The clientele had become huddles of friends, encircled in the warmth and protection of those they knew. Anybody who accidently knocked into someone carrying drinks would receive a harsh stare instead of having their apology readily accepted. Since the Boxer had been completely revamped, no separate lounge or bar existed – just one large room with a circular-shaped bar and various groups gathered together around it. All sorts were there – young, old, male, female, miners, yuppies.

The group of detectives were so engrossed in their conversation that they hadn't paid any particular attention to the group of West Indian youths standing next to them. It was almost 11 p.m. and Paul Fisher had consumed more alcohol than his brain cells could cope with. 'Stark's a bit miserable, not coming out with us, isn't he?' he said in an over-loud slur.

Ashley agreed. 'Yes, he is a bit: He usually likes a drink, doesn't he?'

Charlie, uncomfortable in his surroundings, contributed to the small-talk. 'I think he's bottling a bit with the Marriott murders.'

Paul gave his opinion. 'He reckons it's Winston Kelly, and I've been thinking about it.'

Ashley warned his colleague, jokingly, 'Don't you detect it and stop the overtime supply!'

Steve Aston wanted to join in the banter, but felt a bit shy, slightly alienated. He had tried to chip in once or twice earlier, but had been shouted down by his loud, confident colleagues. He took another sip of his orange juice and wondered if he would ever fit in.

Paul continued his drawl. 'No, hear me out. It's obvious that there was no burglary, right, so whoever killed her had to know her, otherwise she would never have let them in.'

Charlie tried to rebut the observation. 'He could have conned his way in.'

Paul took another large swig of his pint of bitter before answering. 'Yes, but why at that time of night? And can you see Faye Marriott opening the door to a stranger? She was too streetwise. There wasn't a struggle. She must have known the killer – that's why the burglary was staged, it's got to be!'

Ashley nodded. 'You could be right, Paul.'

The rest offered various tame theories, but it was soon time to depart. Paul enquired if anybody wanted to go to a club with him, but they all declined and went their separate ways. Paul had told them that they were all boring, and so he staggered off in an attempt to seek female solace.

Two of the West Indians from the Boxer went to seek out Winston Kelly.

Kelly had returned to his flat and had stayed there a good half-hour. The RCS had been called away to a firearms incident and had been replaced by the newly founded Force Surveillance Team. The team had been seriously depleted and were at half-strength in order to cut down on overtime payments and to keep some senior officer in the police authority's good books.

Kelly took them by surprise when suddenly he ran at full pelt from his flat towards his car, his dreadlocks flying at all angles as he raced along the pavement. He was in a big hurry. The police radio crackled with urgency as the BMW was fired into action. The powerful car quickly generated sufficient speed to cause the surveillance team great difficulty in keeping close enough without showing out. Kelly raced on to the M1, came off the southbound carriageway and doubled back on to the northbound track. The team knew that this was a tactic to dispose of any followers, but it didn't mean Kelly knew he was being followed; he could just be taking precautions. His car roared around the streets of Nottingham for twenty minutes before he abandoned it near the city centre and took off on foot, leading those chasing a merry dance.

After a further twenty minutes Kelly ran into the Tavern public house. His pursuers lay in wait, then after a while they sent a man in. Thirty seconds later, the scruffily dressed man ran out in a blind panic and garbled into his miniature transmitter: 'You're not going to believe this. The guy we've been following is a Rasta in Kelly's clothes, but it is not Kelly! Repeat, *not Kelly!*'

The killer had seen DC Paul Fisher leave the night club, and he watched him devour a kebab outside the late-night chip shop next door. It was 2.40 a.m. The killer was hidden in a shop doorway a hundred yards away, along the pedestrian area. He watched the inebriated detective slowly stumble towards him. He checked for passers-by: there were none; it was deserted. He lay in wait to the detective's left as Paul approached. He toyed with the four-inch knife blade, which reflected the yellow fluorescence of the street-lamps that stood in silent witness. The killer was sweating profusely and had to make a conscious effort to stop his heavy breathing being heard in the now quiet street. He knew what he had to do.

It took a couple of seconds for Paul to register what had happened. He thought someone had punched him in the chest at first, and it was only as the man drew back the knife for a second blow that Paul instantly sobered up. He twisted slightly to the left, as the second blow struck him to the right side of his chest. Paul was a strong young man who had looked after himself many times during his police career, against some very hard men. But on this occasion he had lost the edge and had been completely surprised by the unprovoked attack. Terror crashed into his brain as he looked into the killer's frenzied eyes, and realisation chased away his intoxication. Paul staggered backwards – half as a reaction and half with the force of the blow. The attack took seconds, but it seemed to Paul as if it were in slow motion. He ducked to avoid the third blow. He tried to summon up enough strength to save himself, but the message sent to his right arm to strike out at the man got lost in the shattered nerve ends slashed by his attacker's first blow. Paul was defenceless and crashed on to the unrelenting pavement. The next blow cut into his face, his left cheek, knocking a tooth out with its force. The killer momentarily got the knife stuck in Paul's face and had to slash upwards to release it.

Paul realised he was going to die and a calmness swept over him – the calmness that would bring eventual unconsciousness. Paul looked up at his murderer sweeping blows upon his own helpless body and he felt an immense sadness as he thought of his mother's and father's reaction to the news of his death. He also thought of the horror his friends would feel at investigating the crime. He imagined himself naked on that white slab, dead, with Tony the mortician telling jokes at his side. He had to give his friends a chance to catch his killer. He used every fibre of his being to reach out at the head of the killer with his left hand; he scratched at him as hard as he could, pulling at his hair. Paul recognised the final blow as it powered into his back. It cut straight through the muscle and punctured his heart. Paul felt his heart explode and a searing pain scorched into him before the black. It was all over.

The killer scurried away into the darkness of a nearby alleyway. Paul Fisher lay dead in the gutter, in the warmth of his own blood, a clue to his killer's identity in his own fingernails which he had known would be scraped and clipped off as he lay naked on the slab.

Stark's fists, like his eyes, screwed tightly together. He stood over the body of the twenty-four-year-old man lying in the gutter. He couldn't stop the tear trickling down his cheek. Death had caused Paul's facial features to relax and Stark had to look twice before confirming the worst. Without the flush of youth, without blood coursing through his veins, Paul looked older and empty; it was just a shell.

Everybody had finished the preliminaries and the undertakers picked up the body. It was rock solid, frozen in time by rigor mortis; the bones would have to be broken to get him into the container.

Stark looked away. The muscles in his neck were tense and he swallowed hard. A sensation swept over him that made him shiver: a hollow, negative feeling of rage, and then sadness, and then – for God's sake why? He leaned against a large glass shop window, his forehead resting on his forearm, still trying to shut out the horror. His shoulders rocked as his sobbing became uncontrollable. After a few seconds he steeled himself and aggressively threw himself off the support. He walked down the paved area, his eyes unseeing, his hands thrust deep into his trouser pockets, and kept on walking.

Birdsong began as a new day dawned. Stark would have to tell Fisher's parents; it was his job.

Terry and Sonia Fisher had got up at the usual time, to the accompaniment of Radio Nottingham. They were a fine couple, married some thirty-two years. Terry, a retired schoolteacher, was a complex, sensitive man. Now his balding head was buried in the *Daily Telegraph*, his pen scribbling away at the crossword. Sonia had always been a housewife and mother to their only child, Paul; her greying hair, neatly pinned back, and pinafore were synonymous with the cosy feeling of home that she had created for the apple of her eye, her policeman son. Friends, neighbours and even slight acquaintances could testify to the pride Sonia felt in the son for whom they had waited so long in the early years.

She hummed to herself in the kitchen as she began to cook bacon and eggs, then she went to knock on Paul's bedroom door. There was no reply, so she went in: the bedroom was empty and the bed had not been slept in. She returned downstairs; her husband remained rooted in the living-room chair.

'He's not been in all night, Terry!' Sonia told him.

'Well, he's old enough, love – he's stopped out before. He's obviously picked some woman up and gone back to her place,' Terry said, smiling, basking in his son's ability to be 'one of the lads', something he himself had never quite mastered as a young man.

Sonia was unconvinced. 'Yes, but he usually rings up if he's

159

going to be out all night. He could be lying in a gutter somewhere!'

Terry laughed and again tried to reassure his wife. 'You can't expect him to break off from a young woman to ring his mummy up. He's twenty-four, for God's sake!'

Sonia busied herself with the breakfast. She knew Paul was a grown man, but to her he was still a boy and the tinge of paranoia that at times haunts every mother bit into her. She knew everything would be OK, but it was only natural to worry a little bit.

'Well, I hope he's being careful, then!' she shouted aloud.

Terry came into the kitchen and they ate their quiet breakfast at the table. They were just returning to the living-room when there was a knock on the front door. Sonia darted a glance at Terry. 'Who's that at this time?'

Terry laughed. 'There's only one way of finding out. It's probably the paper boy.'

Sonia looked shocked and a dull ache hit her stomach as Terry returned with Detective Inspector David Stark.

Terry's mouth had gone dry, but he tried a smile to accompany the introduction. 'This is Detective Inspector Stark, Sonia, the one that Paul's told us about, his boss. He says he wants a word with us.'

Sonia looked at the well-dressed man. His face looked drawn and ashen. Sonia threw her hand to her mouth and spoke through it. 'There's nothing wrong, is there?'

'I just want to have a chat with the two of you.' It wasn't an answer.

'God, there is something wrong, Terry!' Sonia was shaking as she clung on to her husband and they sat down together on the Dralon-covered settee. A thousand thoughts shot through Sonia's mind, one of which she would not allow herself to contemplate.

Stark sat in the armchair. 'As you know, I'm Paul's Inspector and that's why I've come.' His voice was low and sullen; he couldn't look the doting parents in the eyes.

Terry tried to stop himself shaking so that he could support his wife. 'Paul's not in any trouble, is he?'

Stark slowly shook his head. 'No, of course not, but I'm

160

afraid I do have some bad news.' He glanced quickly at the quivering pair on the settee.

Sonia's shaking worsened; she felt she could not, dare not ask the question. Terry did it for her. 'He's not been hurt, has he?'

Stark had to reply. 'I'm afraid so . . .' Sonia let out a sob. Stark continued. 'He's been hurt very seriously.' He felt that the only way to do this was to lower the worry and grief in stages, to give the body a chance to soak up the increasing stages of shock as each phrase sank in. He didn't want to drag it out too long, though.

Terry's grip on Sonia tightened and his voice trembled. 'Well, come on, Inspector, how seriously has he been injured?'

Stark looked at the terrified couple wrapped in each other's arms. 'I'm afraid there is no easy way to say this . . .'

'Oh no, please don't!' said Terry, shaking his head, fighting off the realisation as it seered into his mind. Sonia felt sick; she closed her watery eyes and her chest began heaving.

Stark went on. 'I'm afraid it's the worst possible news. Paul's been attacked. He's been stabbed. I'm afraid he's . . . dead.'

A wail emanated from far down within the mother's breast. The two had lost part of their very soul. They clung to each other in their grief. Stark felt helpless and struggled to control his own emotions. He wanted to tell them that everything would be fine; he wanted to comfort them; but he couldn't. He got up out of the chair and went into the kitchen, unsure what he should do.

In a daze he put the kettle on, then he broke down, crying like a baby. At that moment he made a promise to himself – to find the bastard that had wrought such pain on people who wouldn't hurt a soul, people who only wanted to help others and do good. The sort of people that Paul Fisher had sworn to protect on his very first day as a police constable. His unswerving dedication had cost him his life.

Stark could hear the wailing and the sobbing, and he had to force himself back into the pain-filled room. He felt an intruder, but there were things he wanted to tell them. He stayed with them for most of the morning and told them what he and his colleagues thought of Paul as a man and a policeman. He wasn't sure if they heard him; there would be plenty of time to tell them again in the future. He explained the practical arrangements to Terry, who nodded, and he gave them his card. They could call him whenever they wanted to; he had scribbled his home number on it too.

Stark left the house, feeling drained and tired as he lumbered into the driver's seat of his car. His hands gripped the steering wheel. *'Damn!'* he shouted. He took a long, deep breath, tried to compose himself, and drove off. He had made a promise to himself that he intended to fulfil.

The next couple of days flew by for Stark. All the procedures for a murder hunt had, of course, reeled into action. Control of the enquiry had moved on to Detective Chief Superintendent Davies. Stark had been pleased about this, because it meant that all the responsibilities and underlying problems were taken off him and he could get back to being a detective and doing the job his way.

Paul Fisher had been stabbed sixteen times in the body and face by a four-inch-long blade, which at its widest was an inch. The murder weapon had been removed by the killer. Paul had given his clue, and the blood and skin samples were being hurriedly tested at the Forensic Science Laboratory. Once the killer's body samples had been processed, any suspects could be checked using the genetic profiling system. It was the best clue they had.

The enquiry had been directed on the assumption that Paul's death was connected with the Marriott murders. Scores of people had been drafted in and it was quickly becoming the largest enquiry undertaken in the Nottingham Constabulary for five years. Kelly had been rearrested and behaved in an indentical manner, apart from his readiness to provide a blood sample for comparison. He was bailed pending his DNA comparison with Paul's clue. The surveillance team remained Kelly's unseen companions. He had made one mistake and it was hoped that he would make another. Since Paul's death, the surveillance team had suddenly been given infinite resources to ensure that it would not lose Kelly again.

Stark had revisited the Fisher household and tried to console them in the best way he could. He made absolutely sure they knew that Paul hadn't stood a chance and that his courage and strength had left the legacy of an important clue. It wouldn't bring Paul back, but Stark felt that it might be a comfort to them in years to come. The inquest had been a traumatic experience. Stark had told the Fishers that there was no obligation on them to attend, but they had insisted. The unlawful killing verdict would undoubtedly come later; the coroner had gone through the motions, opened the inquest, taken evidence of identification, released the body for burial and adjourned the hearing pending police reports. The funeral had been set for the afternoon of Thursday, 30 August at St John's Church, with a private burial afterwards.

The little Jamaican boy, in baggy jeans and brown, ripped T-shirt, could barely reach the counter of Nottingham Police Station and it was by standing on his tiptoes that he passed the envelope over to the young receptionist. The girl glanced at the envelope: it simply read 'STARK'. She pressed her switchboard buttons and spoke into the telephone.

'Hello, sir, it's Karen on the switchboard. I've got a young boy here with an envelope for you – Oh! He's gone.'

'I'll come down and see you,' said Stark.

The girl gave the envelope to Stark and explained the mysterious circumstances surrounding its delivery. He returned to his office and opened the envelope gingerly. If its contents were relevant, he would be sending it to be fingerprinted soon and the last thing he wanted to do was destroy any potential evidence. He gently withdrew and unfolded the piece of plain A4 paper. He photocopied it, before placing the paper and envelope in separate bags. The photostated copy could obviously be handled freely. He stared down at it and his furrowed brow indicated his puzzlement.

A riddle was written out in capital letters on the page. It read as follows:

THE WARM BRIDE WHO WOULD HAVE FAME WITHOUT ME,
WHIRLED AND JIGGED IN BLACK,
WOULD TAKE WITH HER A SIGH, THE NIGHT SHE LEFT.
WITH OPEN ARMS, SHE WELCOMED THE COVERED HAND
  THAT SMITE HER DOWN,
THE TRUSTING EYE LOOKS OUT NOT IN.

SIGNED. THE FATHERS SON.

12

'The reverse side also has a reverse side.'
Japanese proverb

Stark knew that one of his officers needed him. His shirt was drenched with sweat; he'd got to get there before it was too late! He chased around the side-streets by the Victoria Shopping Arcade and across the road, avoiding the late-night traffic as the horns, distorted in motion, blared angrily at his crazed figure. He was exhausted; he'd been running a long time. He heard the scream and struggled to quicken his pace. Not far now – the next street. He dodged down the alleyway and watched in horror as the stooped figure delivered the final blow. Stark shouted out at him desperately; the dark figure scurried away and the Inspector reached the lifeless body on the pavement. It was lying face down. He turned it over and saw his own face staring back at him! He screamed in terror: '*No!*'

'David! Wake up, for God's sake!' Carol pushed and pulled at his sleeping body writhing on the sheets. 'David, you're having a nightmare! Come on!'

David's subconscious eventually received the message and he began to awaken from his deep, disturbing sleep.

'Bloody hell! Sorry, love.' He was sweating as he sat up and held Carol in his arms, his heart working overtime.

'What were you dreaming about?'

'Oh, nothing. It's gone now.' He looked over at the clock: 4.13, the liquid crystal display revealed.

Carol was worried. 'You've got to come to terms with this, David, love.'

Dave looked tired. 'I know, I will – it's just so . . . Oh, I don't know.'

Carol squeezed her husband as tightly as she could. 'You

164

haven't had a proper night's sleep since . . . since Paul.' She felt inadequate.

'Give me time, Carol. I've just got to find the guy that's done this and I can't rest until I do.'

She shook her head. 'What if he's never caught, love? You can't carry on like this!'

Dave's response was tight-lipped. 'He'll be caught, don't worry about that.'

Carol brushed her fingers through his now bedraggled hair. 'Are you all right now?'

'Yes, I'm fine, honestly.' He kissed her and gave her a quick hug.

'Come on, let's get some sleep,' she said.

Husband and wife moved down the bed and cuddled close together. Carol closed her eyes. Dave stared into the darkness – the same darkness that allowed the devils of self-doubt and recrimination to escape inside him. Later he fell into a stunted, troubled sleep, the sort of sleep where every noise sends consciousness racing to the surface again.

The alarm woke Carol at 6.45 a.m. She could smell breakfast cooking downstairs and she sleepily felt for Dave; he wasn't there. She bit into her bottom lip. She was afraid, afraid for Dave and afraid for her family. She felt completely helpless; she could only pray that things would improve.

The Forensic Science Laboratory at Huntingdon was over-whelmed with work. The staff were constantly bombarded with clothing, human samples, bits of wood, glass; you name it, they examined it. As with any large organisation working under pressure, mistakes were made, 'dead certainties' dispatched and then returned with a negative result. To their credit, the scientists more often than not came up with the goods.

Daniel Katuna was alone in his own silent world. His labora-tory was completely sealed and had several windows, which, of course, were always shut. The room had separate ventilation to prevent cross-contamination from the outside world or from other laboratories. He wore a white coat and skin-tight rubber gloves as he stood at the high table, his left eye concentrated over his microscope, watching the strands of DNA dancing with the enzyme he had introduced to the sample. There are only two pieces of evidence that irrefutably prove guilt, in set circumstances: good old-fashioned fingerprints, and genetic profiling. Mr Katuna was compiling a DNA profile from Winston Kelly's blood sample, but such is the complexity of the process that it would be an absolute minimum of two weeks before the result could be forwarded to Detective Inspector Stark.

Stark was concentrating hard at his desk. He stared down at the riddle, a thin line of smoke heading skywards from the bowl of his pipe.

> THE WARM BRIDE WHO WOULD HAVE FAME WITHOUT ME,
> WHIRLED AND JIGGED IN BLACK,
> WOULD TAKE WITH HER A SIGH, THE NIGHT SHE LEFT.
> WITH OPEN ARMS, SHE WELCOMED THE COVERED HAND
>   THAT SMITE HER DOWN,
> THE TRUSTING EYE LOOKS OUT NOT IN.
>
> SIGNED. THE FATHERS SON.

He pondered over who could have sent it. He felt it had to be Kelly or Lyon, or the third person at Faye's house that night. The fingerprint department had found nothing on the paper and only a partly smudged print on the envelope. The mark wasn't sufficient for it to be identified, but it didn't look like Kelly's or Lyon's. Stark was annoyed with himself for not having solved the riddle yet. If it was Kelly who had sent it, he thought it would be somewhat crude; and Lyon – well, he had more money than brains. Stark felt sure that Winston Kelly had sent it, because of the black delivery boy. He felt he was getting to know what made Kelly tick. The boy was a hint for Stark to know that it was Kelly that was making him sweat, that he had the answer and he was going to make Stark work hard to get it. Kelly needed a way out and Stark felt this was his sadistic way of doing it. It could always be a hoax. He thought not; it was worth looking at very closely.

He read it out aloud for the twenty-eighth time.

*

Stark adjusted his black tie and preened himself in the mirror hanging on the wall in the police-station toilet. The funeral was to be a full police affair, with a private family burial. Stark had declined the invitation to be a pall-bearer and stepped aside for Paul's closer working colleagues, whom the tragedy had hurt just as deeply.

He stood outside the crumbling old church. He was twenty minutes early. He had nodded to several people as they approached the churchyard entrance. The whole of the road surrounding the church had been coned off, with 'No Waiting' the most popular instruction. Police dress was best uniforms, white gloves, no medals and no canes for senior officers. Stark wore a navy-blue suit, white shirt, black tie and carried a dark blue-and-black overcoat. It was the white gloves of the non-attending officers that waved frantic directions to the car drivers; they organised who parked where, under the watchful eye of the Divisional Chief Inspector. A couple of traffic wardens hovered in the background to ward off any other cars.

The church was over a century old and overgrown bushes sheltered the cobbled path which was now lined with the uniformed guard-of-honour. Sounds came from the wall of pipes that was the organ, the keyboard and the organist invisible behind it. As Stark entered, two PCs muttered his name into a 'memo-cord' recorder. He was then ushered into the main part of the church by a uniformed Sergeant.

From the moment that the Fishers had accepted the option of a full police service, the planning had been intricate. The air was heavy with emotion, and not a sound could be heard from the hundreds gathered in the church. There were four main blocks of pews, with two smaller blocks at the rear. The police mourners occupied the two blocks at the back and the whole of the right-hand side, which stretched up towards the altar. Police were also crammed into the rear pews on the far left, the front of that block being reserved for the pall-bearers. It was here that Stark sat, to enable him to be close to his men when they arrived. Family and civilian mourners occupied the right middle block and the Police Federation sat behind the omnipotent array in the left middle block of pews. Anybody who was anybody was there. The Chief Constable, the Deputy Chief Constable, an Assistant Chief Constable, three Chief Superintendents and a gaggle of Superintendents and Chief Inspectors. Mere Inspectors were forced to squeeze in as and where they could. Even the Chairman of the Police Authority and the Civilian Force Administration Officer attended.

Stark reached down to the white piece of paper in front of him. It was headed 'Service for Thanksgiving for the Life and Work of Paul Fisher – Nottinghamshire Constabulary'. He glanced over the Order of Service. There would be two hymns, a lesson read by the Chief Constable, an address by Detective Chief Superintendent Davies and one from the Reverend Alan Marsden, the Force Chaplain.

Stark and the congregation rose as the Chaplain's voice broke into the hushed assembly: 'I am the resurrection . . .' Stark's men solemnly carried the body of their dead friend and colleague into the aisle of the church, behind the chanting vicar. The coffin was draped in the flag of the Nottinghamshire Constabulary. The video cameras secreted outside searched for the face of the killer amongst the crowd. Did the killer have the gall to attend, urged by some sort of macabre curiosity?

Stark stared blankly at the wooden coffin, envisaging Paul's body inside it. He once again saw the image of the undertakers picking him up, stiff and grotesque. At the front of the church he could see Sonia, dressed in black lace, a white handkerchief held to her mouth, her eyes closed tightly, squeezing tears out of the corners. Terry had his arm around her. He had aged; it was apparent that he had not slept, his face was drawn and white. Stark was angry – angry at the bastard that had caused this; angry at the people that call our society civilised; angry with himself for not solving the riddle. He felt so helpless: this was one of those rare occasions that he simply could not do anything about. He could swear vengeance, he could thump his desk another ten times, he could catch the killer, but Paul would still be dead. He shook his head as the strangers pontificated on the dais. It was all so pointless; he had been a mere boy. It was too late to do anything, other than something Stark felt had become an imperative need with him: to put the bastard that did this behind bars.

The Last Post stirred Stark's thoughts and he looked around him at the congregation, seated for the minute's silence. The optimistic notes of Reveille echoed from the rafters and Paul

Fisher was taken to his place of rest. Stark had heard little of what the speakers had said; his service had been a private one – he didn't need anybody to tell him how to feel.

After a while he filed out of the church and into the heat of day. The last white-gloved salute of Chief Inspector Turley shone in the sunlight as it bade a respectful farewell to the cortège. The hubbub of traffic quickly resumed after its temporary pause. The world would continue, for the fortunate ones.

Stark shook the outstretched hand of Mr Turley and accepted his condolences, before he left for the police station and a swig of his desk whisky. Something was niggling at him, tapping away at his brain. Something was wrong.

The Reggae Beat Club was a writhing mass of sweaty bodies and screamingly loud reggae music. Winston Kelly was stepping out boldly around the dance floor to the rhythm of Bob Marley's 'Buffalo Soldier', his exaggerated motions causing quite a stir. His shiny black tracksuit and gold bracelet were an odd mixture, accompanied by the bulbous dreadlocks. He held a can of Red Stripe lager, which spilled out because of his loose grip on it and his jerking body. It soaked into the bare wooden floorboards, ensuring that any joints of cannabis deposited on it, inadvertently or otherwise, would be extinguished. The noise of the reggae sound caused parts of the furnishings to vibrate. The crowd, black with an occasional white woman, revelled in Kelly's motions. They mimicked his movements and started to chant cries of support for the latest hero. They were close to fever pitch: 'Babylon die! Babylon defeated!' The West Indians shouted in unison, some slipping and falling on the wet floor in the mêlée. Kelly whirled around the room, his smile as wide as his face. Kelly was overjoyed. He had cause to be: he had made Stark sweat, he had asked a question of the questioner, he had sent a riddle and they would soon be off his back for good!

Stark sat at his desk. He couldn't rest. The day's events danced around his mind: the funeral, the desolate grief of a family, the grief that no amount of sympathy, no matter how well intentioned, would heal. He remembered his vow to track down

169

Paul's killer, a murderer who had brutally cut down an entire family, wiped them out as if they didn't matter.

He tried to expel his emotions and concentrate on the job in hand. He cleared his mind and stared down at the piece of paper with the riddle on it. He began to think aloud: 'Fame without me . . . fame without me . . . Of course, you idiot! Fame without me is "Faye"!' He straightened himself in his chair and became a little excited. He was focusing, he was getting on to the right wavelength. He began scribbling on a bit of paper and continued talking himself through the riddle. 'Warm bride . . . Cold veil?' He tutted and shook his head. 'No, that's not it . . . Warm bride . . . Hot . . .' The realisation hit him. 'Oh Winston, that is so crude: Warm bride, hot marry.' Stark laughed. '"Marriott"!' He continued; he felt he was on a roll. 'Whirled and jigged in black . . . Danced, spun, hopped in black?' Stark's mind flashed back to Chantelle Naylor. 'Faye was smooching with a guy at Blitz's, could that be it?' He went on. 'Would take with her a sigh . . . A sigh? God knows what that is . . . The night she left? The night she left Blitz's? The night she left – died? Come on, Winston, give me more than this . . . Would take with her a sigh, the night she left . . . Oh, Winston, that is good for you! That's clever! Take the comma out of it: "Would take with her a scythe the night she left!" A scythe – the sign of death! That's got to be it. Winston is saying that Faye Marriott had smooched with the guy at Blitz's and he eventually killed her. Yes, but who the hell is he? I know I'm close, Winston, just give me a tiny shove. With open arms she welcomed the covered hand that smite her down . . . With open arms? So what are you saying: that she asked for it? Could be. She welcomed the covered hand that smite her down . . . Well, there were certainly no fingerprints . . . Covered hand that smite her down . . . Just a minute! Bloody hell! Christ! No! It can't be him, Winston, surely!'

It was 3 a.m. Stark sat behind his desk, his feet perched on top of it; the numerous balls of screwed-up paper betrayed his endeavours. He was feeling more than pleased with himself. He took another sip of whisky, his mind elsewhere, certainly not in his office. The phone rang.

170

Stark jumped. 'Oh shit!' as he spilled his whisky. He reached for the red receiver. 'DI Stark.'

The man's voice had a surprising West Country accent to it. 'Yes, hello. I wasn't sure whether you'd be in. I'm Sergeant James from the Police Liaison Office at Huntingdon Forensic Science Lab.'

'Hello,' said Stark.

'We've got the final analysis on the Kelly comparisons, the genetic profile. It's negative!'

Stark did not display any surprise. 'So you're telling me that Kelly didn't murder Paul Fisher.'

'That's right, sir. At the moment we don't know who killed him.'

Stark sipped his whisky. 'I know who killed him!'

13

'When ideas fail, words come in very handy.'
                    Goethe (1749–1832)

Dave had stumbled into bed at 3.50 a.m. Despite his excitement, the exhaustion that the whole investigation had brought was finally released and immediately he collapsed into a deep sustained sleep. There were no nightmares. So dense was the veil of black that engulfed him that it was only Carol shaking him vigorously and her raised voice that dragged him awake.

'Dave, it's eight o'clock!'

'You what? Bloody hell! Why didn't you wake me earlier?'

Carol gave her honest answer. 'Well, you were fast asleep for a change, and you've been so tired lately I thought an extra hour would do you good. I mean, what time did you get in? Anyway, you're the boss – who's going to mind?'

Stark staggered into the bathroom, followed by Carol. His tiredness caused the inevitable irritated response. 'Carol. Bosses have bosses. I am going to arrest Paul's killer today, for Christ's sake!'

Carol tried to defend her well-intentioned but unappreciated efforts. 'It'll wait, won't it? If you don't look after yourself, I'll have to do it for you.' She felt hurt.

Stark turned on the shower and placed his hand under the jets of water. 'Carol, I am going to be late!'

She sat on the covered toilet seat. 'Stop panicking. I still cannot believe you've found out who Paul's killer is – I'm so proud of you.'

His hand remained cold as the water streamed out. 'Oh shit! There's no bloody hot water now!' he cried.

Carol stood and put her hand under too. 'I'm sorry. I could have sworn that there would be enough. Mind you, you usually beat us to it: now you know what it's like to have a cold shower.'

Dave screamed and complained his way through the cold shower, his body jerking in the small cubicle, goose-pimples on overtime. Eventually he shivered out from behind the plastic curtain.

'I bet you're awake now!' Carol laughed. Stark dried himself in silence. They returned to the bedroom, Stark still annoyed.

'That was very amusing, Carol, and do you mind not following me all over the damn place! I'm not in the mood, OK?'

Carol looked at him, disappointed. 'God, you're bloody mardy, Dave. A bit of cold water and we all have to suffer!'

He was fuming. He knew inside how petty he was being, but he was tired, very tired, and no matter how hard he tried his nastiness seemed to grow instead of decrease. 'I am not bloody mardy. I just expect basic household necessities to be sorted out properly. I don't go to work to have a cold shower!'

'It's probably a good job. You'd come home wet!'

'I didn't mean that. You know what I bloody meant!' he barked.

Carol sat on the bed. 'Don't be like that, love, it's only a bit of fun.'

Stark was sarcastic. 'Sure, let's all be nice and cosy and happy. Well, I don't feel happy. I'm fed up with you assuming all the time. I am in the police force; if I am late I am in the shit. I can be officially disciplined before the Chief Constable, reduced in rank – Christ knows what else. You should have woken me up, that's all there is to it!'

'Here we go,' said Carol, sighing.

Stark dressed in the uneasy silence, as his wife sat on the bed watching. He turned towards her and she offered a hesitant smile, which he ignored. Once he was dressed he gave her a frosty kiss. 'See you later, if you can be bothered to get your fat arse off the bed!' He thudded downstairs and slammed the door shut behind him.

Nobby's carotid artery stood out at the side of his neck as he paced the floor of the CID office. He was impatient. 'What sort of a carry-on is this, eh?'

173

Ashley tried to appease his Detective Sergeant. 'Sit down, Nobby, he'll probably be here soon.'

The plea fell on deaf ears and Nobby's pacing continued. He raised the piece of paper he was holding into the air. 'Have you seen this note?'

Charlie moved his head to one side as his feet, on the desk, obscured his view of Nobby. 'Yes, we've all seen the note, Nobby.'

He carried on his trek up and down the office. Nobody spoke, the level of expectancy immense. Nobby decided to read the note out loud: '"Nobby. I've cracked it! I'll be a few minutes late, I've got a call to make on the way in. Don't let anybody go out. Cheers. Dave Stark."' He threw the note on to the desk. 'I mean, what sort of a carry-on is that?' he repeated.

Charlie was irritated. 'For Christ's sake, sit down, Nobby, you're making us all feel dizzy!' The atmosphere was tense. Nobby grudgingly sat down, muttering about 'lack of communication skills'. Steve Aston handed out mugs of steaming tea. There was a silence, then Nobby blurted out: 'I hope he has cracked it, because I want to get my hands on the bastard that did Paul!'

'Don't we all?' asked Charlie.

There was another lengthy silence. Nobby shook his head disbelievingly. 'Yes, but what I want to know is what sort of a carry-on is this?' He ducked to avoid the barrage of paperclips and rubbers.

Wagstaff and Davies had been elated by Stark's call in the early hours of the morning. They had fully agreed with his analogy of the evidence gathered as a result of solving the riddle and had instructed him to utilise SOU for the foot-slogging checks that would have to be made.

It was as a result of these instructions that the telephone inside the house rang for a full three minutes. There was nobody in. The instructions were clear. SOU had their warrant; they were to gain access with the minimum of force and search the place thoroughly.

The men forced the front door by smashing a small pane of glass and releasing the Yale lock inside. The damaged window was replaced while the officers searched inside. They were in their boiler-suits and were careful to replace anything moved in its original position. Sergeant Tuckworth's windswept black hair bobbed through the doorways of all the rooms, checking on his officers. The search was completed relatively quickly. He spoke into his radio: 'Sergeant Tuckworth, SOU, to Nottingham Control.'

'Go ahead.'

'Inform DI Stark that the search was a success. I am coming back to brief him.'

'Ten-four, Sarge. That's good news. I'll tell him.'

As SOU left the house, they complied with the law by leaving a copy of the warrant in a 'prominent position'. Sergeant Tuckworth unfolded the blue piece of paper and placed it on the Adam-style fireplace. The warrant fell down the back of the mantelpiece, hidden from view. Unfortunately Tuckworth did not notice this, otherwise, of course, he would have retrieved it. He closed the rear door. It was as if nobody had been there.

Stark waved to Samuel Kelly as he pulled away in his car. Stark was smiling, his faith in human nature restored.

After Charlie's visit, Samuel had spoken to Winston for the first time, man to man. He had asked his son to comply with one wish for his mother's sake: that was to clear the Kelly name, which was being spoken in the same breath as murder. Winston had kept his promise. Stark had been right – Kelly had sent him the riddle. It would never be mentioned between the two men, but Kelly had cleared his name and assisted the police in finding the identity of the real killer.

Stark was still smiling as he climbed the steps and walked along the corridor where his men were in heated discussion.

Charlie was confident. 'I'm telling you, it's that wimp Lyon. It's the oldest motive in the book – sexual ridicule!'

'I've got to go for Winston Kelly,' said Nobby.

'I agree,' said Steve Aston.

Steph shuffled her backside further on to the desk she was sitting on. 'Yes, but how can we prove it?' she asked.

Stark's large frame filled the doorway of the office and the talking stopped. Nobby was the first to speak. 'Where have you been, boss? It's a bit naughty, keeping us in suspense like this.'

Stark threw the piece of paper on to the desk. It was Kelly's riddle. 'It's all in there,' he said.

'What is?' asked Nobby.

'The killer's name, everything.'

The detectives all gathered round and Nobby read the riddle out. Stark explained the meaning behind it, line by line. Groans and comments of agreement emanated from the group, then Stark asked the sixty-four-thousand-dollar question. It was so easy it was hard. Who killed Faye Marriott and her mother and father? Stark explained.

'I couldn't believe it at first. You see, *The covered hand that smite her down*. The covered hand killed her, don't you see? What's a covered hand? A glove. Glover killed her!'

The group was startled. Ashley thought aloud: 'I don't believe it. Pete Glover . . . It can't be him: he's an ex-copper!' The others agreed.

'That's just it,' Stark said. 'You see, *The trusting eye looks out not in.*'

Nobby's scepticism rose to the surface. 'That's what the riddle says. Who says the riddle is right?'

'I do, Nobby,' said Stark.

Ashley asked the important question. 'So who is the note from?'

'Winston Kelly,' said Stark.

Nobby laughed. 'You're joking! And you are taking it seriously? He's just done that to throw us off the scent.'

Stark gave Nobby a sideways glance. 'Don't you think I've thought of all this? The checks have been made. SOU have contacted me. I can prove it, Nobby. He's the bastard that killed the Marriotts, and he killed Paul!'

There was a momentary pause, before Ashley asked how they could prove it. Stark explained. 'Glover said that he had broken down on the way home from Traditions Night Club on the night of the murders.'

Charlie agreed. 'That's right. It was Paul who took the statment off Glover.'

'He then says that he saw a figure running with a box, that he had too much to drink, so didn't give chase. He then went to the nearest garage and bought some petrol. He put that in the car, which did the trick and so he drove off.'

'I've got the receipt somewhere,' said Nobby.

'No, you haven't, mate: it's here.' Stark produced the receipt, which had been recovered from the garage, from his pocket. He handed it to Nobby. 'See anything unusual about it?' he asked.

Nobby studied the small square of paper. He shook his head. 'No, not at all.'

'One pound eighty-eight for a gallon of petrol?' Stark hinted.

'What's wrong with that?' asked Nobby.

Stark smiled. 'Nothing, apart from the fact that on the night Glover bought the petrol that supposedly fired his Sierra into life, diesel from that garage was one pound *eighty*-eight: petrol was one pound *ninety*-four! He'd put the wrong sort of petrol in his can, so his car couldn't have been driven away. But, of course, it could be driven away, because it had never broken down!'

There was another pause.

Charlie made a sensible comment. 'It could be a mistake by the garage.'

'They don't think so, Charlie. Anyway, that's just a starter for ten. I've got a list of evidence here to choose from. Mistakes that prove that Glover is our man.'

Ashley looked puzzled. 'Why on earth would Glover want to kill the Marriotts and then Paul, for God's sake?'

Stark surmised. 'I don't think that Glover intended to do anything untoward. I think events took over. What makes somebody become a killer? It is apparent now that Peter Glover met Faye Marriott in Blitz's Night Club. He smooched with her and she promised more, so he took her home. She, of course, invited him in for coffee and played soft music on the hi-fi. The kissing turned to groping, Faye teasing and getting Glover excited so that he didn't want to stop. Faye decided to play one of her old tricks and tried to stop Glover at the last moment. He thought she didn't really mean it and carried on. She started to protest as he began sexual intercourse, so he covered her mouth with his hand. Remember, there were no strangulation marks on her neck. Unfortunately for her, he had covered her nose also so that she couldn't breathe. He must have noticed that she had died before he ejaculated. Death is a big passion-killer. He

177

had killed her; he hadn't meant to, but he had. He began to panic, and it was at this time that the unfortunate Walter and Audrey Marriott could be heard hastily approaching the door. Instead of running out the back, he quickly picked up the brass clown ornament and hid behind the door, on the stairs. You know the rest.'

Ashley was amazed. 'Surely he could have just run out of the back, if he thought about it?'

Stark replied. 'Is a man who has killed a girl by accident just thirty seconds before thinking straight? Not only that: I checked on Glover. He got kicked off the force for breaking a woman's jaw. The woman just happened to be Bernadette Kelly – Winston Kelly's cousin. I've seen Bernadette, who maintains that Glover simply punched her in the face for no apparent reason. Winston obviously knew about this and checked Glover out. When we did our checks he had no convictions, correct, but there have been unproved allegations made against him that wouldn't show up on our computer. One allegation against him was a complaint of GBH. A group of youths cornered him one night at the side of Blitz's about a year ago. Glover took a knife out and cut one – twenty-two stitches! Glover was cornered by Walter and Audrey Marriott!'

Ashley spoke to Nobby. 'I can't believe it, can you?'

'I'll believe anything on this job, but there is still a lot of proof needed to convict, that's for sure. What else have you got, boss?'

'Well, Glover, having been a policeman, thought he could fool us. He tried to cover his tracks. Fortunately for us, he hadn't been a copper long enough to know what he was doing.'

Nobby's brain was almost visibly churning. 'What about the phone call to Bernie Squires that you picked up?'

Stark was ready with the answer. 'Terry Banner had got rid of thirty-five video recorders which were nicked from a warehouse the night before, out of town. He was just letting Bernie know in his half-cocked way. The two of them and a couple of other idiots have been arrested for a series of warehouse breaks all over the Midlands.'

'We could still use some proof,' said Nobby.

Stark laughed again and drew back a playful punch. 'You won't have it, will you? Look at this.' He put his hand in his trouser pocket and threw a piece of paper on the desk. 'Have a read of that.'

Nobby picked it up and read the piece of paper aloud. 'Squires Turf Accountants is the heading and it has a telephone number on it – 425675.'

Stark continued. 'Remember on the statement Paul took off him he denied any knowledge of the Marriott family at all. Guess whose phone number that is.'

'Faye Marriott's' came the chorus.

'It was found in Pete Glover's pocket diary, in his house, stuffed loosely in it with twenty-two other similar scraps of paper with phone numbers on.'

Nobby tutted. 'What a prat. Why didn't he get rid of it?'

Stark gave his opinion. 'I don't suppose it would have crossed his mind, Nobby. You see, as always, Faye would have given him her telephone number early on in the night, before there was a hint of any problem, when everything was cosy. I bet he put it in his diary there and then, with the others, and never gave it another thought. It was several hours after that that he turned murderer, the telephone number long forgotten.'

'What about Paul – why him?' asked Ashley.

The night that Paul got drunk was the night he was killed, if you remember. After he left you he went on to a night club. Traditions was the only club open that night, it being the start of the week. This was Pete Glover's local haunt too. In fact, I suspect that Glover was using his former association with Paul to keep in touch with him to find out how the murder investigation was going. Paul was pissed and, as I understand he did in the pub, he would be mouthing off some theories about the Marriott murders. The ideas meant nothing to Paul, but they obviously struck a strong chord with Glover. He must have left early and lain in wait.'

Ashley was interested. 'How do you know all this, sir.'

Stark replied, 'The riddle prompted me to double-check everything we'd done that involved Glover. Faye's telephone number wasn't the only thing that SOU found. There were two spots of dried blood on an old sheet on the garage floor, about the size of a ten-pence piece; enough for us to check genetically. My bet is that the blood is Paul's. After the attack on Paul, Glover would have been absolutely soaked in blood. This would have dripped in the garage as he walked through it. He would have got rid of the clothing. He's been fairly clever in that he appears to have disposed of the carpet in his car boot, which he undoubtedly put the clothes in, from both sets of murders, to dispose of them. Unfortunately for him, he's missed traces of blood, and fibres from the clothes he wore when he killed the Marriotts. These will be matched up with those at the Marriott house.'

There was a stunned silence.

'The bastard!' Charlie thought out loud.

Stark continued. 'There is enough evidence both forensically and otherwise to convict him for both murders, and that's before we've even had a chance to talk to him.'

Steph shook her head. 'Fancy killing Paul, though. They were old mates.'

Nobby spoke. 'Well, it looks as though you've cracked it, boss. All that police work and it's a riddle that gives us the killer!'

Stark looked serious. 'We've all cracked it. It was a team effort. The police work enabled us to prove it. Glover's made other mistakes as well. The cloakroom attendant at Blitz's – for some reason she hadn't been seen until she was knocked out of bed in the early hours. She distinctly remembers the man who left with Faye Marriott that night asking for his very attractive bright-red jumper from her. She'll identify him. Basically, he's bollocksed!'

Nobby sighed and shook his head. Charlie repeated himself. 'The bastard!'

Stark went on. 'SOU haven't found the video, screwdriver or knife, so he could still have the knife on him. He must have been carrying it the night he killed Paul.'

'Good!' said Nobby. ''Cos I'm going to make him eat the bastard!'

Charlie joined in. 'Yes, let's go and get the little shit!'

'Hold on, hold on!' Stark gestured for them to sit down. 'I want this bastard as much as you do, but we owe it to Paul to get it right. We don't want to lose it on a technicality, or lose him because we rush things. Let's not forget that he's already killed one copper. That's one too many. Now, I'm going to be in on the strike when we nick him. Who's coming with me?'

180

'I will!' The cry was simultaneous and unanimous.

Excitement and anger were welling up inside Stark. He had to keep his head. The arrest of Pete Glover had to be done right or another copper would die.

Stark was surrounded by computer screens, telephones and radio equipment as he sat in the control room and gathered his thoughts. He regretted the tiff he and Carol had had before he came out. He wanted to call her and make things right, but he simply had too much to do and he didn't want to risk floating back to the safe world of family life until this was over and the job was done. He needed to keep his resolve and his concentration.

The plan was basic. After everything had been considered, it was decided to take Glover within the confines of his own house, where there was less danger to the public. After all, he probably still had the knife with him. RCS were to follow Glover, and once they had 'housed' him they would inform Stark and his men, waiting in the nearby streets, who would strike and arrest him.

Stark walked into the general office. It was empty. He couldn't bear it any longer: he had to phone Carol. He went to the telephone: all the outside lines were engaged. He would wait; he had to speak to her before they left.

The door opened; it was Nobby. 'We're going to have to get going, boss,' he said.

Stark again glanced at the still illuminated lights on the telephone. He winced as he stood up. 'Come on, then, Nobby. Let's do this for Paul.'

Stark led his loyal troops out of the station. The lights on the phone went out. Paul Fisher's friends drove off in their cars to capture his killer, each of them excited and taut. None of them was sure how they would react on seeing Glover. All of them were a little frightened: he had killed, and he would kill again if trapped – he had nothing to lose!

The phone in DI Stark's office rang. There was no reply. She was just about to ring off when it was answered. 'David?' she enquired.

'DI Stark's office, PC Winters speaking.' The young voice was alien to Carol.

'Oh, I'm sorry. Can I speak to DI Stark, please? It is rather important.'

'I'm afraid he's out at the moment. Who's calling?'

'It's his wife, Carol. Do you know when he'll be back?'

'I'm afraid I don't. Can I take a message?'

'No . . . er, OK, yes, if you would. Have you got a pen?'

The young PC extracted his black biro from the top pocket of his blue shirt. 'Yes. Fire away.'

Carol felt a little embarrassed, but it had to be done. 'Just put, "Sorry, I love you, Carol."' The PC smiled to himself and added a kiss at the end for good measure, before leaving the note on Stark's desk.

Carol felt unusually uneasy, nervous even, as she paced around her living-room. 'Stop being silly,' she muttered to herself. 'He's probably out in the bloody pub. He'll ring later, when it suits him, I bet.' A shiver shot down her spine. She bit into her nails and stared out of the window at Christopher and Laura, talking on the lawn. The children saw her and waved. Carol waved back. 'He'll be OK, won't he?'

14

'Are you going to come quietly,
or do I have to use earplugs?'
from *The Goon Show*

Pete Glover sat in the small, makeshift kitchen in his insurance company offices. The kitchen consisted of a sink, a microwave oven, a kettle, and that was it. He sipped at his cup of tea. He still couldn't believe what had happened. He reconstructed the events of that fateful night in his disturbed mind. She'd offered it him on a plate. She had begged him to go in for a coffee; any normal red-blooded male would have gone in. Her tongue had played with his in a passionate kiss, supporting her request. She had squeezed his erect member as it strained to escape from his trousers. He had decided that it might be a good idea to go in for a 'coffee'. Their passion continued inside on the soft settee, spilling over on to the floor. He was just about to enter her, the end of his penis was between her lips, and then she said 'No! You can't do that.' It was too late; he entered her. She started squirming and then shouting protests; things were turning nasty. He did what a lot of men do when they begin to lose control of a situation: he used violence. He knew that after all her teasing he wouldn't be long, so he thought he would carry on and just cover her mouth to shut her up, and then – oh God! Why did he have such a temper? Why did those idiots have to come home when they did? Why did he have to panic? He should just have run away . . . and then what? Do life imprisonment? No way!

Glover got off his chair and began pacing the kitchen. He had to remain calm. He hadn't slept since he . . . since Paul. It had to be done, he thought. It was either him or me. What did he have to go all clever for? Saying that he knew who the killer was. He looked so serious, grim, when he told me. 'Is your car diesel or petrol, then, Pete?' he had asked. 'Seen any good videos lately?' Sarcastic bastard. He had said that there was nothing he could do about it. What did that mean? He must have known it was me. I couldn't risk it. He had to die.

Glover threw the plastic teacup into the kitchen bin and pondered his next move. If he stayed calm everything would be OK. In a couple or three weeks the enquiry would start to wind down. Some police chief would start looking at his budget and officers would return to their divisions gradually, when the general crime rate started to rise. Everything would be just fine. He had to keep his wits about him. He had covered his tracks well enough, hadn't he? He cursed himself for opening that window before chiselling away at it. If it wasn't for that they'd still be looking for a burglar, wouldn't they? He took a deep breath. Still, stay calm and confident and forget that any of it ever happened . . .

Glover glanced down at his watch: 12.30. He would go home for his lunch, he couldn't stand the thought of dining with the crowd today. He had shared a lift to work, so it would have to be a cab home. As he stepped out of the offices into the street, he didn't look twice at the man sitting on the bench, eating chips. The man was thirty-eight years old, with long straggly hair and a stubbled chin. His single ear-ring gave him a gypsy look. He had tattooed arms and grubby fingers that concentrated eagerly on stuffing in the chips as quickly as possible. His T-shirt was stained with beer and his jeans were oily. His general scruffiness belied his true identity: DC 1219 Sumpter of the Regional Crime Squad. He was the footman to begin with, and as he disposed of his chips he followed his quarry, giving off the surreptitious hand-signals that informed his associates of his intended direction.

Glover stopped a cab and headed for home. Tommy Sumpter was picked up and the convoy commenced. It led to the door of Pete Glover's house.

He let himself in. There was an odd feeling to the house. He took off his jacket and prepared to cook his under-the-grill pizza. He opened the cutlery drawer and felt for a knife and fork – he froze! A tingle shot down his spine. He knew the compartmental plastic container inside the drawer should be, from left to right, knives, forks and spoons – *not* forks, spoons and knives. If nothing else, Glover was a creature of habit.

Somebody had been in the house. He looked out of the window and saw two men on the street talking. 'Fucking hell!' His panic rose to fever pitch. He ran upstairs and changed into jeans, white T-shirt and leather bomber jacket. He didn't bother packing; he simply collected his passport from the dressing-table drawer. He had all his credit cards on him. He put the passport in his jacket pocket, vaulted downstairs, grabbed a large kitchen knife and ran out of the back door to his car. RCS had to draw back: there was a killer on the loose!

Stark and his team had started their engines and were waiting for the call to strike. They were only in the next street and nerve-ends jangled. RCS had reported that Glover had returned to his house. This was the moment of truth.

Stark's foot revved the engine. 'Come on,' he said to himself more than to anyone else.

Nobby was impatient. 'What the pissing hell is going on? We should be going in now!'

Ashley spoke from the back seat. 'Can't we radio them up, sir, and see what's going on?'

Stark revved the engine again. 'Just bide your time, lads. They've got the eyeball, they can see what's happening, we can't.' The tension in the car had caused the windows to steam up.

Nobby was not convinced. 'We know he's in there. Why can't we just hit it?'

'It's not as simple as that. They've got to make sure that he isn't just going to come straight back out as they approach.' He revved the engine again. The silence made the seconds drag out like minutes. 'They've obviously seen him doing something in the house, or there's a complication,' Stark observed.

'RCS to DI Stark,' crackled the radio.

Stark snatched at the handset resting on his lap. 'Go ahead.'

'The target has left the house and is moving. We'll continue with the follow.'

'Ten-four. Keep us posted.'

'Yes, yes. He's changed his clothes. I hope he hasn't clocked us.'

Stark replied, 'If he has, we'll have to take him wherever we can, in the safest place possible.' His brow furrowed. He spoke aloud: 'Shit! Now what?'

RCS followed Glover's Sierra along the streets of Nottingham and on to the motorway, close by. The convoy followed him the short distance to East Midlands Airport, then attempted to contact Stark. The radio contact wasn't working well, so they had to get the force control room to contact the local control room to contact Stark and update him.

Stark replied through the same chain. 'He's obviously sussed that we want him. Contain him at the airport; we're on our way. If he tries to board a plane, arrest him for murder!'

Carol's mind was troubled as she stood at the sink, washing the lunchtime dishes. Dave still hadn't phoned. She finished the last plate and reached for a towel. As she did so she noticed the old framed photograph of a young David, still in uniform, which stood on top of the side-cupboard. She reached for it to admire it more closely; the smiling face somehow reassured her. Her wet, soapy hands couldn't hold the silver frame and it slipped on the floor with a resounding crash. Pieces of glass were strewn across the linoleum. Carol screamed, before composing herself again. 'Damn!'

Glover was sweating. The carving knife was uncomfortable in the inside pocket of his leather jacket. He was a wanted man. He had to appear quite normal, but he felt that everybody was staring at him. He approached the British Midland Airways desk, went through the booking process and clung on to his one-way cancellation ticket to Paris. It was the furthest he could get away at such short notice. He would have to travel overland to a non-extradition country. Brazil seemed the best location; all he had to do was evade the Airport Police at Paris. He looked at the clock: 2.22 p.m. His departure time was 2.45. Only around twenty minutes to go. The information board indicated that there would be no delays and that he should board at Gate 3. He considered hiding in the toilet, but if the police saw him go in there he would be trapped. He decided on the safer option of mingling with the crowd, until the very last second, when he would jump on to his flight and away. He stood at the row of telephone hoods and pretended he was making a call. He didn't want to leave the country, but it was this or a life in prison. He scrutinised every face, his mind scrambling with fear and paranoia. He stole a glance at the uniformed policeman standing near the passport desk. He felt as if everybody knew who he was, as if there was a big sign above his head with MURDERER displayed on it. He looked at those assembled in the foyer of Gate 3. There were about a thousand people milling around and Glover felt uneasy, jumpy; he felt cornered.

He saw a quick dart of movement to his right. It was the figure of a man appearing in the doorway, then deftly stepping aside to hide behind a wall. Glover recognised the face: it was Detective Inspector David Stark. Glover's heart was pounding. He had to do something quickly. He glanced at his watch: 2.42. He had to cause a diversion and he had to do it now! He reached for his knife.

Glover's days were numbered, but human nature dictates that one fights for one's life, and it was with this in mind that Stark decided to arrest Glover immediately. They had done enough softly-softly policing. The time had come to hit the bastard and hit him hard.

Stark felt that Glover might have seen him when he arrived in the doorway; but if he had, he hadn't shown any signs of it. Stark was with his detectives near the doorway and the RCS contingent were spread out, but were mainly near the bar area. Their radios were useless in the hubbub of the engine noise, trolleys and a thousand goodbyes.

Stark surreptitiously started to walk across the foyer to inform RCS that they were going to move in and hit Glover now – but he never got there. Initially when he heard the shrill sound he thought it was an aeroplane reversing. He was wrong: it was the fire alarm.

What followed was bedlam. Men, women and children panicked *en masse*. They were rushing everywhere, and mainly towards the area where the detectives stood. Glover had created his barrier and Stark could only watch as he crept through the doors that led to a safe passage to Paris.

Dave Stark fought with all his might against the full force of the tide of people, all believing that death was imminent. The others were stuck. Stark alone had a chance of catching the killer. He used all his strength to push through the crowd, eventually reaching the double doors behind which Glover had disappeared. A porter stepped in Stark's way: 'I'm sorry, sir, the fire escape is . . .' He didn't finish the sentence: Stark had knocked him flat on his back.

Once through the doors, he could see Glover in the queue of people entering the jumbo jet on the tarmac airfield. The two men's eyes met. Glover was about a hundred and fifty yards away: he knew that he would never make it. He turned on his heels and ran, simultaneously producing the carving knife from inside his jacket. The blade shone in the sunlight as Glover's arms moved like a bee's wings to escape the Inspector who was quickly gaining on him.

As Stark ran, his mind raced, creating slow-motion images of his own family, Carol and Chris and Laura, of a family brutally murdered and a young man cut down in the prime of his life. Stark was angry, the sort of mad-dog angry that makes men kill. He saw the blade, he thought of Nobby's threat to make Glover eat it: it seemed like a good idea. Stark knew he was going to catch him. Glover also knew he was going to be caught. He was scared. He stopped and turned round, brandishing the knife. Stark stopped. They had reached the end of the runway, near a shrubbery. They stood fifteen feet apart. From the area of the boarding gate, rows of open-mouthed faces stared down at the two men on the tarmac. Both were breathing heavily. Stark stood with his fists clenched at his sides, his face grimacing. Glover stood with the knife in his right hand, his left hand outstretched, palm face down.

'Just you and me, then, Stark!' he said, puffing and panting.

Stark didn't speak; he just stared into Glover's eyes. His anger intensified the grimace on his face and he bared his teeth. His heavy breathing and his contempt forced grunting noises from his mouth. He didn't want to talk. He lunged at Glover. The knife cut into Stark's left upper arm, but he felt no pain. Glover was knocked to the ground, with Stark on top of him. The Inspector got hold of his right arm, holding the knife against the tarmac. Stark looked into Glover's eyes and smiled. Glover was afraid; now it was his turn to taste fear.

'Drop it, you bastard!' Stark punched Glover in the face, breaking his nose. Glover clung on to the knife, but he was powerless to resist. He was petrified; he had never seen such hate and it scared him shitless. He pleaded for mercy: 'All right, all right. Let me get up.'

Stark punched him in the face again. 'You bastard! Did you give Paul a chance? You killed a fucking good man!'

An image of young Paul's cut-up face seared into Stark's brain. Glover released his grip on the knife and Stark threw it to one side. He had lost control. He placed his strong hands around Glover's throat. Glover fought and struggled, but to no avail, as Stark squeezed hard, forcing a gurgle out of Glover's gullet.

Stark's eyes were wide. 'Why don't you kill me, eh, Glover? Why not kill me, you fucking coward?' he screamed through clenched teeth. Glover's eyeballs were starting to protrude and his body began to relax through lack of oxygen. His body was like a rag doll in Stark's hands.

'Sir, *no*! For Christ's sake don't!' Ashley shouted as he raced towards the two figures, his colleagues close behind. Stark heard the young man's pleas. His hatred started to subside and he again thought of his young children. He released his grip on Glover. 'You're not fucking worth it!' He threw him down on the floor, with the contempt he deserved. His body was limp. Stark stood up and after a couple of seconds Glover rolled on to his side, in a ball, clutching at his neck and whimpering. The others arrived and Charlie manhandled Glover to his feet.

'Get him out of my fucking sight!' said Stark.

The men led Glover away, still coughing and spluttering. Stark sat on the floor and buried his face in his hands.

Nobby looked at Ashley, and flicked his head to one side. 'Go on, Ashley, we'll join you in a minute.' Ashley picked up the knife carefully and jogged away to catch up with the others. Nobby sat down next to his Detective Inspector in silence. Stark felt the pain of the cut for the first time. 'Bloody hell! That hurts, Nobby.'

The DS put his hand on Stark's shoulder. 'Are you OK, sir?'

189

Stark let out a heavy blow. 'I think so, Nobby.' He blew again, obviously shaken. 'I should have killed that bastard!'

Nobby laughed. 'I think you almost did.'

Stark laughed too. 'If Ashley hadn't come when he did – ' he began.

Nobby interrupted him. 'Ashley did come. It's over with now, Dave. Paul can rest in peace.'

'Yes, you're right. Thanks, Nobby.'

Nobby shrugged and smiled. 'What for? Come on, let's get your arm seen to. It's pissing blood.'

Nobby helped him to his feet and assisted him in the walk back. Stark picked up Glover's airline ticket with his blood-stained hand. 'I wonder if it's too late?'

'What for?' asked Nobby.

'Well, I could use a holiday in Paris!' The two men's laughter was drowned out by the siren of the fast-approaching ambulance.

Stark lay on the couch in the medical centre. The attractive young nurse with blonde hair smiled at the brave policeman as she bandaged his wounds. Stark had fulfilled his promise to himself to catch Paul's killer; he had thought he would be elated, but he just felt empty – drained of all emotion. He shook his head. Why did all this have to happen? What was the point of it all?

After the nurse had finished attending to the police's latest hero, Nobby complained of slight bruising to his groin and asked the young nurse to examine him. Stark struggled off the couch, his arm now in a sling, his white shirt bloodstained. He shuffled to the call box near the door and rang his wife. 'Hello, love, it's me . . .'

He didn't get a chance to finish. Carol interrupted. 'About time, too. All you do is swan about in the pubs all day, while I'm stuck here with the kids hassling me every ten minutes. Well, it's not on! Why didn't you ring me back? . . .'

Stark smiled. It was good to be alive.

190